10/14

D0378129

TWISTED ties

BOOK TWO IN THE TIES SERIES

NEW YORK TIMES AND USA TODAY BESTSELLING AUTHOR

K.A. ROBINSON

OTHER BOOKS BY

NEW YORK TIMES AND USA TODAY BESTSELLING AUTHOR

K.A. ROBINSON

THE TORN SERIES

TORN
TWISTED
TAINTED

THE TIES SERIES

SHATTERED TIES
TWISTED TIES

Coming April 2014

BREAKING ALEXANDRIA

Visit my website at www.authorkarobinson.blogspot.com or www.facebook.com/karobinson13

ISBN-10: 1495269655

ISBN-13: 978-1495269653

CONTENTS

PROLOGUE
EMMA

Two Years Earlier

I took a deep breath as I passed the sign indicating I was entering the Santa Monica trailer park. I knew what I would probably find here, but I couldn't help from holding on to just a small piece of hope. I was still so angry with *him*, but I wasn't sure how I would feel if I knew he were truly gone. As much as I hated him, I still loved him. I was such a stupid, stupid girl.

I'd thought that I'd found true love with Jesse Daniels, but all he'd managed to do was break my heart. *Why did it have to be her?* Of all the girls in the world, he had cheated on me with Ally—the one person who despised me.

Looking back at everything that had happened, I now knew that she was the reason for all of it. I'd known from the start that she didn't like me, but I could never understand why. Now, I did. *She loved Jesse.* It was so obvious to me now that I wasn't sure how I'd missed it in the beginning. But as that old saying went, hindsight was twenty-twenty.

I couldn't change what Ally and Jesse had done to me. I could only accept it and learn from it. They had certainly made me grow up, that was for sure. I wasn't the naive little girl who trusted anyone and everyone anymore. I was jaded, and I was pissed.

I pulled up to Jesse's house. My heart dropped when I saw the *For Rent* sign hanging from the porch banister. It felt like a slap in the face to see it there, but I shouldn't have expected any less. In my heart, I knew he was gone. A small part of me had hoped he'd simply unenrolled from my highschool, Hamrick High, and gone back to his old school instead of leaving California completely. Now, I knew. He was thousands of miles away from me in West Virginia with his mom and her boyfriend.

A tap on my window startled me, and I screamed. My heart was beating like crazy as I looked over to see Andy standing there with a frown on his face. *Thank God.* I wasn't exactly in the best part of town, and I had been afraid that it was a stranger who wanted to rob me. I knew my expensive car could bring me some unwanted attention around here. I rolled my window down as I willed my wildly pounding heart to slow down. I knew Andy, and he wasn't someone who would hurt me.

"What are you doing here?" he asked once my window was down.

"I don't know."

He looked at me like I was nuts.

"I mean, I know *why* I'm here. I just don't know why I even wanted to see if he was still here. He hurt me, yet here I am, checking in to see if he's really gone."

"I get it, I do. You cared a lot about the asshole."

"Asshole? I thought he was your best friend."

"He was—until he slept with my sister and then kicked her out of his bed the next day. He's lucky I didn't beat the shit out of him."

"Oh, so you know?"

He nodded. "I do. I'm sorry that he hurt you so badly. You're a sweet girl, Emma. You didn't deserve that."

"Why do you care?" I asked.

Andy seemed like a good guy, but we'd never been friends before. I'd assumed that he was only nice to me because I was with Jesse. Plus, he had never tried to hide the fact that he slept around a lot. Usually, guys like him were assholes.

"Because Jesse hurt you and my sister. I'm not the best guy in the world, but even I have morals. There are two things you don't do—cheat and screw your best friend's sister. Jesse managed to do both at once. We're no longer friends, and I made sure to let him know that before he left."

"And here I thought you were the womanizing asshole. I think I had you two backward. You're the nice one, and he's the asshole."

Andy laughed. "No, I'm still a womanizing asshole. I just don't think it's okay to cheat. That's the reason I've never had a girlfriend. I know how I am, and I wouldn't want some poor girl to have a broken heart, thanks to me."

At least he was honest. I felt tears filling my eyes. I wish Jesse could have been as honest as Andy. Instead, Jesse had used me and broken me. I had given him everything because I thought he loved me when he was actually laughing at me behind my back.

"Hey, don't cry. I was trying to make you feel better by telling you that I'm a complete asshole," Andy said.

"I wish Jesse were as honest as you."

"He normally is. I don't know what happened with you two and Ally, and I don't want to know. Why don't you come over to my house? I'll feed you ice cream or something like that. Ice cream always makes girls feel better, right?"

I laughed. "I'd prefer alcohol at this point, but I think I'll pass. I don't know what I'd do if I saw Ally."

"Ally is never home anymore. You have a better chance of seeing Jesse there today than you do of seeing Ally. Come on, let's get you some ice cream. Maybe if you're extra nice, I'll give you some alcohol, too. I'm not usually this sweet, so you better take me up on my offer."

I studied him carefully. Andy had always seemed like a nice guy, but I wasn't sure if I could stand to be around him. He was just another reminder of Jesse, and right now, I didn't need one of those.

"I don't know…"

"It's cookie dough ice cream," he said as he smiled down at me.

"Well, how am I supposed to say no to that? I can't stay long though. I don't want to take a chance of seeing Ally there." I smiled up at him as I wondered what the hell I was doing.

"Fair enough. Just park your car beside mine in my driveway. I'll see you in a second."

He turned and walked down the road to his house as I started my car and backed out of Jesse's driveway.

It's not Jesse's anymore, I mentally reminded myself. Jesse is gone.

I followed behind Andy, still unsure of whether or not this was a good idea. I wanted to forget that Jesse ever existed, and if I ended up being friends with Andy, there was no chance of that. In my head, Andy and Jesse were one since they'd been around each other so much when I was with Jesse.

I pulled in beside an old rusted Chevy Cavalier and stepped out. After locking my car, I stepped up onto Andy's porch and followed him inside his house. The layout was identical to Jesse's. The kitchen was off to the right with the living room to the left. Past the living room was the hall that I knew led back to the bedrooms. Jesse and his mom had always kept their house spotless, and while Andy's wasn't gross, it was messy. It was obvious that two teenagers lived here.

"Sorry for the mess. I was going to clean today, but then I went surfing."

"You sound like Jesse. He liked to surf all the time, too."

"We're California boys. It's in our blood."

"I guess it is," I said as I walked to the couch and sat down.

Andy came out of the kitchen with a tub of cookie dough ice cream and two beers. I thanked him as I grabbed the tub and one of the beers from him. I sighed happily as I took the first bite of ice cream. Andy was right—ice cream always made things better.

"Want to watch some TV while you eat?" Andy asked as he grabbed the remote.

"Sure."

"We don't have a DVD player, but we do have cable. I'm sure we can find something to watch." He turned on the TV and started flipping through channels.

I groaned when he stopped on a channel with one of the *Saw* movies playing. "I hate scary movies."

"This isn't scary. It's all about mind games."

"I've never seen any of them, but I've heard they're gory."

"Whoa, wait a minute. You've *never* watched a *Saw* movie before?"

I shook my head. "Nope, never."

"Okay, now, we have to watch it. You'll love it."

"I seriously doubt that." I popped the top off my beer and took a drink.

"Trust me, you will. And it looks like you're in luck. They're doing a *Saw* marathon day. You can watch them all."

"Lucky me," I grumbled as I nursed my beer.

"Chicken," he coughed out under his breath.

"I am not! I just don't want to watch people die and stuff."

"And stuff? Really?"

"Shut up, and watch your damn movie."

He laughed as he threw the remote down onto the coffee table and leaned back into the couch.

As we watched the first movie, I had to admit that it was pretty good. I would cringe from time to time when something was too gross, but other than that, I was fine. I put away my ice cream halfway through the first movie and grabbed us both new beers from the fridge. I had to admit that hanging out with Andy was actually kind of fun, and he was taking my mind off of everything happening in my life.

By the time the third movie started, the coffee table was littered with beer bottles, and I was starting to feel the effects of the alcohol coursing through my blood. Andy seemed to still be sober, but I wasn't sure. I didn't want to look like a lightweight, so I kept my mouth shut.

"I'm tired," I mumbled as I rested my head against Andy's arm.

"You can't fall asleep on me. We have to finish the movie!" Andy said as he pulled me against him and wrapped his arm around my shoulders.

"I'm not going to fall asleep, I promise. I just need to rest my eyes." I closed my eyes and relaxed into Andy. *God, he smells good.* I had no idea how I hadn't noticed this before. I inhaled deeply, breathing in his scent.

I dozed on and off as the movie played. I would jump and snuggle in closer to Andy when someone on TV screamed in terror. I must have finally fallen asleep toward the end because when I woke up, the house was dark, and the TV was off.

I could feel Andy rubbing my lower back underneath my shirt. I knew I shouldn't like it, but it felt so damn good. I'd been so alone this past month, but I didn't feel that way with Andy next to me. I took another deep breath, instantly regretting it. Between his scent and his hand rubbing my back, I felt myself starting to become aroused. I knew this was a bad idea and that I needed to leave, but I couldn't bring myself to do it.

His hand slipped lower until he was teasing the top of my shorts. My breathing grew heavy as I tried not to pay attention to what his hand was doing.

"Emma? Are you okay?" Andy whispered in the darkness.

1

EMMA

Present Day

Life sucks. It had taken me a while to realize that, but it finally hit me like a ton of bricks. *The only positive is that you learn from your experiences, and you grow.*

Two years ago, I'd certainly grown up when I walked in on the boy I thought I loved in bed with one of his best friends. I'd learned to let him go as time passed—or at least I thought I had.

Now, I wasn't so sure. There are people who pass through your life who forever change you and everything you thought you knew about yourself and the world. Jesse was one of them.

It had been two years since I'd left him standing in his driveway, but I'd never been able to let him go completely.

I'd debated this decision for months. I'd told myself over and over that it was stupid and pointless, but I think I always knew that I would end up here. I knew that Jesse had been a part of my old life, my old self, but I couldn't get my heart to accept that little fact.

I gripped the steering wheel tightly as I drove down I-79 from the Pittsburgh airport to my new school. Up ahead, I saw the sign welcoming me to my new state. It was ridiculous to be nervous at the sight of a simple sign. The chances of him ending up at the same school as me were slim to none.

Then, why am I here?

I took a deep breath as I glanced up at the sign just before I drove past it.

Welcome to West Virginia.

"You okay?" Andy asked from the passenger seat.

"Yeah, I'm just nervous."

"Don't be. This is a whole new experience for you. You can be whoever you want here, and no one will know you're the rich girl from Santa Monica. You can tell them you've been living in a box or something."

"I'm not nervous about anyone finding out who my dad is. I'm nervous about the fact that I might see Jesse again."

"I know. I was being sarcastic. I know it's pointless to tell you not to stress, but I'm going to—again. Don't stress. If you and Jesse were meant to be together, things will work out. If you two weren't meant to be, you'll find someone else."

"You make it sound so easy. I just want to find him, so I can at least apologize for assuming the worst. He tried to tell me, but I wouldn't listen."

"If I'd walked in on my girlfriend in bed with another guy, I would have thought the same thing you did. You can't be angry with yourself. You were trying to protect yourself from being hurt."

"I'd still like to punch Ally."

Andy snorted. "I'm her brother, and I want to punch her for what she did."

After Jesse had left, Andy and I became good friends. Ally hated that little fact, and she'd refused to speak to her brother for months. When she finally had, she'd dropped a bomb on him. I still felt sick to my stomach every time I thought about that day.

Andy called me one afternoon just as I was leaving school. "Hey, Emma. Can you come over to my house for a while? I need to talk to you."

"Yeah, I'll head over now. What's wrong?"

"I'll see you when you get here," Andy said before he ended the call.

All the way to his house, I was terrified of what he wanted to tell me. I had no idea what it could be, but I was afraid that it had something to do with Jesse. I was just starting to let him go, and I wasn't sure what I would do if I found out he had moved back.

Out of habit, I glanced at Jesse's old house when I drove past.

A new family was living there now. They'd moved in just over a month ago. The first time I'd driven by and noticed cars in the parking spaces, I'd nearly had a panic attack. I'd run into Andy's house, freaking out about it, until he'd calmed me down enough to tell me that it wasn't Jesse.

"What's up?" I asked nervously after walking into his house.

Andy had become one of my best friends, and I never bothered to knock anymore.

"Sit down. I need to talk to you," Andy said.

"You're starting to freak me out. What's wrong?"

"Ally finally decided to talk to me."

"And that's a good thing? Should I throw a party?" I asked sarcastically.

"She told me something that I think you should know."

"And that would be..."

"Jesse didn't sleep with her," Andy said quietly.

I froze. "What?"

"Ally admitted that Jesse didn't sleep with her. I guess he was upset because you two got in a fight, so he got trashed. Ally brought him home and stayed with him. She said she did it in case you came looking for him. She didn't want you to hurt him anymore. Of course, you did come to his house, and we know what happened after that. I'm so sorry, Emma. I'm so fucking pissed off at Ally right now. I have no idea how she could do that to either of you."

"He didn't cheat on me?" I whispered.

"He didn't."

"He tried to tell me, and I wouldn't listen. Oh my god, I destroyed everything." I was glad that I was already sitting down, or I would have fallen to the couch.

"Anyone in your place would have assumed the same thing."

I put my head on my knees and started sobbing. I'd destroyed everything.

"Hey, don't cry. This isn't your fault," Andy said as he rubbed my back.

"It is my fault. I should have listened to him. I have to find him!"

I tried to stand up, but Andy held me down.

"How do you plan to do that? He's thousands of miles away, Emma. The chances of you finding him are slim to none."

"I have to try. I can't let him think that I hate him. He has to know that I know the truth. Maybe if he does, he'll come back."

"Emma, it's been months. The chances of him coming back are even less than you finding him. You have to let him go."

"I can't. Please tell me that you'll help me."

He sighed. "We'll try. I just don't want you to get your hopes up."

Over the next month, we'd tried. Neither of us knew the last name of Trish's boyfriend, but we knew her last name and Jesse's. We also knew they were in West Virginia. We'd tried everything that we could think of, starting with social networks. I had gone through pages and pages of Facebook profiles, and I'd ended up with nothing. I'd looked on Twitter next and then MySpace. I'd known it was a long shot, and I had been right. Absolutely nothing had come up.

We'd searched the Web for his mom's name, but we couldn't find a thing. It was like neither of them existed online. Andy had checked with the post office and his landlord to see if either had left a forwarding address. Of course, they hadn't. It was like neither of them had ever existed, period. I'd cried when Andy told me that it was time to let it go. I had known he was right, but I hadn't wanted to accept the fact that Jesse was really gone.

When it had come time to begin submitting applications for universities, I'd started looking at a few in West Virginia. It was obvious that West Virginia University was the biggest. I knew that Trish's boyfriend had money and that Trish had expected Jesse to go to college. I was grasping at straws, but it was all I had.

My mom had been pressuring me to pick from one of the colleges she wanted me to go to, but I'd refused to give her an answer. I'd hidden my acceptance letter from my mom, not wanting her to find out that I was leaving until the last minute. I'd never even told her about Jesse, and I hadn't planned to. I'd started to leave her house when I turned eighteen, but then I couldn't bring myself to do it. I'd already felt so alone, and I hadn't been ready to go home to an empty apartment every day. My mom might not have been home much, but our staff had been. I'd been around most of them my entire life, and they were the closest thing I had to a family.

My dad had known about my relationship with Jesse, and I'd finally broken down and told him what had happened between us right before I graduated. He'd thought I was nuts to leave everything I knew in hopes of finding Jesse, but my dad had tried to understand. He'd helped me get everything ready without my mom knowing a thing.

When I'd finally told my mom where I was going, she'd flipped out on me. She'd screamed that she would cut me off and take my car. I'd calmly handed her my keys, and I'd told her that I was leaving, and she couldn't do a damn thing about it.

When she'd called my dad, he'd explained that he would take care of me financially, so she'd kicked me out. It hadn't seemed to bother her that I was her only daughter, and I hadn't been surprised by her reaction. She had never cared for me like a mom should, so why should she start now?

My dad had arranged for someone to pick me up, and I'd spent the rest of the summer in his apartment in L.A. Andy had become one of my best friends by this point, so he'd spent most of his summer at my house when he wasn't working.

He'd refused to let me go all the way to West Virginia on my own, so we'd looked at apartments close to campus where he could stay. He'd claimed that he had nothing to stick around for in California, but I wasn't so sure. He couldn't afford the plane ticket to go with me, so I'd used that knowledge to blackmail him into letting me pay for his rent for the first few months until he could find a job. He hadn't been happy about it, but he'd finally agreed. He hadn't had any other options.

Ally had disappeared the day after she graduated. She hadn't been around much anyway, but Andy was worried. He would get a text message here and there from her, but that was it. It was enough to let him know she was alive, but it wasn't enough to make him stop worrying. I knew I was being a cruel bitch, but I didn't care if she dropped off the face of the earth. She'd destroyed my life, and I hadn't been able to do a thing about it. I had wanted to go after her when Andy told me what she had done, but he wouldn't let me. I knew that she would kick my ass in a fight, but I hadn't cared. As long as I could make her hurt a little bit, I would be happy.

I'd fought with Andy over it, but he'd finally convinced me not to hunt her down. I'd understood where he was coming from, but it hadn't made me feel any better. She was his sister, but she'd hurt me. I just wanted to make her hurt, too.

"I think that's our exit," Andy said, pulling me from my memories.

I glanced up to see that he was right. I was nervous as I followed the signs pointing me to the university campus. The roads were clogged with students moving in for the school year, so it took a while to get through.

After what seemed like years, we finally arrived. This was it. I was finally here. I pulled into a parking lot directly across the road from a large brick building with my dorm name displayed on the front of it. Tons of students and their parents were unloading cars in the parking lot and along the street.

I felt a pang of jealousy as I watched a mom and dad hug their daughter a few cars in front of mine. I wondered what that would feel like—to have a dad around and a mother who actually cared. I tried to ignore my hurt feelings, but they wouldn't leave. Kids were supposed to have their parents around to take care of them. Instead, I'd snagged a dad who cared from thousands of miles away and a mom who didn't give a damn about me.

"Come on, let's get you checked in," Andy said before stepping out of my car.

My dad had known that my mom had taken away the car she'd bought for me, so he'd had a brand new SUV waiting for me at the Pittsburgh airport. I knew it made me a spoiled brat to accept it, but I didn't care. I needed a car, and my dad had helped me out. I honestly thought the only reason he was helping me with all of this was because he felt guilty for leaving me alone with my mom for so long.

Andy kept his arm around my shoulders as we walked to the dorm. He'd become protective of me after Jesse left, and I was secretly glad. It was nice to have someone there for me just because he wanted to be. In this world, there were too few genuinely kind people to let one disappear from my life.

A line of students was waiting to be checked in when we walked into the lobby. I tapped my foot impatiently as the line slowly moved. I hated to wait.

When it was finally my turn, I gave the girl behind the counter my name and showed her my I.D. Once everything was checked off, she gave me a map of the campus and my key. I was instructed to go up to the third floor and turn left. She eyed Andy warily as she informed me that this was not a coed dorm, and no men were allowed after nine at night. I rolled my eyes, but I said nothing before we turned and walked away. I noticed several girls eyeing Andy, like they wouldn't mind having him in their dorm room after hours. He smiled back at a few of them, but he didn't stop to talk.

"If you want to flirt, go ahead. You need to remove your arm from my shoulders though before someone thinks you're my boyfriend. I don't want people to assume I'm the idiot girlfriend who stands around while her boyfriend eye-fucks the girls around them."

He laughed. "You worry too much. I won't eye-fuck anyone."

"You can eye-fuck all you want. Just don't act like my brother or boyfriend while you do it."

"Maybe I want to pretend I'm your boyfriend." He bent down and gave me a sloppy kiss on the cheek.

"You're an ass," I growled as I wiped his kiss away.

"I know."

He finally dropped his arm from around my shoulders once we made it to the third floor. I wasn't sure if it was because he really was looking for someone to hook up with or because we had to walk single file down the hallway since girls were everywhere, trying to carry boxes. Either way, I was glad.

Once Andy and I had started hanging out a lot back in California, we'd had to fight off the rumors within his circle of friends. Everyone had assumed that we were a couple since we were together all the time, but we'd finally managed to convince them that it wasn't true. Andy and I'd talked about whether or not there was anything between us, and we'd both agreed that there wasn't.

We were nothing more than friends, and I was relieved. I wasn't over Jesse, and I wasn't sure that I ever would be. Andy kept up with his man-whore ways, and I moped by myself, wishing daily that Jesse would come back.

"Hey, I think this is your room," Andy said from behind me.

I turned back to see that he was right. I'd been so preoccupied that I hadn't even realized that I'd passed right by my room. I unlocked my door and threw it open. It was ten times smaller than the room I'd had at my mom's house, but I loved it anyway. My dad had called the school and arranged for me to have a private room since I was his daughter, so I knew my room was smaller than most since it only slept one.

A small closet was only a few feet away from the main door. A desk was against the far wall, next to the one and only window. I could see from here that the window's view was of the parking lot out front. A twin-sized bed sat on the opposite side of the room, and another door was in front of the bed. I walked over and opened it to see that I had my own bathroom. It was small, but it was more than I'd expected. Now, I wouldn't have to fight with every other girl on the floor to shower daily.

"What do you think?" Andy asked as he sat down on my bed.

"I love it," I said as I smiled.

"Really? It's kind of tiny. I've seen your room at your dad's house, and this is the size of your closet there."

"I don't care. It's mine, and my mother has no say here. I love it."

"You're so weird," Andy said as he spotted a stack of boxes beside the desk. "At least your stuff made it here safe and sound."

"Yeah, it would have sucked if they had lost my crap."

"You want to get unpacked before you take me to my place?"

"Nah, I can do that later. I need to make a quick stop before we go to your place though."

"Okay…"

He eyed me suspiciously, but I ignored him. He was going to kill me when he realized what I'd done.

I locked up and led the way back downstairs. I had to hug the wall more than once as girls passed by me with their arms full of boxes. Once we made it outside, I walked to my car and unlocked it. I double-checked my directions as I waited for Andy to get into the car.

"Where are we going?" he asked.

"You'll see."

"Emma…"

"Don't use that tone with me. You'll see soon enough."

I drove through the congested traffic as I searched for the street signs I needed. Once we were off the main drag, the traffic thinned, and it was easier to watch for my destination. I spotted it and quickly pulled into the driveway of a two-story brick house.

"What are we doing here?" Andy asked.

"I have to pick up something."

"What?" He spotted a car in the yard with a *For Sale* sign on it. "Emma, you didn't."

"Shut up." I stepped out and started walking toward the house just as the front door opened.

"Can I help you?" an older lady asked.

"Hi, I'm Emma. We spoke on the phone about the car you had for sale online."

"Of course. Let me grab the keys, and I'll be right out."

I walked across the yard to where the car was sitting. It wasn't the nicest thing out there, but as long as it ran, I'd take it. I knew asking my dad for money to get Andy a car would be too much, so I'd saved some of my monthly allowance from my dad until I had enough to get him something decent. He only planned to stick around for a few months, but he still needed something to drive while he was here.

"I'm going to kill you," Andy whispered in my ear.

I jumped, not realizing that he'd followed me. "You need something to drive."

"I'll take the bus."

"You'll take your car," I countered.

"Here are the keys if you want to start it up," the elderly woman said from behind Andy.

I turned and took them from her hand before walking over to the car. After unlocking the door, I started the car, and I was relieved when it took right off.

"Can we take it for a drive?" I asked.

The lady seemed unsure. "If you do, I'd like to go with you. It's nothing personal. I just don't want it to disappear."

"Of course!" I said.

I got out and then sat in the backseat. Andy and the lady sat down in the front. I knew nothing about cars, so I figured it would be better if Andy did the test-drive. Andy put it in drive and pulled onto the street. We circled the block a few times before he parked it back in her yard.

"It seems to be in good shape. How much are you asking?" he asked.

"I wanted three for it. It was my husband's car, and he recently passed away. I hate to sell it, but I need the money."

"We'll take it," I said before Andy could say anything. I pulled my wallet from my purse, counted out thirty-five hundred dollars, and handed the cash to the lady.

She looked confused when she finished counting it herself. "Sweetie, you overpaid me. I only wanted three."

"And I think it's worth thirty-five," I said calmly.

Her eyes filled with tears, and she hugged me. "Thank you. You have no idea how much this helps me. I've barely been able to afford food since my husband died."

"You're welcome," I said as I hugged her back.

It was so unfair how some people struggled day after day while others rolled around in millions of dollars. I knew it wasn't my money to give, but I didn't care. My dad wouldn't miss a few thousand, and this lady needed it more than we did.

We finished up with the paperwork, and the lady walked back inside her house.

"That was nice of you," Andy said.

"She needed it, and I wanted to help her," I said as I walked to my car.

"You're a good person, Emma. I hope you know that."

I didn't answer as I got into my car before heading in the direction of Andy's apartment. After what I'd done to Jesse, I didn't feel like a good person.

2
EMMA

Jesse was on my mind as I drove to Andy's place. I wondered how different he would be since the last time I'd seen him. Two years was a long time, and people could change a lot in that amount of time. I knew I had. *What if I find him, and he's completely different? What if he isn't someone I could love anymore?* I wasn't sure how well I would handle finding him, only to lose him again.

I saw Andy's apartment complex up ahead. It looked exactly like it did on the website. I'd set everything up through emails and phone calls, and I had to admit that I was a bit nervous about renting something without actually seeing it for myself first. I only hoped that his apartment was how it had been described.

The manager had instructed us to use the parking lot around the back of the building, and we did as he'd said. I parked in the visitor parking area while Andy parked in the space reserved for apartment tenants. After exiting our cars, we walked through the back entrance and up to the front desk. A young guy was sitting behind the desk, looking bored out of his mind.

When he saw us, he took his feet off the desk and stood up. "Can I help you?"

"I'm supposed to move into 2B. I think everything was taken care of over the phone," Andy said.

The boy sat down and started typing on the computer in front of him. "Driver's license, please."

Andy pulled it from his wallet and handed it to the guy. After a few minutes of typing, he returned the driver's license and handed over a set of keys to Andy.

"You're all set. My name is Josh, and if you need any help getting settled in, just let me know."

"Thanks, I will," Andy said.

We turned and walked back toward the rear doors. After locating the elevator, I pushed the button to take us up. The doors slid open instantly, and we shot up to the second floor. Andy's apartment was right past the elevators. When he opened the door, I was shocked at how nice it was. It was even better than the website had described. I'd selected this place because it was one of the few where I could afford to pay rent until Andy saved up some cash. I couldn't spend too much money, or my dad would know that something was up.

The apartment was the perfect size for one person. When we walked in, we were standing in the living room. The apartment came fully furnished, so there was already a blue couch and chair along with a coffee table and end table. A medium-sized plasma television was mounted to the wall directly across from the couch. To the left was the kitchen with the standard white appliances. There wasn't a ton of counter space or cabinets, but it was enough for a single guy to work with. Across the living room, a door led to the bathroom that included a single sink, a toilet, and a small shower. Next to the bathroom was Andy's bedroom with a full-sized bed beside the window and a dresser.

"This place is awesome. Thanks, Emma," Andy said as we finished checking the place out.

"No problem. I'm not going to lie. I'm slightly jealous here. I felt bad for putting you here because I thought it would be a dump, but it definitely isn't. I feel like I should move in here, and you can live in my dorm."

"It's nicer than anyplace I've lived in before, and I doubt your school would want me in a dorm full of college girls."

"You're right. I'd get kicked out of school if I left you there alone. Well, enjoy it here."

"I will. I should have moved to West Virginia years ago. Compared to California, this place is cheap."

I laughed. "You can stay here for as long as you want. I might not even go back to California once I finish school. I'll just go wherever feels right."

"I don't blame you. I know enough about your mom to understand why you'd want to stay far away."

I frowned as I thought about my mom. Even though she had known where I was, she hadn't tried to contact me once since she kicked me out. It was like she didn't even care.

"I didn't mean to make you sad. I'm sorry."

"It's fine. I need to get back to my dorm and unpack though. I have freshman orientation tomorrow morning. I don't want to miss that. Maybe…maybe I'll see him there."

"Just don't get your hopes up, okay? I don't want to see you get hurt again."

"I won't, I promise," I said.

He didn't need to know that my hopes were already up.

I didn't see Jesse at orientation or anywhere around campus during the next week. Andy was hell-bent on finding a job as soon as possible, so I walked around campus by myself while he was off job-hunting.

It was strange to be on my own, but I kind of liked it. After Jesse had left, nothing had changed at school. I had still been the perfect princess who everyone crowded around, so being alone now was refreshing.

I spent the entire week exploring campus to find my classes, and I also checked out downtown Morgantown. One thing was for sure—this was definitely a party town. Bars were everywhere. It was too bad that I didn't have a fake I.D. to get into any of them.

West Virginia was very different from California. Back home, you didn't talk to strangers. You went about your business and avoided eye contact with anyone you didn't know. Here, it was the complete opposite. People would start a conversation with you while you were in line at Starbucks or while you were waiting for the light to change to cross the street. It was cool to hear the Southern accents coming from everyone's mouths. Most of their accents weren't strong, but a few had a serious twang.

It was a complete culture shock, and I loved it. I'd been here for less than a week, and I already felt at home.

I'd made a few friends at the dorm, too. While we weren't painting each other's nails and talking boys, it was nice to have a conversation with another human being besides Andy. The girls across the hall from me weren't very friendly, but everyone else seemed to be. They all asked where I'd moved from and were shocked when I told them. They couldn't imagine wanting to move to West Virginia from California. I didn't agree though. There was just something about the down-to-earth nature of these people that made me feel ten times more welcome than I'd ever felt at home.

I was nervous as I got ready for my first official day of classes. I straightened my hair until my natural waves were completely gone. After making sure that my makeup was perfect, I grabbed my bag and headed for the door.

I texted Andy to let him know I'd meet him for lunch after I finished my second class. We'd stumbled upon a cute little family-owned restaurant one evening, and we had decided to meet there for lunch today.

Nervous butterflies made my stomach churn as I walked to my first class. I hated the fact that I didn't have Andy with me, but he wasn't enrolled as a student. I had to suck it up and do this on my own. I was a big girl. I could do this.

My mouth fell open when I walked into my first class. It was huge, seating probably close to two-hundred students. It wasn't even a classroom. It was a small auditorium. I should have expected as much since it was English 101, and all freshmen were required to take an English class.

All of the seats in the back rows were already filled. I slowly made my way down the steps, my eyes searching for an empty spot. Almost halfway down, I found one on the end. I darted down the steps and fell down into it, relieved that I wouldn't be stuck up front. Even after all this time, I still hated to sit in the front row.

"Hi, I'm Abby," the girl beside me said.

I turned to look at her and smiled. "I'm Emma. It's nice to meet you."

"Likewise," she said as she returned my smile.

Even sitting down, I could tell that Abby was a tiny girl. She was stick thin but not in a way that looked unhealthy. Her skin was porcelain white and went perfectly with her bright red hair and the freckles across her nose.

"So, where are you from?" she asked.

"California. And you?"

"Tennessee."

"Your accent is one of the strongest I've heard so far."

She laughed. "Yeah, I've noticed that, too. You have a bit of an accent, too…or maybe it's a lack of an accent. It's strange hearing all of these different dialects after growing up in Tennessee and then coming here."

"I'm still trying to adjust to the dialect here, too. I'm the odd one out."

"Not at all. I've heard a few different accents around here. You'll fit right in, except you're a bit more tan than most of the people I've seen."

"My friend Andy and I pretty much lived on the beach all summer. We both like to surf."

"That's so cool. I've only been to the ocean one time, but I loved it. I hope I can go back sometime."

This girl was so sweet. Between her personality and her tiny appearance, I wanted to pick her up and hug her.

Preparing for class, I pulled my book and a notebook from my bag. Once I had everything out, I turned in my seat and searched the sea of faces behind me. After a week with no sign of Jesse, I didn't expect to see him, so I wasn't disappointed when I didn't. I sighed in defeat as I turned back to face the front, and I slouched down into my seat.

I knew I shouldn't, but I couldn't help but feel disappointment each time I looked for him and found nothing. From the beginning, I knew that there was a good chance he wouldn't be here. West Virginia was a small state, but he could be at any college.

The professor walked in and greeted us. The room was so large that he had to speak into a microphone clipped to his suit jacket. One thing was for sure—if I were looking for a one-on-one education, I definitely wasn't going to find it in this class.

After introducing himself as Professor Vernon, he handed out a stack of papers to each person on the bottom row and had them pass the papers back to the rest of us. Once I got it, I saw it was our class syllabus. I flipped through it quickly, skimming over the rules and going straight to the assignments we would have for the rest of the semester.

I wanted to groan out loud when I saw that almost our entire grade would be based on three twenty-page papers and our final. I didn't mind writing, but twenty pages seemed a bit extreme. *What happened to those damn worksheets we did in high school that made us circle the noun? I liked those.*

We spent the next ninety minutes going over the syllabus from front to back. It was obvious that I was going to hate this class. Once we were dismissed, I packed my papers and book into my backpack, and then I followed everyone up the stairs and back outside. I didn't realize that Abby was still beside me until she spoke up.

"What's your next class?"

"History with Professor Cale."

"Me, too. Is it okay if I walk with you?" she asked.

"Nope," I joked.

"Oh…okay. I'll see you later," Abby said quietly as she hurried ahead of me.

"Abby! Abby, wait! I was kidding!" I yelled as I raced to catch up with her.

She looked surprised. "I'm sorry. I thought you were serious."

I laughed. "No, I was just messing with you."

I found it strange that she would flee like that, but I didn't ask questions. Something told me that she'd been picked on before. She was timid, like most kids who had been bullied.

We walked the rest of the way to our next class in silence. I was afraid to say anything else to her. I didn't want to hurt her feelings.

Our history class was smaller but not by much. We found seats a few rows from the back and sat down. I waited until most of the seats were filled before scanning the room for Jesse. Again, he was nowhere to be found. I sighed in defeat, causing Abby to look over at me.

"You okay?" she asked.

"Yeah, just looking for my friend. I haven't seen him in a long time, but I thought he might be at this school."

She nodded. "I see. Well, this campus is huge, so he might be here, and you just haven't crossed paths yet."

"I hope that's what it is," I said as I pulled out my book.

The professor entered the room and introduced herself. The class went exactly like the last. I groaned again as I realized I would have to write at least one paper for this class, too. *I better learn to type fast, or I'm gonna be screwed.*

Abby invited me to sit with her at lunch, but I declined. She seemed sad until I told her that I had plans with my friend to eat off-campus. After I promised to eat with her on Wednesday, she perked right back up. I waved good-bye, and then I walked back across campus to where my car was parked.

After fighting the lunch traffic, I finally pulled into the restaurant's parking lot. I didn't spot Andy when I walked in, but after searching the room a few times, I finally noticed him in the back corner. Once I spotted him, I was shocked that it had taken me so long to find him. While most of the residents were tan, they had nothing on Andy. With his darkened skin and sun-kissed hair, he stood out from everyone else.

If things had been different from the beginning, I wouldn't have thought twice about crushing on him. Instead, all I could see when I looked at him was Jesse. They were so much alike, both in how they acted and how they looked.

"What are you doing all the way back here?" I asked.

"There weren't any other tables when I came in. It's actually kind of nice to be away from everyone else." He said through a mouthful of food. *How polite, Andy.*

"I guess so." I sat down and picked up a menu. I still had a few nerves leftover from this morning, so I wasn't really hungry.

When the waitress came over, I ordered a grilled cheese and an iced coffee. It wasn't the most appealing mix, but I didn't care. Grilled cheese was the only thing that looked even remotely appetizing. The waitress gave me a strange look, but she said nothing as she took my order and left.

"So, how was school?" Andy asked.

"It was okay. I'm not looking forward to all the papers I'm going to have to write this semester though, and I'm sure it'll be worse once I get through my classes tomorrow. I have a laptop, but I need to get a printer, so I don't have to constantly run to the library to print stuff."

"Then, go get one, moneybags."

I stuck out my tongue. "You're hilarious. When do you start your new job?"

"Tomorrow. The guy I talked to seemed pretty nice. He had me draw a few things, and he was pretty impressed. I think I'm going to like it there."

"I'm glad," I said as the waitress put my food down in front of me.

I'd learned that Andy was as talented as Jesse when it came to drawing. He just wasn't interested in tattooing, like Jesse was. Instead, Andy used his skills to design custom surfboards for some of the surf shops back home. Obviously, West Virginia wasn't a surfing kind of place, but Andy had managed to snag a job at a local skateboard shop. Neither of us had expected him to find anything even close to his old job. When he'd called me to tell me that he'd found this job, we'd both been ecstatic.

I started nibbling on my grilled cheese as Andy talked about some of the guys he'd met at the shop. It took me a minute to realize that he'd stopped talking. I looked up to see his mouth hanging open in shock.

"Andy? What's wrong?" I asked.

He just shook his head as he continued to stare over my shoulder. I was terrified to look behind me, but I did anyway. My mouth dropped open in shock as well. There was no way she could be here, yet there she was. *Ally*. She had just walked through the door, and she was making her way to the counter. I sat, frozen, as she walked behind the counter and continued into the back room. It appeared that she was not only here, but she worked here as well.

"What the hell? What is she doing in West Virginia?" he asked.

I felt my blood start to boil. I knew exactly why she was here. "I have a pretty good idea," I spit out.

His eyes widened as he realized what—or rather, who—I was talking about. "Jesse."

"Jesse," I confirmed.

"How did she even know where to find him? We searched for months, and nothing came up. There are thousands of people in this town, and we just took a chance and hoped for the best when we came here."

"She obviously came here to find him. I'm betting if she has a job here, then she plans to stay for a while. She must have found him."

"Fuck!" Andy growled.

Nausea overtook me as I realized what that could mean. "Andy, you don't think…"

"What?"

"You don't think she told him what she knows, do you? I never wanted him to know!" Tears were threatening to run down my cheeks, but I refused to let them flow.

"She wouldn't."

"Are you serious right now? Look at what she's already done! There's no way that she didn't tell him."

"Unless…"

"Unless, what?"

"Unless she didn't tell him yet. Maybe she's saving it for when you show up. I never kept it a secret that you were searching for him. Maybe she wants to use it to hurt you if you ever found him."

I paled as I thought about it. He was right. That was something that Ally would do without thinking twice. When it came to her, she always did what she needed to make sure she would come out on top.

"Oh god, you're right," I whispered. "She's going to destroy me as soon as she knows I'm in town."

"Breathe, Emma. It's going to be okay. I'm going to go and talk to her to see if I can find out where Jesse is."

"No!" I shouted, causing a few people at the tables around us to glance our way. "You can't. As soon as she sees me, she's going to go running to him."

Andy sighed. "What do you think we should do then?"

"Let's get out of here. We'll wait a few hours and then come back. We can see where she goes once she leaves here. She might lead us right to him."

"This is nuts. Just let me go talk to her."

"Andy, I know she's your sister, but you can't. She is a manipulative bitch, and she hates me. Anything you do to help will only make things worse. Let's try my plan first and see what happens."

"Fine, but we need to get out of here before she sees us."

"Let's go," I said as I threw a few bills on the table.

I turned to the door while Ally was standing behind the counter. She was in deep conversation with some guy that I assumed was the manager. As long as she kept talking to him, she wouldn't notice our escape.

I didn't breathe until we were out of the restaurant and walking down the sidewalk toward where my car was parked. Andy's car was parked a few spaces behind mine.

"Let's head over to your apartment to wait," I told him as I unlocked my car.

He nodded. "I'll see you in a few."

3
EMMA

I was a nervous wreck all the way back to Andy's house. I'd never factored seeing Ally into my plans, especially seeing her and Jesse together at once. There was no doubt in my mind that she'd found him since she had a job here. If she hadn't, she would have moved on and continued her search. I mean, *come on*. She hadn't come all this way to get a job as a waitress.

How could he even stand to look at her after what she'd put me through? Surely to God, he had to know that she'd played us both. Jesse wasn't stupid.

Oh god, what if she'd come all this way to tell him how much she loved him, and he took her in? What if they are together now? My stomach rolled at the thought of her touching him. I didn't think I could handle seeing the two of them together.

By the time I made it to Andy's, I was on the verge of a full-blown panic attack. He had to practically carry me up to his apartment. Once he managed to get me inside, he put me on the couch and sat down beside me.

"Emma, look at me. You've got to breathe," he whispered as he hugged me.

I relaxed into him, unable to sit up. Every bad possibility that I could think of was rolling through my head. *What if she tells him?* I didn't think I could stand to look at Jesse, knowing he knew just what I'd done.

"I can't handle this," I cried out.

"Yes, you can. You didn't come all this way just to give up. So what if Ally is here? It doesn't change the fact that you still care about him. It's been two years, Emma, since you walked away from him, and you still can't let go. That should tell you something. You still love him as much as you did back then. People search their entire lives to find someone they care about as much as you care about Jesse. You can't just walk away because of Ally."

"What if she tells him?" I whispered.

I felt him tense.

"There's nothing we can do if she does. I told you from the beginning that I thought he should know. I never wanted to hide it from him. Lying to him won't make it go away. It'll only haunt you until you tell him the truth."

"I plan to tell him once we get everything worked out. I'm just afraid that he'll hate me." That was mostly true. Honestly, I wasn't sure if I had ever planned to tell Jesse the truth. I wasn't sure I could handle his reaction.

"Then, he'll hate me, too. What's done is done, and there's nothing either of us can do about it. I wish I could change what happened, but I can't."

"We were stupid," I said.

"We were."

I closed my eyes as the worst mistake of my life played over and over in my head.

"Emma? Are you okay?" Andy whispered in the darkness as we sat together on his couch.

I raised my head to look up at him. "No."

"Me either," he said as his other hand came up to cup my face.

A small amount of light was coming from the kitchen. It was enough to see him leaning down toward me. I only had a second to realize what he was about to do before he did it. I froze as his lips crushed against mine. I gasped in shock, but I didn't pull away.

My head was fuzzy as I opened my mouth to allow his tongue to slip inside. I moaned as he pushed me, so I was lying back on the couch with him on top of me. Fuck, this feels good. My head swam from both lust and the alcohol I'd consumed.

Both of his hands went to my hips and pulled me tighter against him. I could feel him through his shorts, and lust shot through my veins, making me moan. His breath was ragged as he kissed a trail from my lips to my neck. I moved my head to the side to give him better access.

"You smell so good," I panted.

"You taste good," he muttered before running his tongue across my skin.

Goose bumps broke out erupted everywhere as he continued to kiss and lick his way across my skin. He raised me up long enough to pull my shirt over my head before pushing me back down onto the couch. His hands skimmed across my stomach, causing my muscles to jump. His kisses felt like fire as he kissed between my breasts and down my stomach. I wiggled my hips, trying to feel his thickness against me.

"Emma? Emma! Where did you go?" Andy asked.

"Sorry, I was just thinking about…"

"About, what?"

"That night."

He was silent as he studied me. So many things had been left unsaid between us, even after all this time. We'd talked about what had happened but not really. Every time one of us had mentioned it, the other would change the subject. I knew that we would have to talk about it eventually, but I couldn't. If we admitted to what had happened, then it would be true.

"Don't think about it. Think about how you're going to get Jesse back," Andy said as he hugged me.

"You're right. I can't let Ally destroy everything again. I came all this way to find Jesse, and that's what I'm going to do."

I felt like an idiot as I sat outside in my car with Andy, waiting for Ally to leave work. It felt wrong to follow someone, like we were stalking her, but I didn't have a better plan at the moment.

The restaurant had closed almost twenty minutes ago. We'd been sitting here for over half an hour, and there was still no sign of Ally. Surely, she would be leaving before much longer.

I had class early tomorrow, and I didn't want to sit out here all night. I could barely keep my eyes open as it was. More than once, Andy had nudged me when my eyes started to close.

This is getting ridiculous.

I opened my mouth to suggest going home and trying again another night when the restaurant door opened. Ally and a few other girls came out. I watched as Ally waved good night to them, and then she walked over to an older model Ford Escort.

"Showtime," I said to Andy as I started my car.

It was almost eleven, but a few cars were still on the road. As I followed her, I made sure to stay far enough back, so she wouldn't notice me. She had no reason to suspect someone was following her, but it would look suspicious if the same car tailed her the entire way home. She slowed and turned into a driveway next to a one-story white house. I was surprised at just how close to campus she was.

I parked a few cars down the street and watched as she walked inside the house.

"Now what?" Andy asked.

"I have no idea. Maybe wait around for a few to see if someone comes out?"

"Really?" Andy asked in disbelief.

"Do you have a better idea?" I shot back.

"Yeah, let's go knock on the door and see if Jesse answers."

"And what if he doesn't? Just because she's here doesn't mean he is. This might not even be her house. She could be visiting a friend."

"Okay, you've got a point. But do you really think someone is going to randomly walk out of the house this late at night?"

I sighed. I didn't, but I wasn't sure what to do. "Not really."

"Why don't we come back tomorrow? If the car is still there, we'll know it's her house."

"I guess," I said, unwilling to leave just yet.

"Come on, Emma, we need to go. We're starting to act like stalkers."

He had a point. I never thought I'd find myself desperate enough to sit outside a house, hoping that someone walked out.

"Okay. I'll drive by tomorrow before class to see if anyone is around."

No one was outside when I drove by the next morning. I hadn't really expected to see anyone, but it still sucked. I was starting to feel desperate. There was a good chance that he was in that house, and I couldn't even see him. I hated the fact that he might be living with Ally, but I couldn't do a thing about it. I just had to wait and hope for the best.

My two classes were much like the day before. In each one, we went over our class syllabus the entire time. Abby wasn't in either of them, but I managed to meet a few new people who seemed nice enough.

I sat by myself at lunch. I knew that I could sit with one of the girls I'd met earlier, but I didn't want to. I was too preoccupied with finding Jesse to be social. After lunch, I dropped off my books in my dorm room before getting in my car and driving to the restaurant where Ally worked.

Her car was parked out front, so I knew she wouldn't be home. Now was my chance. I had to go while she wasn't at the house. I was terrified as I drove to the house she had entered last night.

Maybe if I knocked on the door, Jesse would answer. Again, I knew I was grasping at straws, but I didn't care.

I parked a little ways down from the house and stepped out of my car. My heart was beating out of my chest as I walked up the steps to the front door. I took a deep breath before knocking on the door. When no one answered, I knocked again. I stood outside, feeling like an idiot, as I waited for someone to answer. After the third time, I finally gave up and accepted that no one was home. I turned and walked back down the steps and to my car. I sat in my car and waited for over an hour to see if someone would come home.

With no signs of life, I finally gave up and drove back to my dorm. I had a small assignment from my math class today, and I needed to get it done before I forgot about it.

After I finished my assignment, I drove to the local mall and purchased the printer I'd mentioned to Andy before. It was sad that I was excited to go out for a printer. I had absolutely no life outside of finding Jesse and spending time with Andy. Since Jesse was still a puzzle and Andy was working late, that left me with my printer.

I returned home and took my time with hooking it up and installing the software. When that was done, I checked my Facebook page to see if I had any new messages. I smiled when I saw one from Lucy, asking how I was.

She thought I was nuts for traveling across the country to find Jesse, but she still loved me. When I'd first told her about my plans, she had gotten mad at me. She'd pointed out that there was no way we would be able to stay close while living so far apart. I'd known she was right, but it hadn't changed my decision.

After messaging her back, I sent my dad an email to let him know that everything was going well. Then, I shut off my laptop and crawled into bed. There was no use in going back out to see if Ally had returned to the same house. Even if she had, it wouldn't mean that Jesse was there with her.

I closed my eyes as exhaustion took over. The last thought I had was whether or not I was insane.

Over the next two weeks, I fell into my new schedule. I only had morning classes, so after I was finished with those, I went back to my dorm and worked on my homework. When that was done, I'd either go to Andy's house on his nights off, or I'd park outside of Ally's house, like a stalker. I knew I was being pathetic, but I couldn't bring myself to care. Occasionally, I'd mix it up by going out for dinner with Abby, but that had been rare. I considered her a friend, but we weren't close enough for me to tell her why I was really here.

When I went to Andy's, we'd order something to eat and watch movies. Once in awhile, he'd drag me out to see a movie in an actual theater, or we'd do something dorky, like bowling. I had to admit that I was glad he'd decided to come with me.

I'd made a few friends since school started, but I was too focused on Jesse to put much energy into bonding with people. I knew something would have to give, or I was going to lose my damn mind. My stress levels were through the roof at this point.

Things finally did change one night, but it wasn't in the way that I'd hoped. As each day had passed, I'd found myself spending more and more hours outside of Ally's house. More than once, I'd fallen asleep and woken up the next morning, almost late for class. I'd started bringing my Kindle with me to pass the time, and it'd seemed to help most nights.

Unfortunately for me, I'd forgotten my Kindle tonight. Andy was working again, and I couldn't call him to keep me awake. I'd caught myself drifting off several times, only to jerk awake. I must have fallen asleep because the next thing I knew, it was dark, and someone was tapping on my window. I groaned as I looked at the time on my dashboard. It was after midnight.

As I rolled my window down, I expected one of Ally's neighbors to be there, waiting for me, so that they could yell at me for parking in front of their house. Instead, I stared at the face of a shocked Ally.

"What the fuck?" she shouted.

I froze as I stared at the person I hated most in the entire world. We'd never been alone together since everything had happened.

"I can't fucking believe this! I thought I was nuts when I kept seeing this car every night when I came home. What the hell are you doing here?"

"Looking for Jesse," I said defiantly. I knew I was busted, so there was no point in trying to lie.

"You're pathetic. Did you really come all this way to find him?"

"Did you?" I asked. "Because I think you did."

"Maybe I did, but at least I'm not parked outside of his house every night like a fucking psycho."

"So, he does live here," I said excitedly.

She'd given me the information I needed. Now that I knew he was here, there was no way that I was leaving without talking to him. She would have to beat me unconscious to keep me away.

"He does, but he doesn't want to see you. I think you've hurt him enough."

"I did hurt him, but I won't again."

I started to open my door, but she slammed it shut.

"Let me out of the fucking car."

"No. I won't let you go in there and destroy everything I've worked for."

"What? Are you together now?"

"We are."

I felt like I'd been punched in the stomach. The moment I had seen Ally that day in the diner, I'd suspected something like this had happened. I wasn't going to leave until I had the chance to talk to Jesse though. Maybe if he knew I was here, he'd leave her and come back to me.

"We'll see if you are after I talk to him," I said as I tried to open my door again.

Ally refused to budge.

"Move."

"Not until you listen to what I have to say."

"Then, spit it out, so I can go talk to him."

"I'm pregnant!" she blurted out.

My mouth dropped open, and then I froze. "There's no way. You're lying."

"I'm not. It was an accident, but there's nothing Jesse or I can do about it. I have his baby growing inside of me."

Forget being punched in the stomach. I'm going to vomit. This couldn't be happening. There was no way that he could have slept with her after what

41

she had done to us. She'd destroyed us, and she'd destroyed his friendship with Andy in the process.

"Do you really want to go in there and take my baby's father from her? Because that's what will happen if you do. Jesse will leave me for you, and I'll be left alone to take care of this baby. You'll destroy my child's life."

I couldn't believe this was happening. How could Jesse have been so stupid? And how could I have been so stupid that I'd held out hope for a boy two years after he disappeared from my life? I was doing nothing more than chasing a high school crush while assuming it was true love.

I thought about the way I'd been raised. If I were to go to Jesse and he left Ally, I would be putting his child in the same situation I had been in. Ally was a spiteful bitch, and I knew she would never let Jesse see his child if he'd left her. His son or daughter would be forced to live with a manipulative bitch while his or her dad wasn't around. I hated Ally, but I couldn't do that to her child. It was innocent despite the circumstances surrounding his or her parents.

"This can't be happening," I whispered.

"It *is* happening. Look at my stomach."

She pulled her shirt tight and turned sideways to show me the beginning of a baby bump. Bile rose in my throat, but I forced myself not to vomit. I wouldn't give her the satisfaction.

"I guess it is," I mumbled.

"I won, and you lost. It's time for you to accept that and go back to California where you belong," she said with a triumphant grin.

I wanted to get out of my car and smack that grin right off her face. I wanted to so badly that my hand was on the door handle before I even realized what I was doing. I couldn't believe that I was about to hit a pregnant woman. *Dear God, I've lost my mind.* I needed to get out of here and fast if I wanted to leave with my sanity intact.

"Move out of my way," I said as I started my car.

"Leaving so soon?" she asked sweetly.

"Get the *fuck* out of my way, or I swear to God, I'll make you move, pregnant or not."

She laughed as I put my car in drive, and then I tore out of my parking spot.

4
EMMA

I knew Andy had to work tonight, but I hoped he was at home by now.
There was no way that I could go back to my dorm room and sit alone
while all of this was going through my head. I was hanging on to my sanity
by a thread, and I knew that if I was by myself while dealing with this, I'd
lose it.

I nearly cried in relief when I pulled into his apartment complex
parking lot, and I saw his car sitting there. I didn't have to be alone. He
would help me. I ran across the lot, and in too much of a hurry to use the
elevator, I sprinted up the stairs to his floor.

Tears were streaming down my cheeks as I beat on his door. I prayed
that he hadn't fallen asleep yet. I had a key to his apartment, but I hated to
use it this late at night. I didn't want him to think someone was trying to
break in.

The door opened, and Andy was standing there. He took one look at
me and pulled me into his arms.

"Emma, what's wrong?" he asked.

I was crying too hard to speak, so I shook my head.

"Who's that?" an unfamiliar female voice asked.

I hadn't even thought about the possibility of him having someone
over. I looked over his shoulder to see a pretty red head standing behind
him. From the fact that she was wearing his shirt, it was obvious that she
planned to stay the night with him.

"This is Emma," Andy told her.

"Who is she? Is she going to be okay?" the woman asked as she looked at me warily.

Obviously, that my tears were making her uncomfortable.

"She's…she's my family. I hate to cut our evening short, but you need to go," Andy said as he walked me over to the couch and pushed me down onto the cushions.

"It's fine. You'll call me?" she asked as she grabbed her pants off the floor and threw them on.

"I will."

Not bothering to take off his shirt, she picked up her purse and walked out the door.

"I'm sorry." I hiccuped. "I didn't mean to ruin your night."

"It's cool. She was just a hook-up anyway. What's wrong?"

I couldn't look at him. I was ashamed that I'd held out so much hope for Jesse and me. I'd gone as far as moving clear across the country just to find him so that we could be together—and I'd dragged Andy along with me.

"Emma, come on, talk to me. Something obviously happened tonight."

I took deep breaths as I tried to calm myself down enough to talk so that he could understand what I was saying.

"I don't even know where to start."

"Start from the beginning."

"I was waiting outside of Ally's house again. I must have fallen asleep because the next thing I knew, someone was tapping on my window."

"Shit, Emma. I told you to stop going over there so much. Who was it?"

"Ally."

He muttered a string of curse words as he looked me over. "What happened? Did she hurt you?"

I shook my head. "No, I didn't even make it out of my car. One good thing is the fact that I found out Jesse is living at the same house as her."

"Was he home?"

"I think so. I never got out to check."

He looked confused. "Why not?"

I stared at him as tears filled my eyes again. "I think congrats are in order. You're going to be an uncle."

"What are you talking—" His eyes widened. "No. There's no way."

"I saw her stomach. She's pregnant. She also let me know that if I took Jesse away from her, I'd be destroying their family since it's his baby."

Andy dropped down to the couch beside me with his mouth hanging open. He was at a loss for words. I knew the feeling well. I waited as he processed the news. It didn't take long before his look of shock changed to one of anger.

"So, let me get this straight. She ran away from home and came here to find him. Then, she goes and gets pregnant with his kid."

"That pretty much sums it up."

"I want to fucking kill both of them!" He stood up and started pacing the room. "How could she do this? How could *he* do this? She's my fucking sister!"

"Maybe they love each other, Andy. It's been a long time since either of us saw Jesse, and Ally barely spoke to you after Jesse left. You know nothing about either one of them now, and neither do I."

"This is bullshit! Jesse never showed a bit of interest in her when we were all together. There's no way that she came out here, and he got her pregnant in three months. If she's already showing, then it would have had to happen right after she came out here!"

"I didn't think to ask for the exact date, Andy," I said sarcastically.

He looked guilty as he dropped down to his knees in front of me. "I'm sorry. I didn't mean it that way. I'm just so fucking confused by all of this. I can't even imagine how much you're hurting right now."

"I feel like someone ripped my heart out of my chest and stepped on it. I never expected this when I decided to try to find him."

"Neither did I. What are you going to do now? Do you want to stay or go back home?"

"I have no home. I'm going to stay and finish this semester at least. After that, I don't know. I was an idiot for focusing on finding Jesse and not planning for the worst."

"You're not an idiot. You thought that you'd find him, and everything would be okay."

"Well, I've found him." I couldn't keep the bitterness out of my tone.

"Do you plan on confronting him?"

"I don't see the point. He has a family now, and I'd do nothing but screw that up for him."

"I'm sorry that my sister put you through all of this. You're a good person, Emma, and you don't deserve this kind of hurt."

"It was a long shot, and we both knew it. You tried to prepare me for the worst, but I didn't listen. I'm just going to pretend like I never came here to look for him, so I can move on with my life. That's all I can do. I need to forget him once and for all."

He nodded. "If that's what you want, then that's what we'll do. I found a decent job, so I'll stay here for as long as you need me to."

"That means a lot. Thank you for everything you've done for me."

"You're my friend, Emma. I'd do anything I could to help you."

"I guess one good thing came from Jesse and me." I smiled down at him. "I never would have met you if I hadn't been with him."

He grinned. "I am pretty awesome."

We both stood and walked to the door.

"You can stay here tonight if you need to."

"I don't think that's a good idea. I'm going to go home and sleep all day tomorrow. You still have time to call your girlfriend back if you want to. I didn't mean to interrupt."

"Nah, I'll have babies on my mind now. That takes all the fun out of it."

"You always know just what to say."

"I try, Emma. I try."

I stuck to my word and spent the next day in bed. It was Saturday, so I had no classes to get up for. I knew I was moping, but I couldn't help it. I'd had this whole plan to make things right with Jesse, and it had completely blown up in my face.

I couldn't believe that Jesse was going to be a dad. Hell, I couldn't believe that Ally was going to be a mom. She'd never struck me as the maternal type, and I hoped that Jesse would make up for her lack of parenting. There was no way someone as mean as her could be a good parent. It just wasn't in her genes.

While it shocked me that Jesse was going to be a dad, I didn't think that he'd be bad at it. I knew how much it'd hurt him that his dad had abandoned him when he was little. There was no doubt in my mind that Jesse would spend his entire life making sure that his kid never felt unwanted. I still believed that Jesse was a good person despite the situation he was in. Besides the time when I thought he'd cheated on me, I couldn't think of a thing that I didn't like about him. He was a genuinely good person.

The next morning, I forced myself to crawl out of bed. I hadn't showered for two days, and I was starving. After showering, I pulled on a pair of shorts and a tank top, so I could go find some food. The school cafeteria was closed on Sundays, but there were plenty of places to eat at in Morgantown.

I drove around town until I found someplace that didn't make my stomach turn. Instead of going through the drive-through like I'd originally planned, I decided to go inside.

My hopes of being with Jesse were gone, and it was time that I started to move on. I didn't care if it made me pathetic to start looking at a fast-food restaurant on a Sunday morning. I ordered my food and sat down at a table facing the entrance. That way, I could see everyone who came in as soon as they walked through the doors.

I quickly realized that I wasn't going to find anyone unless I was hoping to get a date with an eighty-year-old man who liked to drink the tar they called coffee here. I sighed as I finished my food, and then I threw away my garbage. I didn't even bother to look up as I walked to my car. *I need a life.*

I knew where Andy worked, so I decided to stop by and surprise him. He said that his boss was pretty easygoing, so I didn't think Andy would complain if I stopped by for a few minutes to chat. I knew he was worried about me, and it would help put him at ease if he saw me freshly showered and out in the real world.

I drove downtown and parked in front of the building. A bell dinged above the door as I opened it and stepped inside. Andy was sitting on a couch with another guy, and they were watching an old football game that had happened earlier in the week.

"I see you're working hard," I teased when he looked up.

"Emma! What are you doing here?" Andy asked as he walked over to me.

"I thought I'd surprise you."

"Well, you did. I'm glad to see that you crawled out of bed."

"Is this your girlfriend?" the guy on the couch asked.

"Nah, this is Emma. Emma, this is Sam. He's my boss's younger brother."

"It's nice to meet you, Sam," I said politely.

"Likewise." He looked at Andy. "Where have you been hiding her?"

I blushed as Andy rolled his eyes.

"Back off, jackhole. She's like my sister."

"Too bad," Sam said as he stared at me.

I started to look away, but then I stopped myself. Wasn't I just looking for a way to move on while I ate a hash brown?

Besides, Sam was kind of cute. He looked to be around the same age as me, too. His dirty-blond hair was styled messily, and his eyes were a pretty pale blue. He wasn't as built as Andy, but Sam's body suited him.

"Quit staring at her like you want to lick her. It's nasty. I'll say it again—she's like my sister," Andy groaned.

"Shut it, Andy," I scolded.

"So, are you from around here?" Sam asked.

"Nope, Andy and I moved here from California together."

"I should have known that you're a California girl. You just have the look. Why the hell did you move from California to West Virginia?"

I glanced at Andy. "I just needed a change, and Andy did, too. Besides, I like West Virginia. People are so nice here."

Sam laughed. "You're nuts, but whatever. Do you go to WVU?"

"I do. I'm a freshman."

"I'm a sophomore."

"Cool," I said, unable to think of anything else to say.

I was terrible at this. It had been so long since the last time I tried to flirt that I didn't know how anymore. This used to come so naturally to me.

"I live with a couple of guys, and we're having a party this weekend. You should come," Sam said.

"She's not interested," Andy said.

"Ignore him. I'd love to come," I said as I glared at Andy.

"Great. Let me give you the address."

I ignored Andy's disapproving glare as Sam wrote down his address for me.

"Thanks!" I said.

Andy grew more and more agitated as I talked with Sam. I knew Andy was trying to protect me, but it wasn't his job. I had to move on, and I wasn't going to waste any time.

After about an hour, I decided that I'd stayed long enough. Andy walked outside with me to my car.

"What the hell are you doing?" he asked.

"Nothing. Why?"

"Don't play innocent, Emma. Why did you let him think you were interested?"

"Maybe I am!"

"Bullshit. Look, I know you're hurting, but jumping to some guy who you don't even know will not fix things. You need to take time to heal."

"I'm tired of being alone."

"You're not alone, Emma. Besides, I never took you for one of those girls who needs a guy around constantly. You're better than that."

"I guess I am one of those girls. I'm so sick of being alone all the time. It's been two years, and I think it's time that I started trying to find someone who wants me, someone who doesn't have a kid on the way."

"So, what are you going to do? Sleep your way through Morgantown until you don't feel alone?"

"I never said that! Just because I want to date doesn't mean I'm going to sleep with every guy out there!"

"You're hurting, and you're vulnerable. I don't want you to do something you will regret later."

"Like last time?"

His mouth dropped open.

I took the chance to get in my car and drive away. I hated fighting with Andy, but I didn't need someone to tell me how to live my life. If I wanted to live like that, I would have stayed back in California with my mom.

5

"Hey, I'm leaving school. Is there anything that you want me to pick up for dinner?" I asked as I walked across campus.

"I don't care as long as I get food," Ally said on the other end of the line.

"Okay, I'll be home in a few."

"Love you, Jesse."

I hesitated for a second before answering her, "I love you, too."

I ended the call and continued to walk toward my car. It still felt strange to tell Ally that I loved her. I did love her, just not in the way that she wanted. I was trying my hardest to learn to love her, but it just wasn't happening. I felt like a total asshole for not being able to, but it wasn't something I could control. It was either there, or it wasn't, and in Ally's case, it wasn't.

I sighed as I walked. My life was a fucking disaster. But then again, when hadn't it been? For as long as I could remember, things were always tough—except for when I'd been with Emma. I stopped myself. There was no point in going there again. That part of my life was over, and I needed to accept it.

I continued across campus as I tried to get Emma out of my head. Since I'd been so lost in my thoughts, I glanced up to make sure I was still going in the right direction, and I stopped dead.

This is getting ridiculous.

I'd been thinking about Emma, and just now, I could have sworn I'd seen her walking a few people ahead of me. I shook my head. I needed to get my priorities straight. I had to figure out how the hell I was going to take care of Ally and a baby in a few months, not imagine that Emma was here.

The crowd of students parted, and I noticed the same girl again.

God, she looks so much like Emma.

Her hair was shorter, but other than that, she was identical from behind. Out of morbid curiosity, I followed her, keeping a few people in between us. She seemed to be headed in the same direction as me anyway. The more I stared at her, the more she reminded me of Emma. She even walked the same. She reached the parking lot before me and walked over to an SUV. Before I could stop myself, I called out Emma's name. The girl froze for a second before turning to face me.

I nearly dropped my bag as I stared at her. It was Emma.

What the hell is she doing in West Virginia?

Unable to believe that I was really seeing her, I felt like I was in a daze as I walked slowly toward her. She stood there, frozen, as I approached. I raised my hand to touch her cheek, but she backed away.

"Emma?" I whispered.

She was really here. The girl who'd haunted my dreams for years was standing right in front of me. She had always kept her hair halfway down her back, but it was up to her shoulders now. Something else was different about her, too, but I couldn't put my finger on it. She was still my Emma, but something had changed. It took me a moment to realize that it was her eyes. Emma had always had an open heart, and her eyes were like windows into it. Now, they were closed off, like she had built a brick wall around herself.

"You look different," she said quietly.

I guessed I did. I'd cut my blonde hair not long after I'd moved to West Virginia. Instead of it hanging around my face, it was now only an inch or two long. In the last two years, I'd also bulked up by lifting weights. I'd needed an outlet since I couldn't surf, and it had been my substitute. Other than that, I still looked the same. At least, I thought I did.

"It is you. Shit. What are you doing here? It's been so long since I've seen you."

"I need to go," she said hurriedly.

Before I could stop her, she was in her car and driving away. My brain finally started functioning again, and I ran to my car. I tore out of the lot and went the same direction she had. I was afraid that I'd lost her in traffic, but I finally caught up with her about a mile down the road. I didn't think she even realized that I was following her as she weaved in and out of the evening traffic.

She pulled up to an apartment complex, got out of her car, and ran inside. I didn't think twice about following her as I threw my car in park and chased after her. She ran up the stairs and to the second floor with me not far behind her. She was far enough ahead of me that she managed to get inside apartment 2B just before I made it to the door. I beat on the door as I shouted her name. I had to know why she was here. There was no way that this was a coincidence.

I continued to beat my fist against the door for a good five minutes before it finally opened. I'd expected Emma, but instead, a shirtless Andy stood in the doorway.

What the fuck? Did someone throw me into the twilight zone today or what?

Andy looked exactly like he had the last time I'd seen him. Except now, Emma was cowering behind him. I had no idea why they were here together, but I intended to find out.

"Andy?"

"What the hell do you want?" he spit out as he glared at me.

It was obvious that his opinion of me hadn't changed since the last time we'd seen each other.

"I want to talk to Emma. What are the two of you doing here?"

"You need to leave—now."

"Not until I talk to Emma. I have a right to know why you two are here."

"Stay the fuck away from Emma or else."

"Fuck you. I want to talk to her."

"Have it your way," Andy said just before he pulled back and punched me in the face.

I stumbled back as Emma cried out. I pinched my nose to stop the bleeding as I stared at Andy in shock. He was no longer in the doorway. Instead, he was holding Emma as she cried.

What the hell is going on here?

When I'd left California, Andy and Emma had barely known each other. Now, he was *holding her* and comforting her as she cried. It almost looked like they were together.

I froze as I watched him kiss her forehead. Rage filled me. *They're together. They have to be.* Absolutely nothing made sense right now.

"I thought I told you to leave. Don't make me hit you again because I will," Andy said as he let go of Emma.

Then, he slammed the door in my face. I stared at it for a minute before I finally turned and left. I walked back to my car in a total state of confusion.

I didn't even remember driving back to the house that Ally and I were renting. One minute, I was walking to my car, and the next, I was walking through my front door.

"Hey! Where's the food?" Ally asked cheerfully. She took one look at me and stopped dead. "What happened? Why are you bleeding?"

I sat down in the chair closest to me as I tried to process the last half hour of my life.

"Jesse! Talk to me! What happened?"

"Did you know?" I asked as I looked up at her.

"Did I know, what?"

"That Andy and Emma are here?"

"They're here? I had no idea!"

I would have believed her if I hadn't known her for so long. I knew her well enough to know when she was lying to me.

"I call bullshit. Start talking, Ally."

She bit her lip as she stared down at me. "Okay, yes, I knew. I just didn't tell you because I didn't want to upset you."

"My best friend and my girlfriend are in town, and you decided that I didn't need to know that little tidbit of information?" I asked incredulously.

"Ex."

"What?"

"You called Emma your girlfriend. *I'm* your girlfriend now. She's your ex."

"Whatever. How long have you known?"

"A few days. I guess Andy figured out where I was, and he came after me. Emma came with him."

"Why would she do that? They barely know each other."

"Oh, Jesse, I wanted to tell you, but I didn't know how."

"Tell me, what?"

"Andy and Emma are together now. They have been since right after you left. I came home one night and found them."

My stomach clenched. "Found them doing what?"

"I was mad at Andy for being mean to you, so when I heard him in his room with a girl, I stormed in to ruin his fun. I never expected it to be Emma."

"What were they doing?" I asked again through clenched teeth. I knew the answer, but I needed to hear it from her.

"They were naked. I'm sure you can figure out what they were up to. I never told you because I didn't want to hurt you. Besides, it's been two years since you were with her. I didn't think you'd care."

"You saw my best friend and my girlfriend together and didn't think that I needed to know? Even after all this time, it still would have been nice to know."

Tears filled her eyes. "I'm so sorry, Jesse. I've just been so preoccupied with the baby that it honestly slipped my mind."

I closed my eyes and took a deep breath. I couldn't process all of this. After two years of nothing, the three people I came here to escape decided to bust into my life and fuck it all up. First, Ally had shown up and begged me to help hide her, and now, Emma and Andy were in town. Nothing in my life was ever simple.

"Please don't be mad at me. I'm so sorry," Ally whimpered.

"I'm not mad. I just wish that you would have told me." That was a lie. I *was* mad. I just wasn't sure who I was mad at right now. I thought it was a tie between all three of them.

"I should have. I was just so focused on leaving before anyone found out that I was pregnant."

"I get it. I do. This whole situation just sucks."

"It does."

"How did you know they were here?" I asked.

"They hunted me down and cornered me outside of work the other night. Emma can't stand me, but Andy wanted me to come back to California with him."

"What did you tell him?"

"I stuck to the story that we'd agreed on. I told them that I was pregnant, and it was your baby. I said that I wouldn't leave because you loved me."

I buried my head in my hands. This was all so fucking complicated. When Ally had shown up on my doorstep a few months ago, alone and scared, I hadn't thought twice about helping her. I just hadn't expected her to ask so much. She'd stayed quiet for a few days before the truth finally came out.

"Jesse, I need to talk to you," Ally said as she stood in the doorway of my bedroom.

I'd been listening to my iPod, but I'd paused it and set it aside. Ally hadn't said much of anything since she'd shown up on my doorstep a few days ago. I knew something serious was going on, and hopefully, she was about to tell me what.

"What's up?" I asked.

She walked into my room and sat down on the bed beside me. "I don't even know where to start."

"Just start wherever you want."

"You know that I'm hiding from everyone back home."

I nodded.

"I'm doing it to protect them…and myself."

"From, what?"

"I went to a party on the beach. It wasn't with our usual crowd. Some guy invited me, and I decided that I would check it out. If I didn't like it, I

61

could go home. I didn't know anyone, but everyone was nice to me, and I was having a lot of fun. I was drinking too much, but I didn't care. I just wanted to party. I was about to graduate, and I just wanted to have a little fun before I had to go out into the big bad world." She laughed humorlessly.

"A few of the guys there were older, like in their late twenties. They were part of one of the biker gangs that comes through town from time to time. I knew I should stay away, but there was one who seemed really nice. He went out of his way to talk to me. We hit it off really well, and I ended up staying most of the night. By the time the party started to end, I was trashed. He was sober, so he offered me a ride home. I'd never been on the back of a bike, so I told him yes. We told everyone good night, and he helped me onto his bike."

I had a sick feeling in my stomach. I almost told her to stop, but I knew she had to tell someone.

"Instead of taking me home, he took me to that old motel next to the interstate. I told him I wanted to go home, but he said he was tired. I finally agreed to spend the night with him, and then he could take me home in the morning. Everything was fine at first. He wasn't pushy or anything. He helped me into bed, and I fell asleep. The next thing I knew, he was on top of me, and my jeans were gone."

She was sobbing at this point, so I sat up and pulled her into my arms. Ally was like my sister, and I couldn't stand for her to be in so much pain.

"You don't have to tell me what happened. I can figure it out." I could barely get the words out. I wanted to rip this guy's dick off for what he had done to her.

"He threatened to kill me if I ever told. I swore that I wouldn't, and he let me go. I walked the entire way home. I tried to act like nothing had happened, but it was eating me up inside. A month later, I missed my period. I bought a bunch of tests, used all of them, and they all came back the same. I'm pregnant, Jesse. His baby is growing in me, and I want to throw up every time I think about it. I had to leave before anyone figured out the truth. If Andy found out, I knew he wouldn't stop bugging me until I told him who the dad was. Andy would have gone after the guy, and he would have died. Those gangs don't mess around. I couldn't let my brother die just because I was stupid."

I ran my hand across her hair, trying to comfort her. There were no words for how I felt right now. Someone had hurt Ally, and I wanted him to pay. I understood why she hadn't gone to the police. The gangs ruled California. Even if they had arrested the bastard who had done this to her, one of his brothers would have come for her and everyone she loved.

"I'm so sorry you have to deal with this, Ally."

"So, now you know why I needed to hide. I know it's wrong, but I don't want to get rid of this baby. It's not my baby's fault for what happened to me. It might be half him, but it's half me, too."

"I'll help you in any way I can. Just tell me what you need, and I'll do it."

She grew still for a moment. "I need you to hide me."

"I can do that."

"And I want you to promise me that if anyone from home finds me, you'll say the baby is yours. If Andy finds out the truth, he'll go crazy."

I had no idea what to say to that. I couldn't abandon her, no matter how wrong it felt to make that promise to her.

"I'll tell them it's mine," I said quietly.

Ally hid her face in my chest as she started sobbing again. "Thank you, Jesse. Thank you."

"You're like my family. I'd do anything for you, Ally."

I held her as she cried. I didn't know how long we sat there together, but it felt like hours. Her tears finally stopped, and she fell asleep on my chest. I picked her up and carried her to the room where she'd been staying. It was her room now. This was now her home, too. I watched over her as she slept, wishing I could erase the last few months of her life. No one deserved to go through that. One day, I'd find the bastard who had done this to her, and I'd beat the shit out of him.

Over the next few days, we sat down and figured out all the details just in case anyone showed up. Neither of us really expected that to happen though. What were the chances of someone looking in West Virginia? I'd just signed the lease on this place, so the landlord let me add Ally's name, too.

My mom refused to let me work while I was in school. I'd fought with her over and over about that, but she'd finally won. Ally didn't want to take advantage of my mom's kindness, so she went out and started searching for a job to help cover rent. I didn't like the idea of her working, but I didn't want to upset her. She planned to save whatever she had leftover, so she would have some money for when the baby arrived. I'd tried to get her to apply for local state aid to get insurance and assistance for food, but she'd refused. She didn't want to take handouts from anyone.

When I'd agreed to tell anyone back home that I was her baby's father, I'd never expected it to be an issue. It was definitely an issue now. Emma and Andy were here, and they both thought that I'd gotten Ally pregnant. Now, I understood why Emma had run from me and why Andy had punched me. I'd hurt her again, and he had been protecting her. Of course, he would now that they were together.

"I need a beer," I said as I forced myself back into the present. I didn't need a beer. I needed a keg.

64

"I'll get you one." Ally ran to the kitchen, and she came back a few seconds later with a beer in her hand. "Here."

"Thanks," I mumbled as I popped the top and took a drink.

Ally had done everything in her power not to be a bother since she'd arrived. I knew that she still loved me, but no matter how hard I'd tried, I couldn't love her back. By protecting her, I knew that I was throwing away any chance of being happy, but I had no other choice. She was my friend, and I couldn't abandon her. She'd dealt with enough pain to last a lifetime.

Ally had tried to sleep in my bed after we agreed on our story, but I wouldn't let her. She'd thrown herself at me—literally. I couldn't do it, and I knew that had hurt her, but I couldn't sleep with her. There was no way. I hadn't been with anyone since Emma. I'd had opportunities, but I never took them.

Ally had said she understood and that maybe I'd return her feelings one day. I didn't see that happening, but I wasn't about to tell her that. She'd been through enough without me breaking her heart.

"I'm going to my room," I said as I set my beer on the table and stood up.

If she replied, I didn't hear her. My mind was buzzing too loud for me to process anything happening around me. I closed my door and locked it before lying down on my bed. I stared up at the ceiling as my mind kept going back to the look on Emma's face when she'd seen me.

She had looked so hurt. Now, I understood why. She thought that I'd slept with Ally and gotten her pregnant. I'd be hurt, too, if I'd found out that she was pregnant with Andy's kid. *God, I don't even want to think about that. Emma is mine. No, she isn't. She used to be but not anymore. That had been Ally's fault, too.*

I tried not to be angry with Ally, but I couldn't help it. It seemed like every time she came around, my life turned into complete chaos. There was one thing that was bothering me though. Ally had claimed that Andy had come after her and Emma had come with him because they were together. If that were true, why had Emma been on campus? She'd had a bag across her shoulder, too, like she was a student.

I needed to talk to Emma. I had to tell her the truth even if I didn't think she'd believe me. I couldn't let her think that Ally's baby was mine when she went back to California with Andy. I knew Ally would be angry, but I couldn't stand the thought of Emma hurting because of me. I also wanted to know why she had been on campus if they were only here for Ally. That made absolutely no sense to me. Something wasn't right, and I was going to find out exactly what was going on.

An entire week passed without a word from Emma or Andy. I was driving myself nuts, thinking about the two of them together. I should have let go of Emma a long time ago, but I never had.

It wasn't that I hadn't tried because I had. I'd done everything possible to block her from my thoughts when I first moved here. I'd felt so angry with her for thinking the worst of me that I'd been able to force her out of my mind for a while. She'd slowly started to creep back into my thoughts though. It was like my memories of her were a disease slowly killing me inside. Every little thing had reminded me of her. No matter how hard I'd tried to push her away, she was always there.

I'd been doing better since Ally had shown up due to the fact that I was constantly worried about her and the situation she was in. Now that I'd seen Emma again though, even Ally's predicament couldn't distract me.

Emma was eating me alive and I doubted if she even cared.

Ever since the night I'd run into Emma, Ally had been driving me nuts. She had been clingy before, but she was ten times worse now. It seemed like I couldn't take a piss without her standing outside the bathroom door, waiting for me. I would savor the times when she worked the night shift. It gave me time to myself to just breathe. It seemed like I could never breathe when she was around. There was never enough oxygen in the room. She was suffocating me.

"Hey, what are you thinking about?" Ally asked as she set a plate of food in front of me.

"Nothing." I picked up my fork and started eating.

I had no idea what I was eating. She could have been feeding me rat poison, and I wouldn't know. I was too far gone into my own thoughts.

"Jesse, something is obviously on your mind. Talk to me about it. That's what couples do. They talk about what's bothering each other."

I bit my tongue to keep from telling her that we weren't a couple. It took every ounce of willpower I had, but I managed. I had no idea why Ally kept pushing a relationship when we both knew there was nothing between us.

"I'm fine. I was just thinking about school," I said as I glanced up at her. I was surprised to see anger radiating off of her.

"You're lying."

"No, I'm not," I said each word slowly as I tried not to lash out at her. *She needs to mind her own damn business.*

"You're thinking about *her*—Emma," she said, spitting out Emma's name like it was a curse.

"What is your problem with her?" I asked angrily.

"What is my problem? Are you fucking kidding me?" she shouted. "Everything was perfect until Andy and that bitch showed back up! We were connecting, and I know you were starting to feel something for me. Since you saw her, you've barely said a word to me. You were finally falling in love with me, and she ruined everything!"

"Ally, calm the fuck down!" I shouted back. "I love you, but it's not the way you want. You're like my sister, and that's how I'll always feel about you. I'm helping you with the baby because I want to protect you. It's not because I love you."

"I want my child to have a family!"

"I hope that happens for both of you, but it won't be with me. I'm sorry. I'll protect you for as long as you need, but that's all I'll do."

"It's her fucking fault!"

"Emma has nothing to do with this!" I shouted, losing my cool.

"Bullshit. Everything always comes back to her!"

"I'm not dealing with this." I shoved away from the table and started walking to my room.

I slammed my bedroom door behind me, and I locked it, so Ally couldn't get in. I collapsed on the bed as she beat on the door and called me every name that she could think of. I refused to answer as she screamed out my name. She needed to calm down and act like a rational human being. Until she did, I was going to ignore her.

"Fine, Jesse! I'm out of here. Fuck you!" she shouted as she hit my door one last time.

I sighed in relief as the house went quiet. I was slightly worried that she was just faking me out so that I'd open the door, so I waited for almost an hour before I walked out. Ally was nowhere to be seen, and her keys were missing from where she would hang them by the door. She really had left. I knew I had been a dick, but damn, there was only so much crazy shit a guy could deal with before he snapped.

I walked into the kitchen and grabbed a beer from the refrigerator. I chugged it down and opened another one. I didn't want to get drunk. I just wanted to relax for a while. I was tired of my life being nothing but girl drama. I wasn't sure if all women were like Ally, but I doubted it. When Emma and I had been together, she'd never acted the way Ally had. Emma had been the complete opposite actually. She'd kept me calm instead of winding me up until I couldn't take anymore.

Just in case Ally came home, I kept an eye on the door as I walked from the kitchen to the living room. If she did, I was going to haul ass back to my bedroom. I wasn't in the mood to watch TV, so I sat on the couch and stared at the blank screen in front of me. After a few minutes, I heard a noise coming from outside. I walked to my front door and opened it to see what was going on.

As soon as I opened the door, I could hear music coming from a few houses down. I'd forgotten that Sam was having a party this weekend. I didn't know him that well, but he'd invited the entire street. I wasn't sure if he'd done that to be nice or to suck up so that none of us called the cops on him.

It was obvious that the party was huge. He lived two houses down from me, and people were standing on *my* lawn. I shook my head as I listened to the music blaring. The guy apparently knew how to throw a party.

I started to close my door and go back inside, but something stopped me. Why the hell should I lock myself away to mope about all my problems when I could be drinking with a bunch of people who I didn't know? They didn't think I'd knocked up my best friend's sister, and they didn't expect me to take care of a kid who wasn't mine.

I closed my door and walked down the sidewalk to Sam's house. People were everywhere, and I pushed through them as I made my way into the house. It was even worse inside. If he planned to have parties like this, he might want to consider getting a bigger house.

The music was loud enough to make my ears bleed. Jesus, how did anyone expect to have a conversation? Looking around the room, I realized that talking was the last thing on most of these people's minds. Most were paired off with their lips glued to each other. Those who weren't attached were dancing in the living room. I didn't bother to apologize as I bumped into people while trying to get to the table covered in alcohol across the room.

I'd thought a party was just what I needed, but all this place was doing was pissing me off. There were just too many people. I was used to having parties on the beach where there was plenty of room for everyone without being smashed together. Obviously, Sam had a different idea of what a party was.

I stood off to the side, drinking my beer and watching people. I recognized a few faces from some of my smaller classes but not many. I hadn't made much of an effort to make friends, and it was glaringly obvious that nobody gave a flying fuck about me as they walked past me without a second glance. A group of girls standing across the room seemed to notice me, but I paid them no attention. I had enough problems without one of those girls trying to talk to me.

One of them finally broke away from the group and started to approach me. Before she could even make it halfway across the room, I was gone. There was no point in staying here. I was getting annoyed with everyone. I set my beer down on a table and started walking toward the door.

I noticed Sam standing close to it. He had a strawberry-blonde girl pushed up against the wall, and he was kissing her like he wanted to eat her alive. I walked two more steps before I realized that the girl looked familiar—well, what I could see of her looked familiar. I told myself that I should keep walking, but something stopped me. I came to a standstill a few feet away from them and waited for Sam to move. My blood boiled when he pulled away, and I realized it was Emma.

What the hell is she doing with Sam if she's dating Andy?

I was torn between getting the hell out of this house and checking on Emma. I knew I needed to talk to her, but now was definitely not the time. My protective side won, and I closed the space between them and me.

I grabbed Sam's shoulder and pulled him off of Emma.

He spun around. "What the hell?"

"She has a boyfriend."

71

"She never mentioned him, so I think you have her confused with someone else. Mind your own business."

I laughed. "Emma is my business."

"This is *my* house. Get the fuck out."

"I'm not leaving until you let Emma go."

He lifted his hand so that it was no longer wrapped around Emma's waist. She stumbled a bit, but she managed to catch herself before she fell. It was obvious that she was drunk.

Where the hell is Andy?

"See, I'm not touching her," Sam said sarcastically.

"She's fucking wasted. She's leaving with me."

"I don't think so. Get the fuck out."

I ground my teeth together, trying to keep my cool. "She's leaving with me."

Sam stepped closer until we were inches apart. "I'm going to tell you one more time—get the fuck out of my house."

I knew I shouldn't have done it, but I was pissed off. I drew back and hit him as hard as I could. He dropped to the ground. I'd knocked him out cold with one punch.

Emma looked at me with dazed eyes as I stepped over Sam to get to her.

"Emma, you need to come with me."

She only nodded as I wrapped my arm around her waist and led her to the door. No one got in our way as we walked out the door and back to my house. I was practically carrying Emma as we went.

I kept my arm around her as I unlocked my door and pushed it open. I stood in the doorway, debating on where to put her. The couch was the most obvious choice, but I didn't want Ally to come home and see her. With the way she'd been tonight, I wasn't sure what she would do if she saw Emma. I had no idea how long Ally would be gone, and I didn't want to take a chance. I had only two other options—Ally's room or mine. Again, things would definitely end badly if Ally came home and Emma was in her bed.

I knew it was stupid, but I carried Emma to my room anyway. I put her down on the bed and placed a trash can beside it in case she needed to puke. Her eyes stayed shut as I covered her up. I sat down beside her and watched as she slept. This was a big mistake, but I couldn't leave her there with Sam. It was pretty obvious what he'd wanted from her. I wondered again where the hell Andy had been while his girlfriend had been out, getting trashed.

She moaned and opened her eyes. They widened in surprise as she stared up at me.

"Where am I?" she whispered.

"My house. You're drunk."

"Am not," she mumbled as she closed her eyes again.

I couldn't help but smile. She was always so damn stubborn. I made sure that she was lying on her side in case she got sick. Once I had her situated with a few pillows behind her to keep her from rolling over, I slipped silently from the room to go take a shower. On my way to the bathroom, I grabbed a pair of shorts from the dryer. After stripping down, I turned on the water and stood beneath the spray.

The simple thought of Emma so close and in *my* bed was enough for me to turn on the cold water.

"Get your head out of your ass. She's drunk," I said out loud to myself as the cold water covered me.

I knew I was avoiding the situation as I prolonged my shower, but I couldn't help it. I loved her, and she was in my fucking bed. Drunk or not, it was enough to drive me nuts.

When the cold shower finally calmed me down, I shut off the water and stepped out. I took my time drying off before finally pulling my shorts on. I took a deep breath as I opened the door and returned to my room. Emma was still in the exact same spot where I'd left her.

I settled down next to her on the bed and moved the pillows so that she could roll over if she wanted to. As soon as they were gone, she rolled until she was facing me. I was silent as I watched her sleep. She looked so damn peaceful as she slept. She looked like the Emma I'd known long ago, not the person she was now. I couldn't forget the look in her eyes when I stumbled across her on campus. In her sleep, her guard was down.

She mumbled something in her sleep. I leaned forward, trying to hear her better.

"Jesse."

My heart started beating faster as she said my name again. She smiled in her sleep as she mumbled something else that I didn't catch. She was dreaming about me—that much I could tell.

Her lips parted, and I couldn't stop myself. I leaned forward a few inches and pressed my lips against hers. I knew it was wrong, but I couldn't help it. I expected to kiss her and move away. What I hadn't expected was her reaction. She moaned and threw her arm around me as she kissed me back.

It was like the last two years had never happened. I was drowning in her as I kissed her with everything I had. My body was on fire, and I pulled her closer until there wasn't an inch of space between us. She fit perfectly against me, just like she always had. I knew it was wrong to do this. She was with Andy now, but I didn't stop. I kissed her lips, her cheeks, and down her neck.

When she pushed her hand between us and cupped me through my shorts, I nearly came right then and there. When it came to her, a simple touch was all I needed. It took everything I had to push her away from me. If I didn't stop now, I knew I wouldn't.

She opened her eyes to look at me. As I saw the tears in them, I felt as if someone had reached into my chest and ripped out my heart.

"Why did you have to ruin it all?" she whispered before she passed out.

I felt my world crumbling around me as I closed my eyes.

7

"Ugh, my head."

My eyes snapped open at the sound of Emma's voice. It took me a second to realize that I wasn't dreaming. She was really in my bed.

She gasped as she opened her eyes and saw me next to her. "Where am I? Why are you here?"

"You're at my house. I found you drunk at Sam's house last night."

"Oh god."

"It's fine. Don't freak out. Sam was getting a little grabby, but nothing happened."

"I don't remember very much from last night. The last thing I remember is Sam handing me a drink. Actually, I remember him handing me a lot of drinks." It was obvious from her tone that she was pissed. "Where was I when you found me?"

I didn't want to tell her. "It's not important."

"Jesse, tell me where I was at." She glared at me.

"You were still at his house. He had you up against the wall." I felt rage fill me again as I remembered how I'd found her. *Sam better hope that he doesn't cross paths with me for a very long time.*

"Fuck," she groaned.

"It's fine. I saw you before anything happened. I bet Sam has one hell of a headache though."

"Why?"

"I punched him."

She smiled for a split second before she winced. "Did you hit me, too? Because my head feels like it's going to explode."

"No, that wasn't me. That was the alcohol."

We were silent as we stared at each other. Emma seemed to realize that she was in my bed because the next thing I knew, she was throwing the covers off and trying to stand up.

"Where are you going?" I asked, afraid that she would run.

"I shouldn't be here. I need to go."

I wanted to ask her if she was going back to Andy, but I couldn't bring myself to do it. I knew the answer, and I didn't need to hear her say it. The thought of her and Andy together made me sick to my stomach.

"At least let me make you some breakfast. You can shower here, too, if you want. You'll feel better once you're clean and have some food in you," I said, trying to get the image of her and Andy out of my head.

She seemed unsure. "I don't know. I shouldn't even be around you."

"Please? We don't have to talk about…anything. Just a shower and food, and then you can leave."

She studied me for a moment before nodding. "Shower and food—that's it. Then, I'm gone."

"Deal." I stood up and walked to my dresser. I pulled out a pair of my sweatpants and one of my shirts. "Here—you can wear these."

I knew it was wrong, but I got some kind of sick satisfaction out of having her wear my clothes. I knew I should back off because she was Andy's now, but I couldn't help myself. I wanted Andy to see her wearing my clothes. I walked out first to make sure that Ally wasn't home. When I was satisfied that she wasn't, I showed Emma where the shower was.

I left her alone and walked to the kitchen to start searching for food. I grabbed a bottle of water and a bottle of pills for her headache, and then I headed back to the bathroom. The door opened silently, and I walked in to put the bottles on the counter. I couldn't help but look at the shower. The glass was fogged over, so I couldn't see anything but her outline. I forced myself to turn and walk away before I did something stupid. I didn't think she'd appreciate it very much if I decided to help her in the shower.

That thought brought back memories that I'd tried to bury. When we had been in London, I'd offered to help her shower. I'd promised to be good, but she hadn't. I felt my body tighten as I remembered what that shower had led to. I focused all of my attention on making breakfast, so I wouldn't think about things that could never happen again. There was no use torturing myself.

I finished making eggs and toast, and I put them on the table. I walked to the bathroom to let her know that the food was ready. I stopped short when I noticed the door hanging open. I knew she was gone before I even checked. Sure enough, when I walked into the bathroom, Emma was nowhere to be seen. Her clothes were still lying on the floor, and the pills and water bottle were gone. I rushed to the front door just in time to see her car go flying by.

Damn it.

"Jesse, what are you doing?" a voice called.

I looked over to see Ally walking up the sidewalk to the house. She stopped in front of me and looked up at me questioningly.

"I was just looking outside," I lied.

She pushed past me and into the house. "Look, I'm sorry about last night. I didn't mean to say those things to you. My body is all screwed-up from the baby, and I blame the hormones. Will you forgive me?"

"I understand you're going through a lot, but damn, it's like you weren't even you."

She hung her head. "I know. I just get so jealous when I think about Emma. I just want you to be mine. I was just starting to break through your barriers. Then, she walks back in, and everything goes to hell."

"Ally, I think we need to talk. Let's sit down on the couch."

She eyed me warily as she walked to the couch and sat down. I followed and sat down in the chair across from her.

"Look, I'm just going to come out and say this. I don't mean to hurt you, but I won't lead you on."

"What are you trying to say?" Ally asked quietly.

"I love you, Ally. I just don't love you in the way you want. I told you that I would help you with this baby, and I will, but I won't be its father. I can't. Once you get on your feet, you'll move on and find someone who cares about you the way you want, and he'll make a great dad. It just can't be me."

"Why? Because you still love her?" she asked tearfully.

"It has nothing to do with Emma. Even if she hadn't come back into my life, I still couldn't do it. I don't want to hurt you, but I don't want to lead you on. I'm sorry, Ally. I can't make myself feel something for you if it's not there."

"If you gave us some time…"

"Ally, no. There is nothing there. Please let it go."

I felt like the biggest asshole ever as tears streamed down her face. I never meant to hurt her.

"I understand," she whispered. "I didn't sleep any last night, so I'm going to take a shower and try to sleep before I have to go to work."

I stayed silent as she stood and walked into her room. A few seconds later, she reemerged, carrying clean clothes. I winced as she walked into the bathroom and slammed the door behind her. It was obvious that she was pissed off.

I stood and walked to the kitchen to clean up the breakfast I'd made for Emma. It was pretty obvious that she wasn't going to eat it. My mind drifted back to last night. I'd kissed Emma even when I knew I shouldn't have. She wasn't mine anymore. She was Andy's. I needed to accept that and let her go.

That was easier said than done. I tried to keep things in perspective. Yes, she'd kissed me back, but she'd been drunk. But she'd said my name in her sleep. That had to mean that she still felt something for me, no matter how hard she tried to hide it. I shouldn't be happy about that, but I was. The part of me that was actually a decent guy kept reminding me that Andy would get hurt if anything happened between Emma and me. The other part of me—the part that was a prick—couldn't bring himself to care. He just wanted Emma. The prick side of me was winning.

Just as I reached down and picked up a plate, I heard Ally scream in the bathroom. I dropped the plate, and it shattered everywhere. I paid no attention as I ran toward the bathroom. I threw the door open to see Ally standing by the sink.

"What's wrong?" I asked.

She turned to glare at me. "Who the hell was here last night after I left?"

I glanced down at the pile of clothes in front of her. I'd forgotten to pick up Emma's clothes after she'd snuck out. I cursed under my breath as I reached down and scooped them up.

"Who was it?" Ally demanded.

"Does it matter?" I asked.

I didn't want to admit that Emma had been here. Ally had enough reasons to hate Emma without this.

"Yeah, it kind of does. It was Emma, wasn't it?"

"It's not what you're thinking."

"Of course it's not. You didn't bring her over here the minute I was out of the house?"

"It wasn't like that. She needed help."

"Sure, she did. Of course, it was you who she called instead of Andy. You remember Andy, don't you? In case you've forgotten, he's her *boyfriend*."

"She didn't ask for my help."

"It doesn't matter!" Ally shouted. "She will always be the most important thing to you!"

"Ally, just stop."

She took a deep breath before she spoke again. "You're right. I'm overreacting. I'm sorry."

I had no idea where the hell these mood swings were coming from, but they fucking sucked. Ally had been acting like she was crazy half the time.

"Just forget it, okay?" I said.

"Yeah, I'll forget it," she said as she glanced up at me.

There was something in her eyes that chilled me to the bone. While she looked calm, her eyes said otherwise. They were filled with hatred so strong that I took a step back. For the first time in my life, I was scared of Ally and what she was capable of.

8
EMMA

I didn't tell Andy what had happened with Sam or Jesse. I didn't want to make things hard for him at work with Sam, and I knew what would happen if I told him. Andy would beat the shit out of Sam for me. One thing was for sure—Andy never passed up the chance to fight. I didn't tell him about Jesse for an entirely different reason. I knew he'd be mad at me for letting Jesse get that close. Plus, if I told Andy I'd ended up at Jesse's, he would want to know how it had happened. Then, I'd have to tell him about Sam. It was a never-ending cycle of screw-ups. Andy and I would both be better off if I kept my weekend to myself.

Besides finding out that his sister was pregnant with his ex-best friend's baby, things were going well for Andy. He really liked West Virginia. He was making friends with the guys at work, and he had even spent a few nights out with them.

I was happy for him. I just hated the fact that it meant I was alone a lot more. I didn't tell him that though. Whenever he asked if I would be okay by myself for a night, I always smiled and pretended like I would be. Just because I was miserable didn't mean that he had to be miserable, too.

I always spent the evening at his house if he wasn't out or working. My dorm room was too quiet, and right now, I couldn't handle quiet. I started thinking when things were quiet, and that always led to tears. I was tired of crying over Jesse all the time.

As hard as I'd tried, I couldn't get that morning out of my head. He'd been cautious around me, like he was afraid that I'd run away, but he'd still been Jesse. It was the first time that we'd actually talked since he'd left

California. We hadn't discussed anything that mattered, but we'd talked nonetheless. I kept telling myself that it didn't matter if we started talking, but my heart clung to that morning like it was something important.

I kept having dreams about the night of the party, too. I dreamed that I would wake up in Jesse's bed, and he'd start kissing me. As soon as I started to move to the next stage, he'd push me away. It seemed so real that I often wondered if it was. I knew it couldn't be though. He was with Ally now, and he would soon be a dad.

"Emma?"

I looked up to see Abby walking next to me.

"Hey, what's up?" I hadn't made much of an effort to get to know Abby better since school started. I'd been so preoccupied with finding Jesse and then trying to accept the fact that he was really gone that I hadn't worried about making friends. I knew it was too late to start trying now. Most of the girls in my dorm had already formed groups, and I wasn't welcome in any of them.

"I was wondering if you were doing anything tonight," Abby said.

"Um, I don't think so. Why?"

She stared at the ground as she said, "Today's my birthday, and I wanted to go out. I just don't have anyone to go out with. You're the closest thing I have to a friend."

"Oh," I said, shocked at her words.

Abby was a sweet girl, and I felt horrible for her. No one should have to spend her birthday alone.

"I understand if you don't want to or if you already have plans. I just thought I'd ask."

"No, I'd love to go out with you. Where do you want to go?"

"I don't know. Clubs really aren't my thing, so I was thinking we could just go watch a movie and maybe grab some dinner?"

"Abby, are you asking me out on a date?" I asked with a serious expression.

Her eyes widened, and she shook her head. "No! I didn't mean it like that. I'm not...you know."

I started laughing. "I'm just messing with you. Do you want me to drive or do you want to?"

"I can drive. I live in the same dorm as you, so we can just meet in the parking lot."

"Works for me. What time do you want to meet?"

"I'm finished with classes for the day, so whenever you're done, I guess."

"I'm finished, too. Can you give me an hour to get changed and do a little bit of my homework?" I asked.

"Sure, that works for me."

We finished walking to our dorm together. I waved good-bye as I exited the stairs at my floor. I spent the next hour trying to get some of my homework done. After I finished, I changed and hurried downstairs to meet Abby. She was already waiting for me at the edge of the parking lot. I'd never seen her look so excited before.

"Ready?" she asked.

I stopped in front of her. "Yep, let's go."

We drove to the mall where the movie theater was. She tried to get me to pick the movie, but I refused. It was her birthday, so that meant that she got to pick. We debated for a few minutes before deciding on one that was about zombies. Her choice surprised me. I never would have picked Abby to be the zombie-movie type.

I paid for her popcorn and drink as a present to her. I couldn't help but frown at how excited she was. It was obvious that she'd never really had a friend. I sat through two hours of zombies popping out of random spots.

The movie wasn't bad. I just didn't like scary stuff. I rolled my eyes as I realized I'd be sleeping with all the lights on tonight.

"That was awesome!" Abby said as we walked back to her car. "Did you like it?"

"It was great," I lied.

"Are you hungry?"

"Starving."

We drove back through Morgantown toward campus. My hand tightened on the door as we pulled up at the restaurant where Ally worked. Abby didn't seem to notice my discomfort as she stepped out of the car. I looked around and saw Ally's car parked a few spaces away.

This is going to be a disaster.

I followed Abby into the restaurant, scanning the place for Ally. I didn't see her anywhere, but I knew she was here. I made sure to take the seat where I could see the waitress station and the counter. There was no way that I was going to let Ally sneak up on me.

"You okay?" Abby asked.

I tore my eyes away from the restaurant to smile at her. "I'm fine."

"You seem kind of nervous. Do you not like this place?"

"No, I love it."

"Okay, I just wanted to make sure. I was going to say that we could go somewhere else if you didn't."

I was tempted to tell her that I hated it, but I decided not to. It was her birthday, and I wouldn't let Ally ruin it for her. If Abby wanted to eat here, we would eat here.

"What can I get you guys to drink?" a familiar voice asked.

I looked up to see Ally standing by our table with a pen and a pad of paper in her hand. I'd been concentrating on Abby so much that I hadn't even noticed Ally walking up.

"A water for me. What do you want, Emma?" Abby asked.

"The same," I said as I stared at Ally. There was no way that I was going to let her out of my sight.

"I'll be right back," Ally said sweetly.

She made sure to push her stomach out as she turned to walk away. I wanted to vomit.

"She seems nice," Abby said, completely unaware of what was happening around her.

"Yep."

My eyes never left Ally as she walked to the waitress station and filled two glasses with water. When she returned, she was just as sweet as before.

"Are you ready to order?" Ally asked.

"Yeah, I want a cheeseburger and fries," Abby said as she handed Ally her menu.

"And you?" Ally asked as she stared at me. Her back was to Abby, so she didn't try to hide the hate in her eyes.

"The same," I answered calmly as I shoved the menu in her hand.

She stumbled back a bit with the force of it, but the smile never left her face. "Great. I'm going on break, but I'll put your order in before I go. I should be back by the time your food is done. I'll be sure to bring it out to you."

There was just something about Ally that made me nervous. I hadn't given it much thought when I'd been with Jesse, but now, the feeling wouldn't go away. She was a hateful bitch. I had no idea why she hated me so bad. She'd won—she had Jesse. That was all that mattered to her.

I sipped my water and chatted with Abby as we waited for our food. Ally had disappeared into the back room as soon as she put our orders in, so I tried to relax while she was gone. If I didn't like Abby so much, I would have left the second I realized Ally was our waitress.

Ally came out of the back room just as our food was placed on the counter. Another waitress walked to the register to ring someone up, blocking my view. I cursed as I tried to watch Ally. I didn't want her to spit in my food or do something gross like that. By the time the waitress moved away from the cash register, Ally was already walking toward us with our food. She placed them on the table in front of us and walked away without a word.

I inspected my food closely before I finally took a bite. It seemed to be okay. I laughed at myself as I ate. I was being ridiculous. Ally was hateful, but she wouldn't do something that could cost her a job that she desperately needed. She had a kid to support after all. I lost my appetite as I thought about her baby. I felt like a horrible person for having any bad feelings for a baby, but I couldn't help it.

We finished our burgers, and I paid. Abby tried to fight with me, but I won. I knew it was mean of me, but I didn't bother to leave a tip. I just couldn't bring myself to do it. Ally smiled as I walked past, but I refused to acknowledge her. *The sooner I get out of here, the better.*

Abby was grinning from ear to ear as she drove back to the dorm. "Thank you for coming out with me tonight. It means a lot."

"No problem. I had a lot of fun," I told her.

Despite seeing Ally, the night had been fun. It had been so long since I'd had any girl time that I'd forgotten just how much fun it was.

"We'll have to do it again sometime," I said.

"That would be great!" Abby said as she pulled up to our dorm.

It wasn't that late, but I was exhausted. I told her good night as I walked slowly to my dorm. As soon as I hit the bed, I was out.

I barely made it to the bathroom. The second I dropped down in front of the toilet, I started throwing up violently. I heaved until there was nothing left in my stomach to expel. After that, I just curled up into a ball and willed myself to die. My stomach was cramping so badly that I honestly felt like I really was dying. I'd never experienced anything like it.

I felt another wave of nausea hit me. I sat up and started dry-heaving into the toilet. I couldn't breathe. Sweat was sliding down my face as I tried to move. I half-walked and half-crawled to the sink to wet a washcloth. My hands were shaking so bad that I could barely turn the knob. I finally managed to get the cold water turned on. I ran the cloth under the water until it was soaked, and then I ran it across my face. I wiped my mouth before tossing it in the general direction of the hamper.

I waited until I was sure that my body wouldn't revolt again before I crawled back to my bed. My stomach was still cramping to the point that it actually hurt to breathe. I took shallow breaths as I reached for my phone. I pushed Andy's speed dial number and prayed that he would answer.

"Emma? What's wrong?" he asked groggily.

"I need help. Sick," I whispered. I bit my lip to keep from crying out as my stomach started cramping again.

"I'll be right over. Stay put," he said before ending the call.

Like I could go anywhere right now.

I pleaded with my stomach to stop hurting as I waited for Andy to arrive. Ten minutes later, he knocked on my door. He obviously had no problem sneaking into the dorm and up to my room.

I stumbled to the door and cracked it to make sure it was Andy. As soon as I saw him, I unlocked it to let him in. I had to lean on the wall. If I hadn't, I knew I would fall over.

"Fuck, Emma, you look horrible."

"Thanks," I whispered.

Andy helped me back to my bed. I cried out when my stomach started twisting again. I was going to die. I just knew it. He ran to the bathroom and returned a few seconds later with a glass of water. He helped me sit up enough to take tiny sips.

"What happened?" Andy asked.

"Woke up like this," I managed to gasp out between cramps.

"Why don't you try to go to sleep? Maybe it'll go away while you're asleep."

Nothing short of someone knocking me out would put me to sleep while I was in this much pain, but I didn't argue. I didn't have the energy. Andy lay down beside me and put my head on his chest. He ran his fingers through my drenched hair and tried to keep me calm as wave after wave of nausea and cramps attacked me.

I finally passed out around dawn when the cramps started to ease. When I woke up, the clock beside the bed said four. I reached for Andy, but he wasn't in bed. I winced as I tried to sit up to look for him. My stomach felt like I'd done a thousand crunches during the night. I'd never been this sore in my life, even during cheer camp my freshman year.

"How are you feeling?" Andy asked from the window.

"Like someone killed me—twice," I groaned.

"That bad?" he asked.

I nodded. "That bad."

"You seem to be better now."

"My stomach doesn't feel like it's going to fall out at the moment, so I'd say I'm better."

"You either had one nasty stomach bug or food poisoning. Either way, that was horrible."

I sat straight up in bed despite the tenderness in my stomach. "That bitch!"

"What are you talking about?"

"Ally! I went to the restaurant with Abby last night. Ally was our waitress."

"Emma, I know you and Ally don't like each other, but my sister wouldn't poison you."

"There's no other explanation for it. Think about it!"

Andy shook his head. "I know you think the worst of her, but she wouldn't do something like this."

"I think she would," I said stubbornly.

I could just feel it. Ally had done this to me.

"Look, why don't you try to sleep some more?" Andy suggested.

"I've slept enough. I want to go to that diner and kill your sister."

"Emma, stop. There's a difference between two girls who can't stand each other and two girls who would poison each other."

"I'm not enough of a bitch to poison her. Obviously, she doesn't have my morals."

"I'm not going to fight with you," Andy said.

I knew I was pissing him off, but I didn't care. It was too much of a coincidence that I'd eaten where his sister worked and then had gotten food poisoning.

"I have to head to work. Is there anything you need me to get for you before I leave?"

I shook my head. "I'll be fine."

He seemed unsure. "Don't be mad at me."

"I'm not," I said as I slowly stood up. Every muscle in my body protested. I ignored my screaming body as I walked to my dresser and pulled out clean clothes. "I'm going to shower. Go to work. I don't want you to get in trouble."

"Call me if you need anything. I mean it."

"I will."

Andy waved as he left. I slowly made my way to the bathroom and pulled off my clothes. I knew Ally hated me, but I hadn't realized that she hated me enough to do this. *There is something seriously wrong with that girl.*

9

Things had been tense between Ally and me since she'd discovered Emma's clothes in the bathroom. She tried to pretend that she wasn't mad anymore, but I could see the resentment in her eyes every time she looked at me. I'd done nothing wrong, yet she was making me feel like I'd betrayed her. Maybe in her eyes, I had.

I had hoped that our talk would help her understand a little better where we stood. It might have helped if she hadn't found Emma's clothes. It seemed like Ally had completely forgotten about the conversation as she focused on being angry with me.

I knew it was a douche move, but I avoided being at home as much as possible. Instead, I spent my days in class and my evenings at the library. The only good thing that had come of this entire situation was the fact that I was ahead in all of my classes. I had papers done that weren't due for weeks. I'd also memorized every song on my iPod. I never thought I'd see the day when either of those things happened.

I was walking across campus to spend yet another night in the library when I saw Emma. I stopped walking, so I could watch her. She kept her head down as she moved in the opposite direction of the library. At least she looked better than the last time I'd seen her. She wasn't battling a hangover from hell at the moment. I wished that she had stayed like she'd agreed to instead of running away when my back was turned.

I knew I should just keep walking and spend the night with my hot date, the librarian. What I knew and what I wanted to do were two completely different things. I wanted to grab Emma and kiss her until she couldn't breathe. I wanted to rip off her clothes. I wanted to feel her body pressed up against mine, skin to skin. I wanted to flip her onto her stomach and take her from behind while she screamed out my name.

I shook my head, trying to push away the image of a naked Emma coming undone underneath me. Andy was no longer my friend, but I felt like I was betraying him just by thinking about Emma that way. He'd betrayed me, too, though. He had known she was mine, yet he had still taken her from me. He got to hold her and kiss her every damn day while all I had were memories.

I turned and started walking toward the library. There was nothing left to save between Emma and me. I had to let her go.

I made it all of ten feet before I turned around and started following her. I had no idea what the hell I was doing, but I guessed I would find out. She was several feet ahead of me now, and I had to hurry to catch up. I stayed back a bit, afraid that she would disappear if she saw me.

She entered one of the dorms, and I waited outside for a second before I followed her. I had to talk to her. I couldn't let her keep thinking that I'd slept with Ally. Even if she was with Andy now, I couldn't stand the thought of her thinking the worst of me. It would change nothing between Emma and me, and I knew that. I knew Ally would never forgive me for telling Emma the truth, but I'd deal with her later.

Emma disappeared into the stairwell just as I walked into the dorm. I followed, still staying far enough away that she wouldn't notice. There were a few people going up the stairs between us but not enough to hide me if she turned around. She never looked behind her as she continued up to her floor. She stepped out of the stairwell and walked down a hallway. I watched her through the glass in the door separating the hallway from the stairs to see which door she went in.

Once she was inside her room, I started moving down the hallway. When I reached her door, I raised my hand to knock. I stopped just before my fist connected with it. If I was going to go through with this, it might not go the way I wanted it to. I knew she was angry with me, and she might not listen to anything that I had to say. She might kick my ass right back into the hallway—if she even let me get past the door. Realistically, she'd probably slam the door in my face as soon as she saw it was me.

I stood there with my hand raised, looking like a complete idiot. Several women were in the hallway, and they were all giving me strange looks. Of course they were because I was lurking outside of Emma's door. I knocked on her door before I lost my nerve again or before someone decided to call security on my ass. Now, I had to go through with this.

Emma opened the door a second later. Surprise registered on her face when she saw me standing there.

"Hey," I said lamely.

"Hey."

She raised an eyebrow when I didn't say anything. "Did you need something?"

"Uh, yeah. Can we talk?"

"I thought that's what we were doing."

"Can we talk inside your room?" I looked around at the women who were still staring at me. "It's kind of hard to talk privately out here."

She stepped back. "Sure, come on in."

I walked past her and into the room. I was surprised to see that there was only one bed. I thought it was a dorm rite of passage to get stuck with a sucky roommate. The room reminded me a lot of her room back home. This one was a lot smaller, but it was still just as bare as her old one. There were no pictures, no posters, nothing. There was a bed, a desk, and a closet. That was it.

I turned back to face her. "I think we need to talk."

"I don't."

I knew she wouldn't make this easy.

"I really think we do."

She stepped closer to me, and I took a step back. The backs of my legs hit her bed, and I went down. As soon as I landed on the mattress, she was on top of me. Her lips were on mine before I could even process what was happening. I had no idea what was going on, and I really didn't care. She was kissing me, and that was all that mattered.

No, I needed to talk to her. No matter how much I liked what she was doing, we needed to talk before anything like *that* could happen.

I put my hands on her shoulders and gently pushed her off of me. "Emma, we need to talk."

"I don't think we do." She smiled down at me. "I can think of something else I'd rather be doing with you."

She reached down and began pushing up my shirt. Surprised, I let go of her. She fell back down onto me and started kissing me again. I groaned as her tongue teased my lips until I opened them. As soon as I did, her tongue slipped inside to caress mine. She ran her fingers across my stomach, causing me to jump.

She smiled as she sat up and started tugging on my shirt. "Take this off."

I sat up and pulled my shirt over my head. She grabbed the bottom of her shirt and lifted it over her head as I threw mine aside. She tossed hers down onto the floor and reached behind her to unclasp her bra. As soon as she had it free, she slipped it off and threw it somewhere behind her.

"Shit," I groaned as I stared up at her.

I leaned up and ran my tongue across her nipple. She arched her back to give me better access. I sucked one nipple into my mouth as I started tweaking her other with my fingers. I lifted her and laid her on the bed beside me before climbing on top of her.

"I've missed you so much," I whispered.

"I missed you, too. Please, Jesse, it's been so long. I can't wait any longer. I need you inside me."

Emma snapped her fingers in front of my face. "Earth to Jesse. Hello?"

I blinked. After I realized that I'd just imagined that, I wanted to beat my head against the wall.

"What?" I asked.

"You said you wanted to talk, so start talking. Where did you just go?"

"Nowhere. I was just thinking."

"Okay…why are you here?" she asked.

"To talk."

She rolled her eyes. "Are you being an ass on purpose? Or does it just come naturally?"

"Sorry, I wasn't trying to be an ass. I came here to talk about what's going on between Ally and me."

Her eyes grew hard. "I really don't need to know the details. I took sex education. I know how babies are made."

"It's not what you think—" I started.

But she held up her hand. "Look, we're not together anymore. You don't owe me an explanation. You can stick your you-know-what wherever you please. It's not my concern anymore, and it hasn't been for a long time."

"So, I guess I should feel the same about Andy and you."

Her eyes widened. I'd struck a nerve.

"You have no idea what you're talking about."

"I got the gist of it. I have to admit, I never saw that one coming." I knew I should shut up, but I couldn't seem to get the message to my mouth. "At least you waited until I left to fuck him. I appreciate that."

"Shut up, Jesse."

"Why? It's okay for you to fuck Andy, but you can't talk about it? Come on, I thought we were having a nice conversation."

"Fuck you!"

"You already did," I shot back.

I instantly regretted my words as tears filled her eyes. I was the biggest asshole alive.

"I knew she'd tell you," she whispered. "She would do anything to make you hate me. It was an accident. We never meant to have—"

"She didn't tell me," I cut her off. I didn't need to know how it had happened. "She just confirmed what I suspected after I saw you two together the first time."

"What are you talking about?"

"Come on, Emma, I'm not stupid. I knew you were together as soon as he hit me. It wasn't that hard to figure out. How did you two end up together anyway? I have to admit I'm curious about that part. Did you guys do it just to get back at me after I left, and then you both realized that you actually liked each other? Or did you already know something was there before I even left? At least I know you well enough to know that you'd never cheat on me while we were together."

I couldn't understand why I kept saying every hurtful thing that I could think of. I *knew* I was hurting her, but I couldn't seem to stop. I'd come here to make her feel better, and I'd done the exact opposite.

"What about you? Don't tell me that the first time you slept with Ally, you got her pregnant. You know what they say—practice makes perfect."

"I didn't—" I stopped myself.

I'd already screwed up my chances of keeping Emma from hating me. After what I'd just said to her about Andy, nothing I told her would make her hate me any less. I wouldn't give away Ally's secret. I couldn't. If I hadn't fucked up royally five minutes ago, I might have. But now, there was nothing left to save here. I'd destroyed it all.

"I should go."

"I think that is the best thing you've said since you walked in here," Emma said as she stomped to the door and threw it open.

I walked by without looking at her. I had just ruined any chance of us even being friends.

"Jesse?"

I turned to look at her. "Yeah?"

"Stay the fuck away from me."

10
EMMA

I slammed the door in his face. There was a whole five seconds where I felt empowered before I slowly slid down the door and curled up on the floor. Tears ran down my cheeks as I thought about everything he'd just said to me.

He'd used every single thing he could think of to degrade me and make me feel like trash. He'd even used my friendship with Andy against me. Jesse thought Andy and I were together. I had no idea how Jesse had come to that conclusion, but if I had to guess, I would bet that Ally had something to do with it. He'd said she'd only confirmed what he'd guessed, so that meant that they'd talked about Andy and me being together. She'd probably told him that Andy and I had slept together, so he would think the worst of me. I'd tried to explain to Jesse that Andy and I weren't together, but Jesse had refused to give me the chance. It was obvious that he had already made up his mind about Andy and me.

I knew I'd screwed up with Andy after Jesse left, but I couldn't believe Jesse would think that I'd end up with his best friend.

Doesn't Jesse realize that every time I look at Andy, I think of him?

Lucy and I had started to grow apart long before I left, and Andy had stepped in and filled her place without either of us realizing what was happening. He was like family to me despite what had happened, and I could never think of him that way. He'd never stopped his man-whore ways either, so I knew there was no chance that he felt that way about me either.

"You smell so good," I panted.

"You taste good," he muttered before running his tongue across my skin.

Goose bumps erupted across my skin as he continued to kiss and lick his way across my skin. He raised me up long enough to pull my shirt over my head before pushing me back down onto the couch. His hands skimmed across my stomach, causing my muscles to jump. His kisses felt like fire as he kissed between my breasts and down my stomach. I wiggled my hips, trying to feel his thickness against me.

He held my hips down as he kissed back up my body. His arms pushed underneath me, and he undid the clasp on my bra. A voice in the back of my head was screaming at me, telling me that this was a bad idea, but I pushed it away. I just wanted to feel his hands on me. I needed to feel wanted.

"We need to go to my room in case anyone comes home," he whispered in my ear as my bra fell away.

He stood and picked me up. I wrapped my arms and legs around him as he carried me to his room. I ran my tongue along his jaw before sucking on his neck. If it bothered him, he didn't complain.

He dropped me down onto his mattress and climbed back on top of me. He pulled his shirt off and threw it down beside the bed. I reached up and ran my hands across his chest. I leaned forward and kissed a trail across his chest. He shuddered as he pushed me back down and started kissing me again. He sat up and reached for my shorts. I lifted my hips, allowing him to slip them along with my underwear off. His shorts and his boxers came off next.

I suddenly felt nervous. No one had seen me like this except for Jesse, and I barely knew Andy. But Jesse had cheated on me. He didn't care about me, and he never had. It was time to move on even if it was for only one night. Andy's body covered mine, and I pushed Jesse from my mind.

I watched as Andy reached over and grabbed a condom from the nightstand drawer. He ripped it open and slipped it on. I closed my eyes as he lowered his body over mine, and then he slipped inside. My breath hitched as he filled me.

This wasn't about emotions. This was about getting off.

Andy started thrusting as I raised my hips. I clung to him as he worked to push me over the edge. My breathing grew ragged as he brought me closer and closer to the edge. I tightened my legs around him to bury him deeply inside me as I came. He groaned as he released with me.

When our heartbeats slowed down, he slipped out and threw the condom away. We were both silent as he climbed back into bed with me. He didn't hold me, and I didn't expect him to.

"Well, isn't this cute?"

I opened my eyes to see sunlight coming through a window. My head was fuzzy as I tried to figure out where I was. The events of the night before came crashing back as my eyes landed on Andy in bed beside me.

"Sorry to wake you."

My head snapped up to see Ally standing in the doorway. Oh god, this couldn't be happening. There was no way that I'd slept with Andy last night. There was no way that Ally had just walked in to see what I'd done.

Andy groaned and rolled over. He opened his eyes enough to see me beside him and Ally across the room. His eyes widened as he stared back at me. It was obvious that he was as shocked as I was.

"I would say I'm surprised, but I'm not," Ally said as she watched us digest everything.

I wanted to slap the stupid smile she was wearing right off her face.

"Get out of here," Andy said quietly.

Ally laughed. "I'm going, I'm going. I just want to savor this for another minute or two. I always knew she was a slut. This just proves that I was right. Jesse has been gone for, what? A month? She barely waited a month before she moved on with his best friend."

"Get out!" Andy roared.

Ally rolled her eyes, and then she turned and walked out. Andy waited until she closed the door before he rolled over to look at me. We both stared at each other, unable to think of anything to say.

"This can't be happening," Andy finally groaned as he looked away and stared up at the ceiling.

"I don't even know what to say."

"I do. We fucked up—big time. I'm sorry, Emma. I wasn't thinking clearly."

That stung a little even though it shouldn't. From what Jesse had told me, Andy slept with everyone without a second thought, but he now regretted sleeping with me. My eyes welled up with tears. This whole situation was a mess.

"Hey, don't cry. I didn't mean it that way. I just meant that you're Jesse's girl—or at least, you used to be. You're an attractive chick, but last night should have never happened. I didn't invite you over with the intention of sleeping with you. I'm an asshole, but I'm not that big of an asshole."

I gave him a weak smile as tears continued to flow. "I feel like I cheated on him. I know it's stupid, but I can't help it."

Andy sighed. "Look, we were both messed-up. There's nothing we can do now. Let's just pretend that it never happened and move on."

"That's a great plan—except Ally knows. She hates me, and she can use this against me. All of your friends know that I was with Jesse. If Ally tells them that I slept with you, everyone will think that I'm a slut. I don't want that to get back to my school. I can't handle that."

"I'll deal with Ally. She can be a hard-ass, but she's my sister. She won't say anything if I ask her not to."

"Are you sure?"

He nodded. "I'm sure."

"Thank you. Andy?"

"What?"

"I need to go, but I'm naked."

"Oh shit." He laughed. "I'm so torn between embarrassing the fuck out of you or being the nice guy."

"Andy, I will kill you."

"Fine." He threw the covers off of himself and stood.

My cheeks flamed as I stared at a naked Andy. "You're an ass."

"What? I'm just getting up, so I can get dressed. I'll leave you alone to find your clothes."

I stayed silent as he grabbed a pair of shorts and threw them on. He grinned as he walked to the door and opened it.

"See? I'm just being a nice guy."

"Out!" I yelled.

He simply laughed again as he closed the door behind him. I waited a few minutes to make sure that he was really gone before I stood and started searching for my clothes. My bra and shirt were in the living room, so I searched until I found a baggy shirt of his to wear home.

When I opened his door and walked into the living room, he was nowhere to be seen. I grabbed my shirt, bra, and keys before slipping silently outside to where my car was parked.

I shook my head to push the memories away. *What was done is done, and there isn't a thing I can do to change it.* I'd regretted sleeping with Andy for the last two years, but I'd accepted it. We'd made a mistake while drinking—that was all. We'd rarely talked about it since, and we had become really good friends after that night. Everything happened for a reason, and I knew that we never would have ended up as friends if I hadn't gone over there that day.

I just hated that Jesse knew.

No, I didn't hate that he knew. I hated the fact that I wasn't the one who had told him. If things had worked out the way I'd hoped, I would have told him eventually…maybe. Of course, things never worked out the way I wanted. I'd never factored Ally into the equation, and she was the one who had screwed up everything. She always did. It was her fault that Jesse and I had split in the beginning. It was her fault that he'd left. It was her fault that he knew about what had happened between Andy and me. It was her fault that I couldn't be with him now.

It was all her fault.

No, that last part wasn't her fault. Jesse obviously *wanted* to be with her, or he wouldn't be. She might be the reason that we weren't together, but it was his choice to be with her now. I hated her for everything that she'd done, but I hated her for what she couldn't control most of all. No matter how much she schemed, she couldn't control his feelings for her. She couldn't make him love her, but he did anyway.

I wanted this all to go away. I wanted to go back in time, to be back in California, living the life I'd had before Jesse had come into it and changed everything. I wanted to be the girl I had been before, the girl who had never been hurt. It was amazing how one person could walk into my life and change everything. I was tired of hurting over a man who had moved on. I wanted to move on, too. I just wasn't sure how. It was obvious that going to Sam's party hadn't helped. It had only made things worse. I just wanted to forget everything that Jesse had made me feel. If I could do that, I would be okay.

It was time that I figured out what I wanted to do with my life instead of hanging on to the past. There was nothing left for me from back then. I needed to accept that and figure out where I wanted to go from here.

West Virginia was great, but I wasn't sure that I could stay here. There was always a chance that I would run into Jesse or Ally here, and I didn't need that. I needed to be far away from both of them. I knew Andy would understand. He always had. The only question was whether or not he would follow me if I didn't go back to California. I knew he'd come to West Virginia to help me with Jesse, but if I left, there was no reason for him to go with me. I wasn't sure how I would handle being on my own and starting over completely.

I knew I couldn't stay here, but I didn't want to go home either. *So, where do I want to be?* I knew my dad would help me get to wherever I wanted. I just wasn't sure where my destination would be.

I thought about the colleges I'd applied to last year. There were several that I'd been interested in despite my need to find Jesse. I could go to one of them. I smiled as a plan began to form in my head. I would stay here until the semester was over, and then I was going to transfer to a new school.

I stood and walked to my desk. I grabbed a piece of paper and started writing down the schools that I'd been genuinely interested in—University of California, Washington State University, Florida State University, Boston

University, New York University. The University of California was in Los Angeles - too close to home, so that one was out. It rained a lot in Washington, so that one was out, too. That left me with three choices. I stared down at the paper, trying to decide where my life would take me.

I finally decided on New York. It was pretty much as far away from home as I could get without leaving the country. Plus, tons of people were there. Surely, I'd find a friend and a way to start over.

I tore the sheet of paper out of my notebook and put it in my desk drawer. I needed to think this through before I made my final decision. Plus, I wanted to talk to Andy. I wanted him to come with me, but I knew the chances of that happening were slim. I still had to try though. After I talked to him, I'd call my dad to see if he would help me. I knew he probably would, but I didn't want to assume anything.

I would figure things out, and when I did, I was going to start living again.

I stared at the door Emma had just slammed in my face. I couldn't believe that I'd said those things to her. I'd never meant to hurt her. I'd knocked on her door with every intention of telling her the truth about Ally, but the whole conversation had gone south before I had the chance. Emma had to think that I was the biggest asshole alive. For all I knew, she still believed that I'd cheated on her with Ally two years ago, and now, she thought that Ally was pregnant with my kid. It was like the entire world had decided that she needed to think the absolute worst of me.

Only Ally and I knew the truth. I'd done absolutely nothing wrong last time or this time. I was just the asshole who had been dealt a shit hand when it came to my relationship with Emma. If things were different now, maybe Emma would have been willing to give me a second chance. My promise to Ally and her relationship with Andy stood in the way. The two people who had meant the most to me for so many years were the ones who were destroying what I wanted.

I turned and walked away from Emma's closed door. I needed to leave before I beat on her door and begged her to take me back. I wanted to take her and run away from this entire situation.

I walked back across campus to where my car was parked. There was no way that I was going to be able to sit in the library and work tonight. I had too much going on in my head. I couldn't go home either. Ally wasn't working tonight, so I knew she'd be there, waiting on me. I couldn't face her right now. I knew it wasn't entirely her fault, but at the moment, I wanted to blame her for all of this. Keeping my temper in check, I had to keep repeating to myself that she didn't ask for this to happen to her.

I aimlessly drove around Morgantown. My mom and Mark lived about an hour south of Morgantown, so I was slightly familiar with it, but not enough to know where I was going. I really didn't care at this point. I just wanted to drive. It didn't matter where I ended up as long as I escaped.

Ally tried calling my cell phone a couple of times, but I ignored her. I knew she would worry if I didn't answer, but I wasn't in the mood to hear her whining. That was all she'd been doing lately—whining or yelling at me. Then, she would apologize a few minutes later, claiming the pregnancy was making her moody. For some reason, I didn't believe her. Ally had always been moody, but it had been worse than normal lately. I thought it had more to do with the fact that Emma was around than anything else.

I did manage to get lost a few times, but I figured out where I was once I started to see familiar buildings. I drove by Andy's apartment complex twice before I even realized what building it was. I slowed down the third time. I parked in the same parking lot where I had followed Emma to the first day I'd seen her.

If I went up and talked to Andy, I knew there was a good chance that it would end the same way it had with Emma. Things were different with Andy though. He'd been my best friend my entire life. He knew me better than anyone else—at least, he used to. After everything that had happened, he probably hated me more than Emma did. As far as he knew, I'd cheated on my girlfriend with his sister and then ended up getting her pregnant two years later.

I stared up at the window I thought went to his apartment. The lights were on, so I knew he was home, if I was looking at the right apartment. I glanced around the lot, but I didn't see Emma's car anywhere. I didn't want to go in and see them together. I couldn't handle that tonight. I couldn't even stomach the thought of what she could be doing with him this late at night.

I opened my door and stepped out into the cool night air. September was already halfway gone, and fall was fast approaching. Even after two years, I still wasn't used to West Virginia's changing seasons. The first winter that I'd spent here had been brutal on me. I'd never seen snow before, and I had to admit that I liked it. I just didn't like driving in it. That was one reason that I'd decided to move close to campus. Driving an hour one way on the snow-covered interstate wasn't at the top of my to-do list.

Who am I kidding? Going to school wasn't exactly at the top of my to-do list either. I was in Morgantown for my mom and my mom only. I would have been happy finding a local tattoo shop to take me in, so I could do an apprenticeship. Any time that I'd talked to my mom about it, she'd shut me down almost instantly. I hadn't even bothered to search for a local shop since I moved. There was no point in torturing myself. It'd been over two years since I'd added any new ink to my skin. That alone was driving me nuts. So, here I was, taking classes for a business degree that I didn't give a damn about.

I pushed my thoughts away as I walked to Andy's building. I didn't need to worry about my career choice right now. I needed to focus on Emma. I just hoped that I could keep my cool long enough to find out what had happened since I left. I knew what Ally had told me, but I wasn't convinced that she'd been completely honest with me.

I still had no idea why Emma was enrolled in school here. I was sure that she was now that I knew she was living in one of the school's dorms. One other thing that didn't make sense was the fact that she was living there instead of with Andy. His apartment was closer to campus than my house, so I knew it didn't have anything to do with travel. I just hoped that

Andy could give me the answers I was looking for. I needed *something*, so all of this would piece together in my head.

I slowly climbed up the steps to the second floor, trying to think of what I would say when I saw him. I needed answers, so I could let Emma go. *Hell, if Andy can explain everything to me, I might even wish the two of them good luck—then again, maybe not.* I didn't think that I'd ever be able to accept the two of them together as a couple.

I stopped in front of his door and knocked. When no one answered, I knocked again, harder this time. A few seconds later, I heard the deadbolt sliding, and then the door opened.

Does he ever wear a shirt? It's not like we're in California anymore, I thought to myself when I saw him standing in front of me, shirtless.

"What do you want?" Andy asked icily.

"I wanted to talk for a few."

"I'm busy."

I ran my hand across my face as I leaned against the wall. "Look, I know you hate my guts, but I need some answers. I'm going nuts here."

"I don't have your answers, and like I said, I'm busy."

He started to close the door, but I reached out and grabbed it before he could. "I won't stay long, I promise."

"Andy, who's out there?" a girl asked as she appeared behind him.

It took me a minute to process the fact that she was wearing nothing but his shirt.

"You've got to be fucking kidding me!" I shouted.

I knew Andy had slept around a lot in high school, but I assumed that he would stop since he was with Emma.

"You're fucking around behind Emma's back?"

"Who's Emma?" the girl asked as she glared at Andy.

He opened his mouth to reply, but I beat him to it.

"She would be his girlfriend."

"You asshole!" the girl shouted as she slapped him.

"Ouch! Damn it, Cassie! Let me explain. It's not what you think."

"I'm pretty sure I get the concept of what a girlfriend is, Andy. I wouldn't have come here if I had known you were with someone." She shoved him out of the way before walking out the door.

I stepped aside to let her pass me. If I wasn't so pissed, I would have laughed at the fact that she was only wearing his shirt and no shoes or pants. As soon as she was out of the way, I pushed through the door and shoved him back. He stumbled back, and before he could regain his footing, I drew back and slammed my fist into his stomach.

"I'm going to kill you for hurting her," I growled as I drew back again.

"Wait a fucking minute! Emma is *not* my girlfriend!" Andy wheezed.

"I'm not buying it. Try again."

"I'm not kidding! Emma is my friend and my friend only. I love her—but not that way."

I dropped my arm down to my side, unsure of what to do. I knew he was probably lying, but I wasn't entirely sure.

"I think you need to explain to me what the fuck is going on," I grumbled as I walked past him and sat down on his couch.

"Make yourself at home," he said under his breath as he righted himself.

"I plan to."

He walked over and dropped down on the opposite end of the couch. "Why the hell do you think I'm with Emma?"

"I saw you two together the night I followed Emma here. You punched me for her."

"No, I punched you because you knocked up my sister and broke Emma's heart."

"But Ally said Emma was with you now. She said that Emma followed you when you came here to bring Ally back to California."

"I didn't even know Ally was here until we saw her one day. We didn't come here for her."

"Then, why did you come all this way?" I asked.

"I followed Emma here when she moved. She came here looking for you."

I was going to strangle Ally with my bare hands. She'd lied to me about them cornering her when she was at work and about Emma being with Andy. I was starting to wonder if every word that had come out of her mouth was a lie. It certainly seemed that way.

"I'm so fucking confused," I groaned.

"It's not that hard to figure out, asshole. Emma has been looking for you since Ally admitted that you hadn't slept with her. Emma came to WVU, hoping that she would find you here."

"She doesn't think I slept with Ally?" I asked, shocked at what he was saying. *Emma came all this way just to find me?*

"She didn't—until we moved here and found out you had knocked Ally up. That kind of ruined Emma's plans to ask you to give her another chance," Andy said as he glared at me.

"Fuck."

"Yeah, you fucked up big time. I can't even process how bad you fucked up."

"I have to talk to Emma. I have to get her back," I said as I stood up.

Andy jumped to his feet and pushed me back down onto the couch. "You're not going anywhere. Did you forget the little fact that you're going to be a dad? I won't let you leave my sister hanging while you run off into the sunset with Emma. Ally deserves better than that."

I stared up at him, debating on what to do. Ally would never forgive me if I told her secret, but she'd lied to me over and over again to keep me from going back to Emma. I'd done everything I could to help Ally, and she'd stabbed me in the back the second she'd had the chance.

This was that pivotal moment in my life that would set everything following into motion. I could tell the truth and pray that Emma would take me back, or I could keep Ally's secret and lose everything. Either way, someone was going to get hurt.

"The kid isn't mine," I blurted out. There—it's out. There is no way I can take it back now.

Andy froze as he looked down at me. "What did you say?"

"I said, Ally's baby isn't mine."

"How is that even possible? She told Emma that you are the dad."

"That's because Ally doesn't want anyone back home to know what happened. She showed up this summer and begged me to help her. I agreed to tell anyone who asked that the baby is mine. I never thought that I'd ever see you or Emma again."

"If you're not the father, then who is?"

I shook my head. "I can't tell you that. You need to ask Ally."

"You're going to tell me."

"I can't. Ally will never forgive me."

"Jesse, if you don't tell me, you're not going to walk out of my apartment. You're going to crawl."

"She's keeping it from you to protect you, and I agree with her. I know what you'll do if you find out."

"Jesse, she's my fucking sister. I deserve to know what's going on." He stared down at me. "Or maybe you're lying, so I'll let you go after Emma."

"I wouldn't lie about this shit."

I couldn't believe that he thought that I would sink that low. If Ally's kid were mine, I would never abandon her like that. I knew what it was like to grow up without a dad.

"I don't know what to think about you anymore, Jesse. Tell me what happened, or I'll make sure Emma never speaks to you again. She hates you so much at this point that it wouldn't be hard to get her to ignore you."

"This is bullshit! You're asking me to tell you something that could get you killed!"

"Tell me what the hell is going on!" Andy roared.

"Fine, but if something happens to you, it's not on my conscience. Ally was raped back in California by one of the bikers. I don't know which one. She never told me."

Andy's mouth dropped open in shock as he sat down beside me on the couch. "Why wouldn't she tell me something like that? I could have helped her."

"There was no way you could have helped. It had already happened."

"Then we should have called the police. Or I could have killed the guy myself."

"We both know how dangerous those guys are. He threatened to kill her if she told. Even if the cops caught him, he has brothers who would have killed her. If you had gone after him, you would have died. When she found out she was pregnant, running was the only option she had."

"I don't even know what to say. I've wanted to kill you for getting her pregnant when I should have thanked you for helping her."

"She's like my sister, too. I would do anything to protect her."

"This is a fucking mess," he groaned. "I still want to kill that fucker. I wish she would have told you his name."

"So, you could go and get yourself killed? I don't think so. There's nothing we can do at this point, except help her. She loves that baby already, so we just have to be there to support her. I would like to kill her for lying to me though. I knew something was up when I realized Emma was a student here."

"So, what are you going to do?"

"I need to talk to Ally first and tell her that you know. She'll be angry with me, but once she figures out that you're not going to go out and do something stupid, I think she'll be okay. After that, I'm going to talk with Emma. I said some really horrible shit to her tonight. I accused her of sleeping with you since that's what Ally told me."

"Shit. Jesse, I need to talk to you about something."

I was instantly on alert as I felt him tense beside me. "What?"

"I...okay, first off, it wasn't something that either of us meant to do."

"Andy, just tell me what the hell you're talking about."

He looked up at me, his eyes filled with remorse. "I slept with Emma."

12

I felt like he'd just punched me in the stomach.

"I thought you said that you two weren't together? Didn't I just see a half-naked woman leave your apartment twenty minutes ago?" I asked.

"We're not together, and we never have been together. It was a one-time thing."

"So, you just slept with her and sent her on her way, like you always do?"

I felt rage boiling up inside of me. He'd used her and then tossed her aside like garbage.

"What? No, of course not! It was an accident."

"How do you accidentally sleep with someone?"

"It was right after you left. She drove to your house and parked outside. I felt bad for her, so I went over to talk to her. I knew she was really upset, so I invited her over to my house. We started drinking, and the next thing I knew, I was waking up with Emma beside me in my bed. Both of us regretted it, but there was nothing that we could do. We never meant for it to happen, I swear. Emma was hurting, and I just wanted to make her feel better."

"It looks like you did a good job. I don't know if I want to hit you or kill you at this point."

"It was two years ago. We've been friends ever since, and nothing else has happened. She's too hung up on you to notice anyone else, and I don't think of her that way. You have nothing to worry about when it comes to me. I don't plan on settling down for a long time."

"I was a complete jackass to her earlier tonight. I thought that you two were together, and I know I hurt her."

"There's nothing you can do now, except apologize. Emma loves you—a lot. You just have to be honest with her and then give her some time to process everything. She's spent the last year and a half searching for you, only to find you with Ally and a kid on the way. She's hurting."

"I need to go. I'm going to talk with Ally first, so hopefully, she'll come visit you tonight. You two have a lot to work through, too. She's pretty messed-up because of everything that happened to her. She's hurting, too, because she loves me, and I flat-out told her that I don't feel that way about her. She blames Emma, but Emma has nothing to do with it."

"I figured out how Ally felt about you a while before you left. I just never told you because I didn't want you to change the way you acted around her."

"I wish you had. Maybe if I had known how she felt before everything had blown up, things would have been different."

"I don't know. Maybe," Andy sighed.

"Are we cool?"

He nodded. "Yeah, we've been cool for a long time—with the exception of when I thought you knocked up Ally. I could never find you before to tell you that we were okay."

"I'm glad. I've missed having you around."

"Likewise. Go talk to Ally, and then get Emma back. I'm tired of seeing Emma miserable all the time."

"Let's see if she'll give me the chance to make her happy again."

I prepared myself for the fight I knew I would get into as I unlocked my front door. Ally was going to be angry with me, but I'd had to do what was right for me. I just hoped that she would understand eventually.

I walked in and set my keys down on the table. "Ally?"

When she didn't answer, I started walking from room to room, trying to find her. I knew she was home since her car was outside. I checked the kitchen first and then her room. I looked in my room next even though I knew she wouldn't be in there. That left the bathroom. I walked to the door and knocked gently. Light was coming out from underneath the door, but Ally didn't answer.

I opened the door and stuck my head in, just to make sure she was okay. I didn't see her by the toilet, so I pushed the door open further. She was standing at the sink in her bra and a pair of shorts with her earbuds in her ears. That explained why she hadn't answered me. I didn't want her to think that I was staring at her while she was nearly naked, so I quickly backed away and started to close the door.

But then, something caught my eye on the sink, and I stopped. It took me a minute to process what I was seeing. Once it hit me, I threw the door open and stormed in.

"You've got to be kidding me!" I shouted loud enough for Ally to hear me over the music coming from her earbuds.

She jumped and turned to face me. As soon as she saw me, she grabbed a shirt and held it over herself.

"Jesse! I didn't hear you come in."

"Obviously not. There's no need to cover yourself. I already saw."

"What are you talking about?"

"I saw your stomach, Ally. It's flat. There is definitely no baby in there, and I'm guessing you've been using that"—I pointed to the band-type contraption on the sink—"to make it look like you are pregnant."

"Jesse, let me explain."

"Explain, what? The fact that you've been lying to me about being pregnant? Tell me the truth, Ally. Was it *all* a lie? Were you even raped in California?"

Tears fell down her cheeks, but I wasn't buying it. I couldn't believe that she had done this to me.

"Jesse…"

"No, answer me. Was it all a lie?"

"Yes," she whispered.

I turned and punched the wall, leaving a hole in the drywall. "Get the fuck out of my house. I can't even stand to look at you."

"Please, let me explain. I did it for you!"

"How the hell did you do this for me? You lied to me! You've been lying to me about everything since you came back into my life!"

"I knew Emma was looking for you! I *knew* she was planning to come here to look for you, so I left first. I wanted to find you before she did, so I could protect you from her. She's a horrible person, Jesse! She doesn't deserve you! She doesn't love you like I do!"

"You don't love me, Ally. With everything that you've done, I'd say you're obsessed with me. This isn't healthy, Ally. Think about it."

"You're wrong. I do love you. I've done all of this to protect you! I've loved you since we were kids. We're meant to be together!"

"I can't even stand to be in the same room as you. Why the hell would you think I love you? I told you from the beginning that I would help you, not that I loved you. I even sat down with you and explained how I felt."

"I thought if I gave you time, then you might start to love me. I know you do even if you don't realize it."

"Ally, get out of my house, or I'll call the police on you. I can't believe that I let you live here. You nearly destroyed everything for me. I almost lost Emma again because of you!"

"You've already lost her. She's with Andy now, and he told me that they're going to get married soon," she said triumphantly.

I laughed. That was all that I could do. If I hadn't laughed, I might have strangled her. "Try again."

"Why are you laughing? How could you think this is funny? You lost her, Jesse. She belongs to Andy now, and you can't do anything about it."

"You're a lying bitch. I talked to Andy tonight. I know everything that you told me about them isn't true."

Her eyes widened in disbelief. "You're lying."

"No, actually, I'm not. I had a nice conversation with Andy, and we managed to get a lot cleared up. I know why they're here."

"She slept with Andy! I saw it with my own eyes! I'm not lying about that."

I shrugged, trying not to show how much that hurt. "I know."

"And you don't even care? You're still going to take her back after she slept with your best friend?"

"We all make mistakes. You living in my house is proof of that. I can forgive Emma for what happened. But you? I will *never* forgive you for what you've done. I want your stuff packed, and I want you out of here in the next half hour. Once you're gone, I never want to see you again. If you ever come near Emma or me again, you'll regret it."

"Please, Jesse, give me another chance. I swear, I won't lie ever again. I just want to be with you."

She threw her shirt to the ground and ran over to me. Before I could stop her, she was kissing me. I felt bile rise in my throat as I shoved her away.

"Stay. Away. From. Me."

"Jesse, please!"

"Get the fuck out of my house!" I roared.

I'd had enough of Ally to last a lifetime. I turned and walked to my room. I made sure the door was locked behind me before I lay down on my bed.

I couldn't believe that this Ally was the same girl who I'd grown up with. *What kind of person lies about being raped and then about being pregnant?* I didn't know if she'd always been this way and I'd just missed it or if something had happened to her to make her change, but I didn't care. I never wanted to see her again. There was something seriously wrong with her to have fabricated everything that she'd told me. If she thought that was what it took to make someone love her, she needed some serious mental help.

I remembered the hatred I'd seen in her eyes before, and I wondered just what she was capable of. I hoped that she packed her things and left not just my house but Morgantown as well. If she stuck around, I would have to make sure that Emma was around either Andy or me at all times. I didn't want Emma to get hurt because of me. If she didn't want anything to do with me, I would still make sure that she was safe. She just wouldn't know that I was there. I knew my plans seemed like I was going to become a stalker, but I couldn't help it. I wanted to keep Emma safe.

Ally started beating on my door as she sobbed and apologized, but I didn't care. She could beat on that door until she died as far as I was concerned. There was no way I was coming out of this room until she was gone.

Ally finally gave up after almost an hour. I could hear her sobbing in her room as she threw things around. I hoped that she was packing her shit. If she refused to leave, I would sneak out of my damn window if I had to.

Maybe if I called Andy, he could get her out of here.

"You'll regret this, Jesse! I'll make sure of it!" she screamed outside of my door, making me jump.

She hit my door one last time before I heard the front door slam shut, and then the house went silent. I refused to get up and check to see if she was really gone. There was no way that I would fall for any more of her tricks.

My eyes started to grow heavy after about an hour of waiting. Unable to fight sleep any longer, I closed them and drifted off. My last thought was of Emma's expression when she slammed the door in my face. I had to get her back.

I opened my eyes to see that the sun was starting to rise. I sat up slowly, trying to remember why I was so pissed off. The night before came rushing back to me, and I jumped out of bed. I had to get to Emma and talk to her. I had to explain everything that had happened. I didn't know if she would believe me when I told her about Ally, but I had to try.

I grabbed my keys and ran out of my house. I knew it was still early, but I hoped that Emma was awake. I doubted that she was though. She'd never been much of a morning person when we were together. I stopped to think as I sat down in my car. I glanced at the dash. It was barely past seven. *Maybe I should give her some time to wake up, so she doesn't bite my head off.* I didn't want to piss her off before I even got started.

I seriously doubted if Ally would go straight to Emma anyway. Ally probably knew that I would go to Emma as soon as I could. Besides, for all I knew, Ally might have left Morgantown already. She had to know that Andy would come after her once I told him what she had done to me.

I made a split-second decision and headed toward Andy's apartment. He wasn't much of a morning person either, but I didn't care if I pissed him off. It wasn't like I hadn't dragged his ass out of bed at ass o'clock before to go surfing.

There wasn't much traffic this early in the morning on a Saturday. Morgantown was a college town, and most of the students were either sleeping in or sleeping off their hangover from Friday night.

I made it to Andy's within ten minutes, and I hurried inside. I had to beat on the door for a few minutes, but he finally answered.

"Do you have any idea what time it is? Some of us like to sleep, you know."

"You can sleep later. We need to talk," I said as I pushed through the door and walked to his couch to sit down.

"I think we did enough of that last night. I really don't need anything else dumped on my lap at the moment," Andy grumbled as he closed the door.

"Have you talked to Ally since I was here last night?"

"No, but Emma stopped over right after you left. Do you have any idea how hard it was to pretend like nothing had changed? She kept asking me what was wrong with me."

"Why did she come over so late?" I couldn't hide the jealousy from my voice. I hated the fact that Emma had gone to Andy when she needed someone to talk to. I hated that he was the one she leaned on now instead of me.

"She mainly wanted to talk about what an ass you are. I started to tell her the truth, but then I thought that you might want to be the one who told her what was going on."

"Thanks for letting me do it. What else did she want to talk about?"

"She wants to leave West Virginia."

"What?" I nearly shouted.

She couldn't leave yet. I needed to explain to her what had happened. I had a chance to get her back, and it was probably my only chance. I wouldn't let her leave until I explained everything.

"Relax. She's not leaving until the semester is over. You have more than enough time to tell her everything."

"Don't scare me like that. Look, I'm going to head over to her dorm in a few, but I wanted to talk to you first. Something happened last night with Ally."

He held up his hand to stop me from continuing. "I swear to God, if you tell me you slept with her, I'm going to kill you."

"Definitely not. I surprised Ally when I came home last night. I saw her without her shirt."

"Dude, really? Why do you need to tell me something like that? She's my sister."

"Let me finish. I saw her without her shirt. She's not pregnant."

Andy froze at my words. "Wait—what? I've seen her, Jesse. She is definitely showing. Emma saw her, too. Emma said that Ally made sure to show off her stomach as she said that she was having your kid."

"Ally had some kind of band thing she was using to make it look like she was pregnant. I saw it on the sink."

"You've got to be kidding me."

"I wish I were. I got into it pretty bad with her last night. She tried to lie and say that you and Emma were getting married soon. She wasn't happy when I told her that I'd already talked to you, and I knew that you weren't with Emma. She lied about everything, Andy. She wasn't raped, and she sure as hell isn't pregnant. It was all part of a plan to keep me away from Emma."

"Are you sure, Jesse? This is my sister we're talking about here."

"I know it is. That's why I came to you. I kicked her out of my house last night, and I'm hoping that she'll just leave town. If she doesn't, I think you'd be the best one to deal with her. I can barely stand to look at her at this point. She's convinced that it's all Emma's fault that I don't want to be with her. I seriously think that she's lost her damn mind. Who the fuck lies about being raped?"

"Ally has always been a little strange. You never saw it because you didn't live with her. I never thought that she'd do something like this though."

"Neither did I. I don't even know what to think about all of this. She destroyed my relationship with Emma before, and Ally did everything in her power to keep me away from Emma this time."

"Ally has been in love with you for most of her life. That's a long time to love someone and end up being rejected—twice."

"That doesn't give her an excuse to go batshit crazy."

"No, it doesn't. I'll go out and look for her today, but don't expect much. If Ally wants to disappear, she'll disappear. She's always been that way."

"Let's hope she leaves. I don't want her anywhere near Emma."

"I don't know if Ally will stick around or not. She has always been a wild card."

"Until we're sure that she's gone, I want one of us around Emma at all times."

"Don't you think you're overreacting here?"

"She lied about everything, Andy. Until I know that she's going to leave, I'm not willing to take a chance."

"All right, all right. We'll drive Emma nuts by babysitting her."

"I don't care if we annoy her. At least we'll know that she's safe. I'm going to go and talk to her now. Hopefully, she'll give me enough time to catch the door before she slams it in my face."

Andy laughed. "She's feisty when she's mad, and you definitely pissed her off. Good luck. You're going to need it."

"Thanks." I waved as I walked out of his apartment.

Then, I headed back down the stairs. I barely paid attention to where I was going as I walked to my car. All I could think about was Emma's face yesterday. I'd hurt her so bad and I wasn't sure if she'd ever forgive me.

As I drove to her dorm, I kept going over what I would say to Emma when I saw her. I'd screwed up royally last night, and I hoped that it wouldn't ruin my chances of getting her back. Surely, if she had come all this way to find me, she would listen to what I had to say. I couldn't lose her now that I had the chance to win her back.

I still couldn't wrap my head around everything that Ally had done. No matter how I looked at the situation, I had no idea how she'd thought her plan would work. *What would she have done when it was time to have her baby?* She had to know that she would get caught eventually.

I remembered the little girl I'd met so long ago. She'd looked so sweet and innocent as she'd watched Andy and me playing together outside of her house. It had taken weeks after they'd moved into the trailer park for her to finally talk to me. Their mom had moved them to the park after their dad died in a car crash. As I had gotten older, I'd come to realize that their mom wasn't much of a parent. She'd spent most of her time drinking, leaving Ally and Andy to take care of their house.

I knew her mom's lack of parenting had to have affected Ally in some way, but this was ridiculous. Andy had grown up in the exact same situation, and he hadn't ended up batshit crazy. Sure, Andy had done the typical teenager stuff, like fighting and drinking a lot, but that hadn't been nearly as bad as what Ally had done.

I pulled up in front of Emma's building and shut off my car. I smiled as I remembered the time she'd fixed this very same car. When I'd first moved here, Mark had offered to buy me a new Jeep. I'd declined, not wanting to give up one of my few reminders of Emma. She'd barely known me then, but she'd still helped. That was what Emma did—she helped others. She was such a good person, and Ally had put Emma through hell repeatedly.

I opened my door and stepped out. I still had no idea what I was going to say to Emma. I would just have to wing it and hope for the best. After trying to figure it out all the way over here, I would have thought that I could have come up with something halfway decent to say.

The dorm was silent as I walked in and climbed the stairs. It was still too early for any college kid to be up on a weekend. I hoped that Emma was awake, but I doubted it. I would just have to deal with the grouchier version of her. After yesterday, I deserved it. I walked up to her door and knocked. A minute later, I heard the lock clicking, and the door opened.

She frowned when she saw it was me. "You've got to be kidding me."

"Can we talk?" I asked as I looked at her.

It was obvious that she'd been in bed. Her hair was rumpled, and it was sticking out around her head. I couldn't help but smile at the princess pajamas she was wearing. They were so her. She was a real-life princess to me.

"I think we did enough of that yesterday," she said as she started to close the door.

I reached out and caught it just in time. "Things have changed."

"What? Are you a bigger douche canoe today than you were yesterday?"

"Look, I said a lot of stupid shit yesterday that I didn't mean. I talked to Andy last night, and he cleared up a lot of stuff for me."

Her eyes widened. "You talked to Andy?"

I nodded. "I did. He knows that I'm here now. He thinks that we need to talk, too."

"What about Ally? I'm sure she wouldn't be happy if she knew you were talking to me."

"Ally is one thing I need to talk to you about. Can I come in?"

She eyed me warily. "I really don't want to see you right now, Jesse. I think you made your opinion of me very clear yesterday."

"I shouldn't have said those things to you. I regretted everything as soon as the words left my mouth."

"I'm sure you did. Just go, Jesse, please."

She tried to shove the door closed, but I held my hand against it.

"You need to hear what I have to say. It changes everything," I said.

"Everything has already changed. I did a lot of thinking after you left yesterday. I was stupid to come here and think that everything could go back to the way it was. Once this semester is over, I'm leaving. You'll never have to see me again."

"I don't want you to leave," I said softly as I pushed the door open enough to step inside. "Just hear me out."

She sighed as she closed the door behind me. "Fine, but you can wait until after I shower."

"I'll wait for as long as you want me to."

She rolled her eyes, and then she grabbed a shirt and pants from her closet. "I'm sure you would."

I sat down in the chair next to her desk as I waited. At least she hadn't kicked me out. I knew she'd wanted to, so I considered myself lucky. I watched her walk into the bathroom, and then I heard the water turn on a few seconds later. I concentrated on the desk in front of me to keep from picturing her naked. If things were different, I'd be in there with her right now. Showering with her had been one of my favorite things to do when we were together. Seeing her naked and wet wasn't something that I could ever forget, not that I ever wanted to.

She reemerged from her bathroom a few minutes later. She looked amazing without any makeup on and with her wet hair hanging around her face.

"You look beautiful," I said before I could stop myself.

She blushed furiously. "Tell me what you came here to say, so you can leave. I have stuff to do."

She refused to look at me as she grabbed her brush off the dresser, and then she started dragging it through her hair. I tried to focus on what I needed to say as I watched her.

God, I've missed her so much.

"A lot has happened since I talked to you yesterday."

"I'm waiting," she said as she sat down on her bed and looked at me.

"After I left here, I drove around town for a while, and I ended up at Andy's apartment. He wanted to kill me at first, but we managed to talk without hitting each other. Well, I did hit him, but I thought I was doing you a favor."

"Why did you hit Andy?" she asked incredulously.

"Because I thought he was cheating on you. When I showed up, a girl was walking around his place, wearing only his shirt."

She laughed. "I've walked in on that a time or two. Andy always has a girl over there."

"I'm glad you find it funny. I didn't. I had no idea that you two weren't together, so I punched him. After we both calmed down, he told me that you two were nothing more than friends."

"And now, you're here because you feel like an ass for saying all of that to me yesterday. Well, guess what? I don't care. I tried to tell you, but you wouldn't listen. You just wanted to make me feel as bad as possible."

"I feel horrible for what I said, but I'm not here for that. After he told me the truth, I realized that Ally has been lying to me—a lot."

"Why do you seem so surprised? That's what Ally does—she lies."

"I know that now, but she was my friend. When she came to me this summer, I tried to ignore the fact that she'd lied to Andy about me sleeping with her. She needed help, and I couldn't turn her away."

"Why did she need help?" Emma asked.

"When she came to me at the beginning of the summer, she told me that she'd been raped back in California. She'd run away because she'd discovered that she was pregnant, and she was afraid that the guy would hurt her if he found out, so I took her in."

"Wait a minute—she told me that the baby was yours," Emma whispered.

I could see the hope in her eyes even though she was trying to hide it.

"I agreed to tell anyone back home that it was mine, so no one would find out that she'd been raped."

"Oh my god. All this time, I thought you two were finally together and that the baby was yours. She made it seem like that was what had happened."

"We've never been together, and we never will be. The only girl I've ever cared about is you, Emma. The minute I saw you, I knew that you were something special."

"Why are you telling me this now?"

"I was angry with Ally for lying to me about you and Andy, so I went home to confront her. She didn't know I was home. I surprised her and caught her without her shirt."

Emma raised an eyebrow.

"Let me finish before you say anything. I saw her without a shirt, and she's not pregnant. She lied about *everything*."

"Are you serious?"

"As a heart attack. Once she realized that she wasn't going to get away with it, she came clean, and I kicked her out."

"And she just left? I don't see her doing that. If she did all of that to hang on to you, she wouldn't just leave."

"She didn't leave without a fight. We got into it pretty bad."

"I don't even know what to say."

"I know what you mean. She even tried to tell me that you and Andy were planning to get married. Imagine her shock when I told her that I'd talked to Andy."

Emma laughed. "Oh my god. I don't even know why I'm laughing, but I can't help it. I fucking hate that bitch, and it makes me so happy to know that she finally got caught. Maybe Andy will believe me now."

"About, what?"

"The other night, I went to the restaurant where she works with my friend. I got so sick afterward that I felt like I was dying. Andy had to come over and help me. When I told him that I thought Ally had poisoned me since she was my waitress, he didn't believe me."

"I bet she did. After everything else she's done, it wouldn't surprise me. I wish I could have been the one to take care of you."

"It's not your job anymore," Emma said quietly.

"I want it to be. I've missed you so much, Emma. I could never get over you, no matter how hard I tried. If I'd known that you were looking for me, I would have come back. I thought you hated me."

"I did hate you for a long time, but I couldn't let you go. I kept hoping that you'd come back just so I could see you again. Once Ally had told Andy that you hadn't slept with her, we started searching for you."

14
EMMA

"I'm so sorry. I didn't mean to abandon you," Jesse said as he stood and walked over to me.

"It was my fault for believing Ally. You tried to tell me," I said, still trying to comprehend everything that he'd just told me about Ally.

He crouched down in front of me. "I don't blame you for that. We'd just had a fight, and then you walked in to see me in bed with another girl. I would have thought the same thing."

"She threatened me that night we went to the party on the beach. She said to leave you alone because you were hers. After I saw you in bed with her, I thought that she meant you were sleeping with both of us at the same time."

"Definitely not. I have never, nor will I ever be interested in Ally, and I definitely wouldn't sleep with her. I knew I was destroying any chance I had with you when I kept her secret, but I didn't want to abandon her. If I had known what she was doing, I would have told you what was going on the minute I saw you."

"Is she gone?" I asked.

"I don't know. I hope so. Andy is out looking for her now. If she hasn't left town yet, she will after he gets through with her. I've never seen him so mad."

"This whole situation is a mess—even more so than I thought originally."

"Tell me about it. She had me fooled, that's for sure."

"So, what are you going to do now?"

He shrugged. "The same thing I've been doing—going to school. Only now, I don't have to focus on her all the time. Now, I can focus on getting you back."

"Do you think that's a good idea?" I asked. It killed me to say it, but one of us had to.

"Of course it is. Why would you think otherwise?" Uncertainty clouded his eyes as he stared at me.

"Think about it, Jesse. So many things have kept us apart. It's like fate is trying to tell us something. Maybe we're not supposed to be together."

"I don't believe that. I agree that we've dealt with a lot, but that doesn't mean that we should give up. I've always believed that if you want something, then you should go after it until it's yours. I'm not giving up on you, Emma—not when I just got the chance to win you back. I spent the last two years without you, and it was horrible. I can't do that again now that I've found you. I know this whole thing sucks, but we can move past it. You didn't come all this way just to let me go."

I wanted to believe him, but I wasn't sure if I could. If I did agree to start over, I would constantly be waiting for something else to happen to us.

"I can't, Jesse. I'm going to New York once this semester is over. We both need to let go of something that isn't there anymore."

"If you leave, *I'll* follow *you* this time. I won't give up without a fight."

I stared down at him. Every cell in my body was screaming at me to throw myself into his arms, but I was so scared. I was tired of hurting all the time. I couldn't deal with anything else Ally might throw at me.

"Jesse—"

"Look, give me one chance to prove to you that I'm worth all the trouble."

"How do you plan to do that?" I asked.

He stood up and pushed me back until I was lying on my bed. He nudged my legs apart with his knees and positioned himself over me.

"I'm going to kiss you. Maybe you'll reconsider after I do."

I stared up at him, unable to think of anything to say. I couldn't think at all with him practically lying on top of me. The heat radiating from his body made me shiver with want. He pushed my damp hair away from my face. My skin tingled where his fingers brushed against it.

"Will you let me kiss you?"

I could only nod. I held my breath as he lowered his lips to mine. The kiss was soft and gentle at first. Jesse had always been gentle with me. As his lips moved against mine, I closed my eyes. I'd missed kissing him so much. He ran his tongue along my bottom lip before biting on it gently. I gasped as fire shot through my body. He took advantage of my open lips and slipped his tongue between them. He kissed me harder as his tongue tangled with mine. I wrapped my hands around his neck to pull him closer. I wanted to get lost in him. Every painful moment had been worth it just to kiss him again.

He pulled away and ran his thumb down my cheek. "I've missed this."

"Me, too."

He didn't move away like I expected him to. Instead, he kept his body pressed against mine as he stared down at me.

"Tell me you don't want this. Tell me that you don't care about me anymore, and I'll walk away."

I closed my eyes as a battle raged inside of me. I wanted him more than anything else in the world, but I was scared.

"I just don't want to get hurt again," I whispered.

"I will never let Ally or anyone hurt you ever again. I promise. Just tell me that you'll stay."

"I'll stay for now. I can't promise that I'll be here forever though. If something happens, I'm gone. I can't stand to be hurt anymore."

He smiled. "Nothing will happen, so I have nothing to worry about. You're mine, Emma. You always have been."

"Jesse, I need to tell you something. I don't want us to finally start to be happy, and then you find out about it later."

He rolled off of me and sat up with a nervous expression on his face. "Okay?"

I sat up next to him and took his hand in mine. "Something happened after you left California."

"What?"

"I slept with Andy. We never meant for it to happen, but it did. Nothing has happened since that one time," I blurted out in a rush.

"I already know. Andy told me the truth last night," Jesse said calmly.

"And you're not mad?" I asked. I hadn't expected him to be so calm about Andy.

"I was pissed when Andy told me, but I'm trying to accept it. I won't pretend that it doesn't suck because it does. But there's nothing that we can do about it. What's in the past is exactly where it should be—in the past."

"I thought you'd hate me when you found out."

"After everything I put you through with Ally, I have no right to hate you. We both screwed up."

"We did."

"I don't want to screw up anymore," he whispered.

"Neither do I."

He leaned over and kissed me. I grabbed him and pulled him back on top of me. I needed to touch him. I needed to feel him against me. He kissed the corner of my mouth and then the tip of my nose. I closed my eyes as he kissed both of my eyelids and then my cheeks. I pulled his face down until he was kissing my lips again. I moaned as his tongue slipped inside my mouth once more. I didn't want him to ever stop kissing me.

He pushed away and smiled down at me. "I'm not asking for anything more than kisses right now… unless you have something else on your mind, then I'll ask."

I grinned. "I have something else on my mind."

"Thank God. I was hoping you would say that. Two years is a long fucking time to be without you."

He started kissing me again. He wasn't as gentle as before, but it was still sweet. I wrapped my arms and legs around him until he was pressed tightly against me. He rested his weight on both of his elbows so that he wouldn't crush me.

"I love the way you smell," he whispered before kissing behind my ear.

I shivered from the sensation. His lips were everywhere after that—below my ear, on my lips, on my neck. I moaned as I felt him pressing against me. He'd done nothing but kiss me, and I already felt heat at my core. I hadn't felt this way in a very long time.

"It's been too long," I whispered.

"I know. All I want is to be inside you, but I'm going to take my time. I want to kiss every inch of you."

He sat up and brought me up with him. He pulled my shirt over my head and tossed it aside. My bra went next. I suddenly felt shy. It had been so long since he'd seen me like this. I crossed my arms over my chest, trying to hide myself.

He smiled as he grabbed my arms and pushed them away. "Never hide from me. I want to see all of you."

He ran his fingers just under my breasts so that he barely touched them, and I felt my nipples harden. I was torn between covering up and begging him to touch me.

"Jesse?"

"Hmm?" he asked as he grazed my breasts again.

"Please don't tease me. I want you to…"

"What do you want me to do?"

"Touch me."

He smiled as he slid his hand between my breasts. "I already am, but I think I know what you want."

I fell back against my pillow as he ran a single finger across the swell of my breasts and then underneath again. He kept up his teasing, circling motion, getting closer to my nipples each time. When he finally reached them, he barely touched them, and I whimpered. I couldn't handle his teasing anymore. I opened my mouth to beg when he finally ran his thumb over one of them. Lightning shot through my body and straight between my legs. My hips rose to grind against him. His breathing hitched as I pressed my body against his.

"Let's get rid of your pants," he said as he moved off of me.

He tugged my pants down, leaving me in only my underwear.

"Fuck. You never wore anything like this before."

"Like, what?" I asked, confused.

"A thong." He pulled me from the bed and turned me around.

"What are you doing?"

"I want the full image of you wearing this seared into my brain. It's sexy as hell. Do you have more like this?"

"Yeah."

"Good."

He hooked his thumb in the fragile string wrapped around my hips. Before I realized what he was doing, I heard a rip, and then my underwear was gone.

Jesus, he just ripped them right off of me.

I should have been mad that he'd ruined them, but I wasn't. It was quite possibly one of the sexiest things he'd ever done.

"There—that's better." He kissed my neck.

"You're still wearing clothes," I whined.

"You're right, my bad." He lifted his shirt over his head and then pulled his pants and boxers off.

When he was finished undressing, he grabbed my hips and pulled me tight against him. I moaned as my sensitive nipples rubbed against the bare skin of his chest. He gripped my ass and lifted me as I wrapped them around him. He fell back onto the bed, and I nearly came then and there as I felt his shaft rub against my clit.

No more teasing. I need this now. I need him now.

He rolled me onto my back and started kissing me again. He broke the kiss and lowered his lips to my breasts. I arched my back as his tongue circled my nipple. He rolled off of me, and his fingers skimmed down my stomach to where I needed them. My legs fell open to allow him access.

"You're so wet," he said as he ran his fingers along my core.

I moaned when he pushed one of them inside me. He thrust it in and out a few times before pulling back out. He flicked my clit with his fingers, and I nearly came up off the bed. Every nerve in my body was on fire.

"I want you so bad," he said in a strained voice as he watched me raise my hips with each flick of his finger.

"Then, do something about it."

"Roll onto your stomach."

I did as he'd said. He stood and positioned me so that he was against my entrance.

"Fuck, Emma. I don't have protection."

"I'm on the pill, and I'm clean, I swear."

"I trust you, and I haven't been with anyone since you."

He pushed in, so just his tip was inside me. He reached around and ran his fingers across my clit. I was going to explode if he didn't stop torturing me.

"Jesse, stop teasing."

"You're tight. I don't want to hurt you."

"You're killing me right now."

He pushed farther in, making me moan. He pulled almost all the way out, and then he thrust in again, going farther this time.

"Fuck, you feel good," he moaned.

He continued his slow thrusts until he finally pushed all the way in. I moaned in pleasure. He pulled back out and thrust in again. He kept his leisurely pace for a minute before finally speeding up.

"You can go faster. You're not going to hurt me."

He said nothing as he started moving in and out faster. He grabbed my hips and pulled me back each time he thrust in so that he could go deeper. I buried my face in my pillow to muffle my moans.

"I want to hear you," he said as he slammed into me.

I shook my head. Someone in one of the rooms around us might hear us.

"Emma, let me hear you. If you don't move that pillow, I'm going to fuck you so hard that nothing will hide your screams."

When I didn't move, he laughed.

"I was hoping you'd make me work for it."

He pulled all the way out and then slammed back into me. I cried out, unable to stop myself. He continued his hard and fast thrusts until I was screaming his name. I was past the point of caring whether or not anyone could hear me. I shattered to pieces under him as I came. He continued to thrust until he found his own release. He shouted out my name as I felt his seed filling me.

When he was finished, he pulled out and rolled me over. I reached up and grabbed him to yank him down on top of me, and his sweat-covered skin slid across mine.

"I love you, Jesse. I always have."

"I love you, too. I've missed you so much. I've missed *this* so much."

He kissed my forehead, and then he rolled to his side and pulled me tight against him. I smiled as he wrapped his arms around me.

This was exactly where I was supposed to be—in his arms.

15

I held Emma's hand as she drove us to Andy's. Now that I had her back, there was no way that I was going to let go of her, not even for a second. We pulled up to Andy's building and stepped out of the car. I walked around the front and grabbed her as soon as she closed her door. My lips crushed against hers as I pulled her against me. I never wanted to stop tasting her.

"Jesse, stop it! We're in a very public parking lot. Someone might see."

"Let them watch. Maybe they'll learn something."

She rolled her eyes as she linked her fingers with mine, and we started walking toward Andy's building.

"I'm sure they would," she said.

Once we were inside, she turned to take the steps.

I tugged on her hand, stopping her. "Let's take the elevator."

"Okay..."

I ignored her questioning look as I walked to the elevator and pushed the button. The doors slid open instantly, and I pulled her inside. As soon as they closed, I pushed her up against the wall. My hands worked to push her shirt up.

"What are you doing?" she cried.

I ignored her as I pulled the cups of her bra down. As soon as her breasts were free, I leaned down and sucked one of her nipples into my mouth. She grabbed my shoulders to hold herself up.

"Oh god, Jesse."

I ran my tongue across her nipple. I wanted her here and now, but I knew that wasn't possible. I was going to take her home as soon as we left Andy's apartment. She wouldn't have to worry about being quiet since no one would be around to hear her as I made her scream out my name.

"I want to take you right here, but I can't. Soon though, I promise." I helped her fix her bra and pull her shirt back down.

I hated the jeans she was wearing as I reached between her legs and stroked her through the material. Her lips parted as her head fell back against the wall.

"Soon."

The elevator door sprang open, causing us to jump apart. I cursed as I realized that I'd forgotten to push the button to take us up to Andy's floor.

"Okay, gross. I don't even want to know what you two were doing five seconds ago," Andy grumbled as he stepped onto the elevator. "I see you two worked everything out at least."

"I worked her pretty good," I said as I grinned at Andy. I knew I was being a jackass, but I couldn't help it. I realized that there was nothing between the two of them, but I wanted to make it crystal clear to Andy that Emma was mine.

"Jesse! Shut up!" Emma said as she blushed.

"It's fine. I knew you two would act like bunnies once you kissed and made up." Andy grinned at her.

When she turned away from us to push the button, he shot me a dirty look, letting me know that I wasn't fooling anyone with my caveman act. I ignored it as I pulled her back against me. I was marking my territory.

"You're both idiots," Emma grumbled as the elevator rose to the second floor.

When the doors opened, we followed Andy down the hall to his apartment. He unlocked his door and threw his keys on the table.

"By the way, if you start acting like bunnies on my couch, I'll kick you both out."

"Oh, shut up," Emma said.

I walked over to the couch and sat down as Andy headed into the kitchen. Emma started to sit down next to me, but I grabbed her and pulled her onto my lap. I wanted her as close to me as possible.

Andy returned a few seconds later with a beer in his hand, and I raised an eyebrow.

"What? If you want a beer, you can go and get it yourself. I'm not your maid." He sat down on the opposite side of the couch.

"I'm your guest. You have to wait on me hand and foot."

"Try again, asshole."

I smiled. It was like the past two years had never happened. Andy and I were back to the way we'd always been.

"Did you find Ally?" Emma cut in.

Andy shook his head. "No, and believe me, I searched everywhere. One of the girls at her work said Ally had come in early this morning and quit. I think she's gone."

"Good riddance," I muttered.

"I feel like an ass for saying this, but I agree. Ally has changed and not for the better. I just hope that she's smart enough to leave the two of you alone," Andy said sadly.

"I think she will. She must realize by now that we all know what she did. I don't think she'll show her face around any of us again. I know this has to be hard for you, Andy. She's still your sister, and despite everything that she's done, I know you still love her," Emma said.

"I'll be fine. I'm more ashamed of what she did than anything. If this is the person she's become, then she's not my sister anymore."

We were all quiet as Andy sipped his beer. None of us really knew what to say at this point. The things that Ally had done were unreal.

"Andy, I really do think that she made me sick that night," Emma said quietly.

He sighed. "I think you're probably right. I didn't think she'd do something like that before, but now, I have no idea what she's capable of."

Emma scooted off my lap and over to Andy. My hands balled into fists as she reached over to hug him. I knew they were friends now, but I wasn't used to seeing them together like this, and it bothered me. I wasn't sure if I'd ever be okay with the two of them alone together after what had happened between them.

"I'm sorry, Andy. I started all of this," Emma said as she pulled away.

He shook his head. "Nah, this is all on Ally. She's the one who fucked up."

"Agreed," I said as I pulled Emma back over to me.

"I hate to cut this short, but I need to get ready for work. Sam texted me and said one of the guys called in sick, so I have to cover his shift."

"Whoa, wait a minute. You work with Sam?" I asked.

Emma tensed beside me. "Jesse, don't."

Andy looked between the two of us. "I do. He's my boss's irresponsible younger brother. Why? Do you know him?"

"He lives a few houses down from me. I caught him trying to maul Emma at one of his parties."

I could practically see the smoke coming out of Andy's ears.

"He did, *what?* Emma, why didn't you tell me?"

"I didn't want to make things awkward for you at work. It was my own fault anyway."

"I'm going to strangle the asshole," Andy said.

"No, you're not. You're going to pretend like you don't know. He's your boss's brother. If you fight him, you'll get fired."

"Is there anyone in this world who isn't an asshole?" Andy seethed.

I raised my hand. "Me."

"No, you're definitely an asshole."

"Please don't say anything, Andy. Please," Emma begged.

He rolled his eyes. "Fine, I won't. But if he so much as mentions you, I'll knock his head off."

"And if you get in a fight, I'll hit you." Emma scowled at him.

He laughed. "You've hit me before. It doesn't hurt."

"Whatever," she huffed as she stood up. "We'll leave you alone, so you can get ready for work."

I stood and started to follow her, but Andy called my name.

"Jesse, hang on a minute." He waited until Emma was out in the hallway before he continued. "Look, I know you're butt-hurt over Emma and me, but you need to let it go. It was a long time ago, and I'm not going to come between you two. Stop trying to make me see that she's yours. I already know it."

I nodded, feeling like an idiot. "You're right. It's just...I just got her back, and I don't want to lose her."

"I've been her friend for a long time now. Trust me when I say that she isn't going anywhere."

"Jesse, are you coming?" Emma asked as she opened the door to look for me.

"Yeah." I glanced at Andy. "I'll see you later."

"Later."

Emma refused to take the elevator back down to the main floor. She said something about not trusting me. I had no idea why she would think that. Okay, maybe I did see her point.

The skies had darkened while we were inside Andy's place. I could hear thunder in the distance. From the way it looked, we were in for a nasty storm.

On the way back to my house, we stopped at a fast-food restaurant to grab something to eat. It was nice to just sit there and chill like a normal couple. I relaxed back into the booth as I realized that there was no crazy bitch hanging over our heads. I wasn't about to let my guard down just in case Ally showed up again, but that didn't mean that I'd let her ruin my happiness.

Emma was mine again, and I planned to keep it that way. I didn't care what I had to do. I would make sure that she was always mine.

"What are you thinking about?" Emma asked as she stared at me from across the table.

"You," I said simply.

"What about me?"

"Just that I'm the luckiest guy ever to have you back in my life. It doesn't matter, but I have to ask you something. What's the situation with your mom now? Is she as bad as she was before?"

"Nah, she's worse. She took my car and kicked me out when I told her I was coming to West Virginia for college. That was in May, and I haven't heard a word from her since. My dad let me stay at his place over the summer."

"She kicked you out? How can a parent do that to her kid?"

Emma shrugged. "It doesn't matter. I'm glad that I'm finally free. All she did was make my life hell."

"Did you ever tell her about me?"

She shook her head. "No, I didn't see the point. You were gone."

"I thought I'd lose you because of her."

"And I was afraid that she'd keep me away from you. Obviously, that isn't a problem now. It's not like she can disown me twice if she did find out."

"That's true. You know, I still have the same fears as before. I'll never be rich, Emma, and I hope you can accept that."

She frowned. "I told you before that money doesn't matter to me. The only thing I ever wanted when I was growing up was to be happy. My family had all the money in the world, and we were miserable. Money doesn't buy happiness. Happiness is something that comes from within. I learned a long time ago that my mother could never be happy. She just doesn't have it in her."

"But you do. You're the happiest person I've ever met."

"You haven't seen me on a bad day," she teased.

"No, I haven't—well, except for that day in your room, but that doesn't count. I can't wait to see it. I bet you're even hotter when you're in a pissy mood."

She laughed. "You're an idiot. So, tell me, what have you been up to since you moved?"

"Not much. We moved here, and I started a new school. I made a few friends but none worth mentioning. I kept my nose out of trouble and graduated at the top of my class. Mom married Mark a year ago, and they're both blissfully happy. It made me want to vomit when I lived there."

"Do you like Mark now?"

"I do. When I met him, I convinced myself that he was going to break her. Instead, he made her happy. I've never seen her the way she is now. Once I got over myself, I actually talked to him, and I realized that he isn't such a bad guy. Before he met my mom, he was married, but his wife died four years ago. I think it really messed him up for a long time."

"I can't even imagine."

"Neither can I. But I think my mom helped him as much as he helped her. They're both really happy together."

"I'm glad. Your mom was always so nice to me."

"She liked you. She never asked why I'd left, but she knows it had to do with you."

"I bet she hates me now."

"Nah. My mom doesn't have it in her to hate anyone, even my dad. She'll be excited to see you again."

"I hope so."

"Why don't we go visit her tomorrow? I could use a day away from here and all the drama."

"If you're sure that she doesn't hate me..." Emma said, obviously nervous.

"I promise, she doesn't. She'll probably bake cookies for you or something."

Emma laughed. "I'd like that. The only person who has ever made me cookies was the chef my mom hired."

I frowned when I noticed how something as simple as cookies could upset her. It was obvious that her mother had never taken a second to actually be there for her daughter.

"I'm sorry that you had to grow up alone."

"It's fine. I'm over it. I'm putting the past behind me and moving on to bigger and better things."

"Like the poor kid from the trailer park?"

"Like the boy who stole my heart and taught me how to surf."

"I miss surfing. It's been a long time since I was on a board."

"I kept surfing after you left. I went to that spot you had taken me to, and I surfed there. Andy and I found a good spot, too."

"You surfed with Andy?" I hated the fact that he'd been there for her when I wasn't.

"Yeah, we surfed a lot this summer."

"I thought you said you moved to your dad's place in L.A."

"I did. Andy came with me."

I sighed. "This really blows."

"What do you mean?"

"I hate the fact that you've spent so much time with him. I know you two are just friends, but it still bothers me."

"Jesse, you have to understand the relationship I have with Andy. He was there for me when I had no one. He's my best friend. Well, he was. Since you are back with us, I think I've been bumped down to just a regular friend. You stole my spot."

"I doubt that. Andy is the kind of guy who will always be loyal once you break down his wall. Once you're in, you're in."

"Good. I don't want to lose him."

"I'll try to work on my jealous side when it comes to him, I promise. Just give me some time. When I left, you two barely knew each other. Now, you're as close to him as I used to be."

"Thank you. And I promise you that you have nothing to worry about when it comes to him. He's nothing more than a friend."

"Good." I glanced outside to see that the storm was getting closer. "I think we should probably get back to my house before that storm hits."

"Sounds like a plan."

I stood and followed Emma back to her car. I couldn't wait to get her alone.

16
EMMA

I hurried back to Jesse's house, trying to beat the storm. Just as I pulled into his driveway, rain started to splatter against my windshield. It was nothing more than a shower, but I knew more was coming. I smiled as I realized that I might be stuck at Jesse's for a while.

We ran up to his house as the rain started to grow heavier. Jesse unlocked the door and held it open for me. Once we were inside, I pulled my jacket off and hung it on one of the hooks by the door. I looked around his house. I'd been in such a hurry to escape the last time that I'd been here that I hadn't paid any attention to it.

His house was small but nice. I could see myself spending a lot of time here. For some reason, it already felt like home.

"Do you want something to drink? I won't be an ass like Andy and not ask," Jesse said as he walked to the kitchen.

I laughed as I followed him. "Nah, I'm good."

He opened the refrigerator and pulled out a bottle of water. I leaned against the island as I watched him. I would never get tired of looking at him. Every little detail about him amazed me. He set the bottle down on the counter and walked over to me.

"I think we have some unfinished business."

"What?"

"We never got to finish what we started in the elevator earlier."

"Oh."

Heat engulfed me as he stared at me. A hunger was in his eyes that couldn't be denied. Thunder rumbled outside, causing me to jump. I'd been so distracted by his gaze that I'd forgotten about the storm that was upon us. He raised his hand and cupped my cheek. I closed my eyes as I felt his skin against mine.

God, I've waited so long for his touch.

I couldn't wait anymore, and the look in his eyes told me that I didn't have to. His other hand went to my waist to pull me closer. I stumbled, but I caught myself by grabbing his shirt.

He leaned down and pressed his lips against mine. I fisted my hands in his shirt as I clung to him. I never wanted to let go. I released his shirt long enough to grab the bottom of it and pull it over his head. His chest and stomach were hard as I ran my hands across him. I couldn't believe how much he'd changed over the past two years. He'd always been in shape, but I could see that he was no longer the boy I'd met. In his place was a man.

I looked up to see him watching me silently as I explored him. His eyes were filled with heat, but he didn't move a muscle. I leaned forward and kissed around his nipple. His chest rose and fell quickly, but he remained frozen. My tongue darted out and flicked across his nipple, my eyes never leaving his face. He closed his eyes and clenched his jaw.

"Why are you just standing there?" I asked.

The Jesse I knew would have thrown me over his shoulder and taken me to the bedroom by now.

"You're in charge," he said simply.

"I like that."

I pulled his head down, so I could kiss him. My tongue slipped between his lips, and I explored his mouth. He grabbed my hips and squeezed as he tried to stay in control. I kissed along his jaw and down his neck. I could feel his heart beating in his chest as I pressed against him.

I reached forward and undid the button on his jeans, making sure to brush my hand against his straining cock. A small moan escaped him despite his attempt to hold it in. I pulled his jeans down, taking his boxers with them. He stepped out of them and kicked them to the side. My eyes roamed his body, taking in every inch of him.

I kissed his chest and then flicked my tongue over first one nipple and then the other. I kissed a trail down the hard muscles of his stomach as I dropped to my knees in front of him. His breath hitched as I took him in my hand and started rubbing up and down his shaft. It was clear just how much he wanted me. I smiled as I leaned forward and ran my tongue along his shaft. He groaned as he grabbed the counter.

"Emma..."

He moaned as I did it again. Before he could say anything else, I wrapped my lips around just his tip, and I sucked gently. He held on to the counter with one hand while he grabbed my head with the other. I expected him to force me to take him deeper, but he didn't. Instead, he simply ran his fingers through my hair as I continued to tease him.

I swirled my tongue over his tip just before I took him deeper. I suctioned my lips tightly around him as I slowly pulled away. As soon as I reached the end of his shaft, I opened my mouth and drew him back in. I did this over and over until he stopped me.

"Emma, you have to stop, or I'm going to come."

I ignored him as I started sucking harder.

"Emma, please..."

I released him only to grab his shaft. He cursed as I squeezed hard. His body tightened, and he came all over my hand.

"Jesus," he groaned as he finished.

I stood and walked to the sink to wash my hands. When I was done, I turned and came face-to-face with him. I hadn't heard him walk up behind me. His lips were on mine instantly. He pushed against me until my back was against the counter. Our bodies were pressed tightly together as he continued to kiss me.

"It's my turn," he whispered in my ear. "There's something I never told you before."

I was almost afraid to ask. "And that would be?"

"You probably figured it out already, but I like rough sex."

"You were always gentle with me," I said, confused by his admission.

"I didn't want to scare you. You were still figuring everything out. Last time, I was rougher than I was when we were together before. I could barely hold it in."

"Nothing you do could ever scare me."

"I hope you mean that because I don't want to hold back any longer."

He picked me up as he started kissing me again. I wrapped my legs around him and moaned as I felt him growing hard against my body. He sat me down on the table and tore off my shirt. My bra followed. He dropped them to the floor, and helped me shimmy out of my jeans and underwear. As his eyes traveled over my naked body, I didn't feel self-conscious like I had last time in my dorm room. Instead, I felt beautiful. He wanted me, and I was going to let him have exactly what he wanted.

Once he had me naked, he pushed me down until I was lying on my back. He wasted no time as he leaned over me and took my nipple into his mouth. He wasn't gentle as he sucked on it. I cried out as he bit down. He didn't do it hard enough to really hurt me. It was just enough to mix pleasure with pain.

His fingers found my core and thrust in quickly. My head fell back on the table as he thrust them in and out again and again. Instinct took over as I tried to close my legs.

"Not a chance." He grabbed both of my knees and jerked my legs apart.

I moaned as his mouth covered my clit. His tongue flicked across it, causing my hips to come off the table. He licked a trail from my clit to my core. I cried out his name when I couldn't take anymore. My body convulsed off the table as I came—hard.

As I unraveled beneath him, he never stopped his attack, prolonging my orgasm. When my body finally relaxed, he stood up and pulled me to the edge of the table. He grabbed my hips, and after he positioned himself at my entrance, he rocked into me. My body was still getting used to having him inside me again, and it hurt a bit at first as I adjusted to his size. He waited until I nodded, and then he pulled out and pushed back into me. He went slow, taking his time with each thrust. Each time he entered, he ground his hips against me, driving me mad.

"Go faster."

"I told you, I like it rough, not fast." He continued to torture me.

"I can't take it," I pleaded. This slow-and-hard was driving me mad.

He slipped out and didn't thrust back in as I'd expected.

"Tell me exactly what you want me to do," he said.

"I already did. I want you to go fast."

"If you're sure…" He trailed off.

He entered me again, and his thrusts were fast but shallow. He was just playing with me.

"Jesse, please!"

"I'm only doing what you told me."

"Fine! I want you to go fast *and* hard!"

"That's all you had to say," he teased.

He plunged deeply into me before pulling out and doing it again. He increased his speed with each thrust until I felt like I was going to explode. My fingers gripped the table to keep me from sliding back with the force of his thrusts. I knew he was close, but he was refusing to come without me. I reached between us and ran my thumb across my sensitive clit. He growled and started thrusting harder as he watched me pleasure myself.

"Fuck!" he groaned as he pulled out suddenly.

My eyes widened, and my hand stopped. "Did I do something wrong?"

"No. I just want to watch you do that."

"Oh." My hand refused to move.

"Please, Emma…" He took my hand and guided it to my core. "I want to watch."

I knew I couldn't do it if I saw him staring at me. I closed my eyes as I pushed two fingers inside me over and over again. It was nothing compared to him, but I was so turned-on that I would take whatever I could get. I moved my hand up to my clit and ran my thumb over it again.

"I just want to take a picture of you as you are now—spread out on my table and playing with yourself—and hang it on my fucking wall. Jesus."

I kept my eyes closed as I continued to rub. I was right at the edge, and all I needed was that little push. The next thing I knew, he thrust hard and deep into me. I cried out as I came around him. He thrust two more times before he came inside of me. My body was slick with sweat as I tried to catch my breath. I'd never experienced anything like that before.

"That was the sexiest thing I've ever seen," Jesse said before he kissed me.

"I promised you a long time ago that I would let you watch."

"You did."

He pushed off the table and helped me stand. I reached down to pick up my clothes, but he stopped me as he grabbed me. He pulled me back until my ass was tight against his still hard dick. He nudged my legs apart as he shoved between my legs with his body.

"You can't possibly want to go again."

"I'm going to fuck you all night. I have two years to make up for. It'll be a while before I can come again though. Let's see how many times I can make you come before then."

I moaned as he rubbed against me. I was still sensitive.

"I don't think I can," I whispered.

"I think you're wrong. Stay bent over, and spread your legs apart."

I did as he'd said. He smacked my ass hard before slipping back into me. I moaned as he leaned over me and tweaked my nipples. He was going to be the death of me. He released my nipples and grabbed my hips as he thrust in and out of me. He'd taken me from behind before, but it had been nothing like this. If he hadn't kept his grip on me, my legs would have given out. I panted as he continued to shove deep inside me. I felt myself building again and fast. He reached between my legs and flicked my clit as he thrust roughly into me. I cried out in ecstasy as I came, but he never stopped.

I rested my head on Jesse's chest as we lay in bed together. We'd finally managed to make it to his bedroom—after we'd taken a shower together, of course. Jesse seemed to like to shower with me—a lot. It wasn't that I minded. I loved exploring his body as I washed it.

"Why don't you have any more tattoos?" I asked as I traced the ones on his right arm.

"Huh?"

"You don't have any new tattoos."

"Maybe I'm hiding them," he teased.

I raised my head to look at him. "I've seen every inch of you in the last few hours. There are no new ones."

"Good point. I guess I didn't think about that." He shrugged. "I haven't stepped into a tattoo shop since I left Rick's."

Rick's Tattoo was where he worked when we first met in California. It was also where he'd given me my first and only tattoo of the word *freedom* on my hip.

"Why? I figured you would have found a shop to work at here."

"What's the point? My mom freaks out every time I mention wanting to tattoo. She wants me to go to college and *do something with my life*," he said the last part sarcastically.

"It's your life. You get to choose what you want. No one else can control your decisions."

"Tell my mom that."

"Not a chance on your life. I stood up to *my* mom. You have to stand up to yours."

"It's not about standing up to her. I don't want to hurt her. She doesn't want me to end up in the same place we were before we moved here with Mark. So, I'm in college, trying to get a business degree. Just think how hot I'll be if I have to wear a business suit."

"I'm sure you'd look awesome in a suit, but do you really want to spend your life in one?"

"I will, if it means I can give you a nice life."

"Jesse, we've been over this a million times. I don't care how much money I have as long as I'm with you. All I want is to be happy."

"You might not care, but I do. I want to make sure that you're taken care of. I know I can't give you what you have now, but I'll try my hardest to get you as close to it as I can."

I dropped my head back onto his chest in defeat. "You're the most hardheaded person I've ever met."

"You like me when I'm hard," he teased as he ran his fingertips up and down my arm.

"Pervert."

"You say that like it's a bad thing."

"Quit changing the subject." I sat up and smiled at him as a thought struck me. "I have an idea."

"Does it have anything to do with my hard head?"

"*No.* I have a solution for your problem. Why don't you get your business degree like your mom wants and use what you've learned to open your own tattoo shop? By that time, I'll be over twenty-one, so my trust fund will be available to me. I can give you the money to get started."

"Not a chance. There's no way I'm going to let you blow your money like that. Plus, I'd have to go through an apprenticeship on top of school."

"First of all, I'm not blowing my money. It would be an investment for our future. And second, so what? It would take a while to do the apprenticeship, but it would be worth it in the end."

"Emma, I don't feel comfortable doing that."

"Just think about it, okay? We have four years to figure this stuff out."

"I like the *we* in there. It's nice to hear it again."

"You'd better get used to it."

He pulled me to him. "It'll be hard, but I think I can manage."

His mouth was on mine before I could respond. I was glad that we didn't have to decide on anything right now. I'd much rather spend the next four years right where I was—in his bed.

17
EMMA

I straightened my skirt in front of the mirror again. I pulled it down a bit, wondering if it was too short. I didn't want to look like a skank.

"How long do you plan to stand there, staring at yourself?" Jesse asked as he watched me from the bed.

"Until I think I look okay," I said as I stared at him in the mirror.

"You look fine. Actually, you look better than fine. You look amazing."

"I'm nervous."

"Why? You already met my mom."

"That was two years ago. She knows something happened between us, and now, we're back together all of a sudden."

"And?"

"I don't want her to hate me."

"Emma, I already told you not to worry. My mom has never hated you, and she's not going to start now."

"You don't know that. She might secretly hate me."

He threw a pillow over his head and groaned into it. "Shoot me now."

I fiddled with my skirt for a few seconds longer before turning to him. "I think I'm ready."

"*Finally*. Let's go before you decide you need to recheck your hair or something."

"Oh, you're right! I should check my hair." I turned back to the mirror and pretended to inspect my reflection. "I think it looks bad like this. Maybe I should straighten it."

He jumped from the bed and grabbed me. I shrieked as he threw me over his shoulder. He laughed as he carried me through the house and out the door while I kicked and tried to get free.

So much for making sure that my skirt is straight.

"If you don't stop freaking out, I'm going to make you walk into their house naked," he threatened.

"Hardy har har," I grumbled as he put me down beside his car.

"We're going to be late for dinner, thanks to you. Maybe my mom really will hate you since it's your fault."

I stuck my tongue out as I opened the passenger door and got in. He could make fun of me all he wanted, but I was still nervous. I'd destroyed Jesse two years ago, and while he might have forgiven me, that didn't mean his mom would.

He turned up the radio once we were on the interstate. I couldn't help but laugh as he sang along with the songs. Singing was definitely not a strong point of his.

"Are you making fun of my singing?" he asked, pretending to be offended.

"Not at all."

"Good—because I sing like an angel. I could have made a career out of it."

"Sure, you could," I said as I rolled my eyes.

He continued to sing as he drove down the interstate. His mom and Mark lived in Weston, which was about an hour or so away from Morgantown. I stared out the window as we went farther south. This was the farthest away from Morgantown I'd been so far.

I couldn't help but notice just how beautiful West Virginia was. The hills went on for miles and miles until a larger one blocked out the ones behind it. It was late September, and the leaves were already changing. The colors were striking. Deep reds and burnt orange colors dominated the landscape. Only a few trees held on to their green leaves at this time of year.

I remembered Jesse saying that his mom had wanted to come back to West Virginia to look at the leaves. Now, I understood why. The landscape was the most beautiful thing I'd ever seen. I glanced over at Jesse and smiled. Okay, after Jesse, it was the second most beautiful thing I'd ever seen.

He hit the exit ramp at the Weston exit and then turned on to a narrow two-lane road. My nerves were shot at this point. I knew we were close. I glanced out my side window to see us passing a humongous barn with *Weston Livestock Auction* written across it. I smiled. That wasn't something to be seen in California—at least, not where we had lived in California.

We continued to drive until the houses started to thin out. They were replaced with wide-open fields. My eyes widened as I stared at the cattle grazing in some of them. It was the first time that I'd ever seen a cow in real life. They were kind of cute.

He gave his signal and turned up a gravel driveway. Trees surrounded us on both sides as we drove down the curvy road. The trees were pretty when they were far away, but it was nothing compared to seeing them up close. Jesse laughed at my excited expression over something as simple as leaves.

"What? I think they're cool. Did you see the cows back there? They're so cute!"

"Oh god. You're starting to act like a girl."

"That's because I *am* a girl."

"I never would have figured that out if you hadn't told me," he said sarcastically.

I opened my mouth to smart off, but I froze as the trees opened up to reveal a large meadow. At the center was a huge house. While it wasn't as impressive as my mom's house, it also wasn't anything to stick your nose up at. Jesse pulled into an empty spot next to a brand new Ford truck.

I looked up at the house. I hadn't expected something like this. I was so used to Jesse living in a trailer, and for some stupid reason, I'd expected him to live in one here. That was dumb because I knew Mark had money. The house was a two-story log cabin with a garage sitting next to it. The banister around the front porch was made of smaller logs. It looked like something out of a movie.

"It's beautiful," I said.

We stepped out of his car and started walking toward the porch.

"It is. My mom loves it here."

"I can see why."

He laughed. "I thought she was going to pass out the first time she saw this place."

"I'm glad she found Mark."

"Me, too. I didn't think I would be, but I am."

He reached for my hand and threaded his fingers through mine as we stepped up onto the porch. The front door opened, and his mom came running out.

"It's about time you decided to visit! I've missed you," she said as the screen door slammed shut. Her eyes widened when she noticed me. "Emma?"

I gave a small wave. "Yeah, it's me."

"Damn. You guys didn't make me go through the whole, 'Emma, this is my mom, Trish,' again. I was looking forward to that," Jesse joked.

"What a surprise! I never thought I'd see you again! What are you doing here?" Trish asked, ignoring Jesse.

I glanced up at Jesse. I wasn't sure how much he wanted his mom to know about everything that had happened with Ally.

"It's a long story. The important part is that she's here."

His mom stepped forward and hugged me. "It's good to have you around again."

I hugged her back, relaxing as I realized that Jesse had been right. It was obvious that she didn't hate me.

She released me and grabbed Jesse to hug him, too. "I missed you, kiddo."

"I missed you, too, Mom."

She pulled away and opened the door. "There's no point in standing out here. I have dinner ready inside. I was worried that I'd made too much, but since Emma is here, we should be fine."

I followed Jesse into the house. The inside looked much like the outside. The walls were made of logs. A large stone fireplace with a television sitting on the mantel was in the living room. The light brown couch and chairs had images of deer across them. I could tell that Mark was very much an outdoor type of person.

The kitchen was a bit more modern even with the walls being the same as the living room. White tiles covered the floor, and the appliances were all stainless steel. As we made our way to the end of the kitchen, I noticed a man, Jesse's stepdad, Mark, I assumed, sitting at a large oak table in the dining room.

"Emma, this is Mark," Jesse said as we reached the table. "I don't think you two had a chance to meet in California."

Mark stood and shook my hand. "It's nice to meet you."

"Likewise," I said as I looked at him.

His hair was a dark brown with a bit of gray starting to show through. His eyes were a soft chocolate color. He was dressed in simple jeans and a flannel shirt. I glanced at Jesse's mom to see that she was also in jeans. I looked down at my skirt and white dress shirt, suddenly feeling overdressed.

"Don't just stand there, you two. Sit down," Trish said as she took the chair next to Mark.

I sat down in the chair between Mark and Jesse. I folded my hands nervously. While I knew his mom wasn't angry with me, I still felt unsure of myself. I hadn't thought to ask Jesse what to say or how much his mom knew when it came to Ally.

I bowed my head as his mom said grace. Once she was finished, we started passing plates full of food around the table. His mom had obviously spent a lot of time on dinner. The table was covered with more food than any of us could ever eat.

"How's school?" his mom asked as she handed Jesse a plate of pork chops.

"It's going good."

"Are you in school, too, Emma?" Mark asked.

"I am."

"Is that how you two found each other again?" his mom asked.

"Kind of," I answered. I didn't want to lie to her, but I also wasn't going to reveal anything about Ally in case Jesse hadn't mentioned it.

"Kind of?" she asked.

"Truthfully, I came to West Virginia to look for Jesse. I knew he planned to go to college, so I enrolled at WVU because I knew it was one of the biggest schools in the state. I figured that it was the best place to look for him."

I didn't mention the fact that the only way I knew he planned to go to college was because he bitched about his mom forcing him to go instead of finishing up his apprenticeship at the tattoo shop.

"That has to be the sweetest thing I've ever heard. You better take good care of this girl, Jesse," Trish said.

"I will, Mom." Jesse rolled his eyes.

"How long have you two been together? I feel like I'm asking a million questions, but since my dear son never calls me, I'm a bit out of the loop."

I smiled as I glanced over at Jesse. I knew exactly why he hadn't called his mom that much. If he had, he might have slipped and told her about Ally.

"Just recently. The campus is huge, and we never ran into each other at school. We met at a party off-campus." I lied smoothly.

"Ah, I see." She smiled at me.

I felt bad for the little white lies I was telling, but I knew Jesse would kill me if I told her the truth. I almost wanted to just so another person would know exactly what Ally was really like.

Mark wasn't much of a talker, but he seemed nice enough. It warmed my heart to see how much love was in his eyes when he looked at Jesse's mom. It was obvious that he thought the world of her.

I glanced down at his mom's hand and noticed her wedding ring. "Wow, that's beautiful."

She smiled proudly as she held out her hand to let me see it better. "It is. Mark picked it out on his own. He has great taste."

"Of course I do. I married you." Mark grinned at her.

Her cheeks went pink, and she looked away.

"You guys are so cute," I told them.

Jesse rolled his eyes. "I was thinking more along the lines of nauseating."

"Oh, shut up," I told him.

I felt myself relax as dinner progressed. It was like the last two years had never happened. His mom was as warm and kind toward me as she had been before. I should have known that I had nothing to worry about. It was just so important to me that Jesse's mom liked me. If she hadn't, it would make things hard for Jesse and me. I'd heard the horror stories about how the mother-in-law made the wife's life hell until she couldn't take it anymore. I didn't want my life to be like that. My own mom hated me enough for everyone.

We spent the rest of the evening with his mom and Mark. It was nice to just relax and spend time with them. When it was time to go, Trish hugged us both tightly.

"Make sure that he comes around more often. I miss him," she whispered in my ear before letting me go.

"I will."

I fell asleep on the way home. When I woke up, Jesse had me cradled in his arms as he walked through his house. He laid me down on his bed and pulled off my shoes. I snuggled down into the covers. I was too tired to try to talk with him. He crawled into bed next to me and wrapped his arms around me.

18

"Happy birthday!" Andy shouted as he walked into my house, unannounced.

Emma and I had finally managed to crawl out of bed right before he showed up, and I wasn't conscious enough to deal with his shouting.

"Fuck off," I mumbled as I reached into the cabinet for a bowl.

All I wanted for my birthday was a bowl of cereal—and Emma naked. That wasn't too much to ask. I didn't need to be tormented by Andy.

Since we had been kids, he'd tortured me on my birthdays. To me, it was just another day, but to him, it was his favorite day of the year. He would run through the halls at school and sing "Happy Birthday" to me until everyone else would join in. He'd gotten a fist to the stomach more than once for that shit.

"Well, aren't you just a ray of sunshine, snookums?" He tried to kiss me on the cheek.

I glared as I shoved him away. "Are you high?"

"I'm high on life." He grinned at me. "It's my two best friends' birthdays. Why wouldn't I be happy?"

For some reason, Andy found it hilarious that Emma and I were born on the same day.

"You're so fucking weird," I grumbled.

We both looked up as the bathroom door opened.

Emma stepped out, wearing nothing but a towel. "Jesse, I have a birthday present for you." She stopped dead when she saw Andy standing there. "Oh shit."

Andy laughed. "Don't stop just because I'm here. You could make it my special day, too."

I elbowed him in the stomach—hard. He grunted in pain as Emma flipped him off and walked into our bedroom.

"Thanks, asshole. You just cockblocked me on my birthday."

Andy laughed. "Mission accomplished."

Emma emerged from our room a few minutes later and walked into the kitchen. "Let's try this again now that I'm wearing clothes. Good morning, Andy."

"It's afternoon," he pointed out.

"We slept in," I told him.

"I'm sure you were sleeping," he said.

He was right, but I wasn't going to tell him that. Over the past two weeks, I'd slowly started to relax when Emma and Andy were around each other. Now that we were all three hanging out together, I could see that nothing was going on between them. But that didn't mean I was going to tell him that I'd spent half the night fucking her on every surface in the house, including the counter that he was currently leaning against.

Best. Birthday. Ever.

"So, what are we doing today?" Andy asked.

"We? If you mean Emma and me when you say *we*, then we're going to watch a movie on the couch and order pizza. If you think you're included in that *we*, try again."

"Oh, come on, I'm lonely by myself at my apartment."

"Call one of your girlfriends to keep you company."

"I got bored with them. I'm currently taking applications for new ones."

I rolled my eyes. "You need help."

"Nah, I need to get laid."

"Really?" Emma asked. "That's more information than I needed."

He ignored her as he looked at me. "Come on, let me in on the birthday fun."

"Let's not and say we did."

"Let him stay, Jesse," Emma said.

I gave her a pleading look. I'd lied about the movie part. I had no intentions of watching a movie with her. I wanted to get her naked. That would be kind of hard to do with Andy around.

I finally gave up and agreed to let him stay. By his reaction, I would have thought I'd told him that Christmas was here three months early. He really did need to get laid.

"I'll be right back," he said as he walked to the door.

"Take your time!" I yelled as he closed it behind him.

A few minutes later, he returned with bags full of alcohol and a birthday cake. I almost laughed at him until I saw the excitement in Emma's eyes. I kept my sarcastic comments to myself as she took some of the bags from him and put them on the counter.

"Damn, Andy. Did you rob a liquor store?" she asked as she pulled bottle after bottle from the bags.

"Nah, I'm friends with a guy who works at a liquor store. He hooked me up."

"Obviously." Emma said.

I finished my cereal as Emma cut the birthday cake. It was obvious that she was way more excited over it than I was. I couldn't help but smile as I watched her dig into a piece. It was good to see her happy again. When Ally had been around, I had been afraid that I would never see her smile again.

I pushed Ally from my mind as I picked up a piece of cake and started eating it. Today had nothing to do with Ally, and I wouldn't let her ruin my birthday. Everything was going great for us right now. I finally had not only Emma back in my life, but Andy as well.

"You could at least pretend to be civilized," Emma said as she watched me eat my cake with my hands.

"What's the fun in that?" I pointed to Andy. "Yell at him, too. He's eating it the same way I am."

"I'm surrounded by cavemen." Emma laughed at us.

Once we finished our cake, Andy started mixing drinks. It was kind of early to drink, but who cared? It was our birthdays, and we had nowhere to be. By the time we finally got around to watching a movie, we were all buzzed.

Andy sat in the chair closest to the couch as Emma snuggled into my side. I was actually kind of glad that I'd let Andy stick around. He was my best friend, and it was nice to have him here.

When the movie was finished, I put another one in and settled back onto the couch. Emma grabbed the blanket off the back of the couch and threw it over us. She snuggled back against me and sighed.

Even though we'd done nothing special, this was the best birthday I'd ever had. Things were finally coming together for me, and I couldn't be happier.

19
EMMA

I stretched and yawned as I glanced at the clock. I'd been studying for almost two hours, and I felt like my brain was about to explode. Jesse was still in class, so I'd taken advantage of the quiet to get ready for a big test on Monday. Whenever Jesse was around, things were rarely quiet.

I decided to take a break and find something to eat. As soon as I thought of food, my stomach growled loudly. I laughed as the sound seemed to echo around the quiet room. *Yeah, I definitely need food.*

I threw my book down on the living room table and walked to the kitchen. I opened the cabinet to grab a bowl. I rolled my eyes as I dug through Jesse's eight-million cereal boxes until I found something that looked good. I swore that he lived off that stuff.

I poured some cereal into a bowl and sat down at the table to eat. I looked into the living room and smiled as I noticed that my things were everywhere. Since Jesse and I had gotten back together, I rarely spent any time at my dorm room. Without even realizing it, I'd managed to move half my stuff over here. If Jesse had noticed, he didn't seem to mind. In fact, he was always the one who insisted I stay the night.

I was rinsing my bowl out in the sink when my phone rang. Thinking it was Jesse, I answered without looking at the screen to see who it was.

"Hello?"

"I'm surprised you answered," my mother's cold voice replied.

It took me a moment to get over the shock of hearing her voice.

"Mom?"

"Who else would it be?"

"What do you want? I mean, why are you calling?" I asked as I sat down at the kitchen table.

"To see if you've wised up yet."

"What are you talking about?" I asked.

"Don't play stupid, Emma. You know exactly what I'm talking about. I want to know if you're bored with that *school* yet." The way she'd said *school* made it sound like it was a dirty word.

"No, I'm not bored with it yet. I'm actually really happy here."

"You've got to be kidding me."

"Why do you always do that? Anytime I'm happy, you always act like I shouldn't be. Why can't you just be happy for me?"

"You don't belong there, Emma. You need to come home where you're supposed to be."

"So you can control my life again? No, thank you."

"Where did I go wrong with you? I made sure you had everything you ever wanted, and you do this to me."

I ground my teeth together to keep from yelling. I hated how she always tried to make me out to be the bad guy. She'd done it to me my entire life.

"Yeah, you gave me everything I wanted—except for a mom."

"What on earth are you talking about?" she asked angrily.

I really didn't want to do this with her. I was finally happy, and I knew she would only try to tear me down.

"You never acted like I was your daughter. All I wanted was for you to be a mom to me."

"This is ridiculous."

"No, it's not. I'm tired of pretending that we have a relationship because we don't. We never have."

"I'm done with this conversation, Emma, and I'm done with you. Don't bother to call me when the world comes crashing down around you."

With that, she hung up on me. I sighed as I put my phone down on the table in front of me. Tears slid down my cheeks as I realized that I would never have a normal relationship with my mom. Things would always be tense between us. She wasn't capable of being the kind of mother that I wanted. I wiped my tears away as I vowed not to let it bother me any longer. I wouldn't let her destroy whatever life I'd built for myself here.

I picked my phone back up and deleted her number from my Contacts list. She would never know about Jesse. She would never know when I graduated from college and found a job. She would never know when she was a grandma. She would know nothing about me from this day on.

I stood and started walking to the bedroom when the doorbell rang. My forehead creased in confusion. I had no idea who it could be. The only person who ever stopped by was Andy, and he never bothered to knock, let alone ring the doorbell. I walked to the door and looked through the peephole. Not seeing anyone, I opened the door, but no one was there. I stuck my head out and looked both directions, but there wasn't a soul around.

I assumed it was just kids messing around as I closed the door and walked back into the bedroom. As soon as I made it there, the doorbell rang again. I ignored it, but whoever it was rang it again. Afraid that someone was actually out there this time, I turned and made my way back to the door.

I opened the door to see that no one was around—again. This was starting to piss me off. I walked out onto the porch and looked around the yard.

"Okay, whoever you are, you're hilarious," I said sarcastically.

When no one appeared, I turned and started to walk back inside. As soon as I turned toward the door, I was shoved from behind. I stumbled through the entryway and grabbed the chair to keep from falling. I spun around to see who was behind me, and I stopped dead. Ally was standing in the doorway with the most chilling smile I'd ever seen. The hairs on the back of my neck stood up as I stared at her.

"What? No hello?" she asked sweetly.

"You shouldn't be here," I told her.

I'd never liked her, but I'd never been afraid of her like I was now. Something in her eyes told me that I should be *very* afraid. I glanced at the clock on the wall to see that it would be another hour before Jesse came home.

"Why shouldn't I? I live here. My name is on the lease," she said as she continued to smile at me.

"You're not welcome here," I told her, refusing to show that I was afraid of her.

"No, *you're* not welcome here. This is my home."

"It's Jesse's."

Her eyes lit up at the sound of his name. "Where is Jesse anyway?"

"He will be here any minute," I lied.

"Tell the truth, Emma. I know what time he gets home. I lived here, remember?"

"So you keep saying."

I needed to get her out of here—now. She was slowly inching her way into the house and away from the door. The farther away from the door she walked, the less chance I had of getting her out.

My eyes scanned the room, looking for something to use as a weapon if I needed one. My eyes landed on my cell phone. It was still on the kitchen table. It was so close yet so far away. I knew Jesse wouldn't be able to answer if I called him, but Andy wasn't working today. If I could just get to my phone, I could call him to help me.

"Why are you really here?" I asked.

"Can't I just come to visit you guys? I mean, you've pretty much moved in, and Andy is here whenever he isn't working."

"You've been watching us." It was a statement, not a question.

"I have. It's funny how blissfully unaware you three are. I mean, I was practically part of the party on your birthday. I have to say, I liked the second movie a lot better than the first."

"You were here?"

"Well, I wasn't in the house, if that's what you're asking, but I was around."

She was seriously starting to freak me out. It was clear that she had been stalking us. She'd never left.

"Why didn't you leave, like Jesse told you to?" I asked.

She laughed. "Jesse is just confused. He'll come around eventually."

"He's not confused, Ally. He hates you for what you did to him, to us."

"You're being silly. Jesse could never hate me. He loves me."

"Ally, something is seriously wrong with you. You need help."

She just laughed as she stepped closer to me. If she came much closer, I wouldn't be able to make it to my phone. I needed to distract her, so I could either make a run for it out the door or get to my phone. Right now, she was still between the door and me, so I needed to make a move toward my phone.

"So, why do you think Jesse loves you?" I asked, trying to distract her.

She smiled. "You wouldn't want to hear why."

"Of course I do. If something happened between you two, I should know about it. That would mean he lied to me."

She studied me for a minute. I tried to look like I was genuinely worried about what she would tell me. I knew she would probably say the most horrible thing she could think of just to hurt me. I wouldn't believe anything she might say.

"He told me he did," she said quietly.

That wasn't what I'd expected at all. I'd assumed that she would make up some story.

"When?"

"The first time was when we were just little. There was a boy at school who liked to pick on me. It was before I started taking up for myself. Jesse saw me crying on the playground, and he tried to make me feel better. He told me that he loved me and that he would always protect me, no matter what. Besides Andy, he was the first person to tell me that he loved me."

My heart broke for her. It was obvious that her childhood hadn't been that great. I knew I shouldn't feel sorry for her, but I did.

"Ally, I think he meant that he loved you in a different way than you think. He loved you like a sister."

She glared at me. "You have no idea what you're talking about! Jesse loves me! He loves me, not you!"

I shrank back as she screamed. "I didn't mean to upset you."

"Yes, you did. You always try to hurt me, but you can't. Jesse loves me, and he is mine!"

I crept closer to the kitchen and to my phone. "Ally, he loves you. I know he does. It just isn't the way you want. He loves me. I know it hurts to hear that, but you need to understand. You're obsessed with him, and it isn't healthy."

"He loved me until *you* came around. I knew as soon as I saw you on the beach with him that day that you would be trouble."

"On the beach?" I asked.

"When he was teaching you how to surf. He was so caught up in you that he didn't even notice me, but I was there. I'm always there."

I felt a chill go down my spine. Ally's obsession with Jesse wasn't new. It wasn't due to the fact that he'd left her in California. No, it was much older than that. If she had watched us that day, then she had been watching him before that, before I even knew him.

"I saw the way he touched you that day. I wanted to drown you in the ocean. Then, he started bringing you around. I tried to warn him about you, but he wouldn't listen. I only wanted to protect him."

"Ally, I would never hurt him."

"You destroyed us."

She closed her eyes, and I scooted closer to the kitchen. I was almost close enough to sprint to my phone.

"If you left, he would come back to me."

"You can't really believe that. You hurt him when you lied about being pregnant."

"I know now that it was stupid to lie to him like that. Once I apologize to him, he'll forgive me."

"I don't think so, Ally. You really hurt him."

"I wouldn't have had to do that if you hadn't screwed everything up. Once you're gone, he'll need someone to help him get over you again, and I'll be there. I'm always there when he needs me."

"When I'm gone? I'm not going anywhere, Ally."

She smiled. "Yes, you are."

I was as close as I could get to the kitchen without tipping her off to what I was about to do. It was now or never.

"Oh, thank God! You're home!" I said as I looked over her shoulder.

She spun around, thinking Jesse was behind her. As soon as she turned, I shot across the kitchen and grabbed my phone. I unlocked it and started

185

to push Andy's speed dial number when she plowed into me. I dropped to the floor, and my phone went flying across the room.

"No!" I shouted as I watched it land several feet away from where I was.

"You sneaky little bitch!" She climbed on top of me.

I thrashed around as I tried to push her off of me. I managed to grab her hair, and I yanked as hard as I could, making her scream in pain. It gave me the opportunity I needed to shove her away from me. As soon as I was free, I scrambled to my feet and ran for the door.

I almost made it. Just before I reached it, she tackled me from behind. My forehead slammed against the floor as I went down. Black dots danced in front of my eyes as I tried to crawl toward the door. I had to get away from her. If I didn't—well, I didn't want to think about what she might do.

"You're not going anywhere!" She grabbed me and flipped me onto my back.

Her fist connected with my face, and the black dots became larger. I could barely see past them. I reached out blindly and tried to push her away.

She laughed as she slapped me across the face. "Come on, you can do better than that."

"Please let me go, Ally. Please," I begged.

"Why? So you can go running to Jesse to tell him what a mean, horrible person I am? I don't think so."

I felt like the world was spinning off its axis. My stomach lurched, and I fought to keep myself from throwing up. Ally's fist connected with my face again, and I raised my hands to try to protect myself. She laughed at my feeble attempts as she delivered another blow. My eyes closed, and darkness took over.

I welcomed it. I'd do anything to escape the pain.

20
EMMA

My head felt as if it was going to explode. I refused to open my eyes as pain shot through my forehead to the base of my skull. Everything was fuzzy. I took a deep breath as I tried not to cry out. I'd never felt such pain in my life.

I cracked one eye open to look around me. There was very little light in the room, but it still hurt to open my eye. I was in a room with no windows. Nothing was in the room, except for the floor lamp across from me.

Where am I?

I tried to remember how I'd ended up here, but I had no idea.

I was eating cereal, and then my mom called. What happened after that? Someone knocked on the door. Neighborhood kids were playing a prank. No, that wasn't it.

Pain shot through my head, and I clenched my jaw as I waited for it to pass.

Danger...I tried to reach for my phone.

Ally's face slammed into my mind like a hammer. I gasped as I finally remembered.

She came to the house and attacked me. I tried to escape, but she tackled me. I hit the floor, and then Ally hit me. Black dots. After that? Nothing. I must have blacked out.

I tried to stand, but something stopped me. I forced my eyes open to see that my legs were tied to a chair. My arms were tied up behind me. *I am so fucking screwed.* Ally was crazy, and I was alone and defenseless.

"It's about time you woke up, princess." Ally's voice came from behind me.

I turned my neck to look for her, but I didn't see her anywhere. Suddenly, she was beside me. She slapped me across the face, and I cried out in pain. The pain in my head increased until I couldn't bear it anymore. I wanted to black out again. I'd do anything to escape that pain.

"How are you feeling?" she asked sweetly as she pulled a chair in front of me.

She must have grabbed it from somewhere behind me because there was definitely nothing in front of me.

"Like someone cracked my skull," I spit out as I looked away from her.

She laughed as she raised her hand. "Guilty."

"Let me go, Ally. Just walk away, and no one has to know what you did. You got your anger out. It's over."

"Oh, it's far from over, dear Emma. I'm just getting started."

There was a coldness to her voice that made me wonder if she would actually kill me. I looked up at her. As soon as I looked into her eyes, I knew she would kill me without a second thought. Her eyes were cold, and there was no kind of emotion behind them at all.

"Please let me go," I quietly begged.

"But we're just starting to have fun. Don't you want to see everything else I have planned for you?"

I ignored her question and looked away. She could hurt me all she wanted, but I wouldn't give her the satisfaction of me begging a second time. I already knew that she was planning to kill me. That was all I needed to know. The less I knew, the better. Maybe if I didn't fight, she'd get bored and make it quick.

Jesse would lose it when he found out what she'd done. I had no idea how long I'd been out, but I knew it had to be a while from the pain shooting through my skull. He had to know by now that I was gone. Maybe he was searching for me. Hope swelled in my chest as I pictured him rushing in to save me.

My hope was crushed when I realized that even I didn't know where I was. I might not even be in Morgantown anymore. Hell, I might not be in West Virginia.

"Where did you bring me to?" I asked.

"My house."

"And where exactly is your house?"

She studied me for a minute. "I guess it won't hurt to tell you. It's not like you can call someone for help." She laughed as if she'd said something funny. "You're still in Morgantown. Actually, you're only about twenty minutes away from Jesse's house."

If I was still in Morgantown, Jesse stood a chance at finding me. It was a slim chance, but I needed to hold on to something.

"You've been staying this close to us the entire time since you left, haven't you?"

She nodded. "Yep, and you guys had no idea. It's kind of funny when you think about it. I've spent a lot of time watching you at Jesse's house since he kicked me out. I'd give you some advice about closing your curtains, but I don't think you'll need to worry about that anymore. There are no curtains where you're going."

I turned away from her. I couldn't even stand to look at her right now. I felt sick. She'd been stalking us for weeks, and we had been clueless.

"Get away from me."

"Why? Did I say something wrong?" she asked innocently.

"You're a fucking psycho," I told her.

I tried to break free of my restraints. The rope dug into my skin, but I ignored the pain as I struggled.

"You might want to stop before you hurt yourself," she said happily.

I stopped struggling once I realized that the ropes weren't going anywhere. "Just do what you're going to do, and get it over with."

"Oh no, I want to draw this out," she said quietly. She placed her finger under my chin and lifted my face to look at her. "And I can't wait to watch you cry out in pain."

"You won't get away with this, Ally. The police will catch you. Jesse will know that you had something to do with this. He hates you now. You know how I told you that he'd meant he loved you like a sister? You don't even have that from him now. Even if I die, he will *never* be yours."

"Shut up!" she shrieked as she slapped me again.

I clenched my teeth to keep from crying out. One thing was for sure—the bitch was strong. Even her slaps were enough to make my head spin.

"You know nothing about how Jesse feels about me. You have some kind of power over him. Once you're gone, he'll realize that he loves me. We'll be happy together, and he'll forget all about you."

It was my turn to laugh. "Think whatever you want. You'll see."

"You know what the worst part is?" she asked suddenly.

"That I'm tied to a chair?" I asked sarcastically.

"When I watched you guys, I saw you…together. It made me sick to see him touch you."

My stomach rolled at the thought of her watching while Jesse and I'd had sex. "You're sick."

"I didn't want to watch, trust me."

"Then, why did you?"

She shook her head. "You wouldn't understand."

She stood and walked behind me. I could hear her moving things around, but I couldn't turn around far enough to see what she was doing. I glanced around in front of me, hoping to see something that would help me. There was nothing. The room was as empty as before.

I tried to hold my tears in as they filled my eyes. I wouldn't give Ally the satisfaction of seeing me cry. While I knew something was wrong with Ally after everything she'd done to Jesse, I never realized that she was capable of something like this.

She silently walked back over to me. I met her gaze head-on. Fuck her, I wouldn't shy away.

"I overheard Jesse talking to Andy about you one day at our old house. Jesse told him how beautiful he thought you were." Her eyes were so cold as she spoke. "You and I both know that I'm prettier than you, but Jesse doesn't seem to realize that. I'm going to change that. When they find you, he'll realize that you could never be as pretty as me."

I had no idea what she planned to do, but I knew it wasn't going to be pleasant for me. She had kept her hands behind her since she walked over. I watched silently as she finally moved them. My stomach dropped when I saw the knife in her hand.

"Ally, think about what you're doing. We can still work something out. If you use that, then you're done."

"I think you're confused as to who is tied to the chair and who has a knife. I'm in control, Emma, and I always have been." She ran the dull side of the knife across my face. "You're not pretty in the least, but you obviously have something that Jesse likes. We need to fix that."

"Ally, let me go. You don't want to do this," I pleaded, forgetting my earlier promise to myself that I wouldn't beg.

"Trust me when I say I do. I want nothing more than this. I want to hurt you as bad as you hurt me."

She turned the knife, so the sharp edge was pressed against my cheekbone. I held my breath as I waited for her to kill me. I wouldn't scream. I would never let her know how much pain she caused me.

Despite my determination not to cry out, a small whimper escaped me as she ran the knife down my cheek. The cut didn't hurt as bad as my head, but it stung. I shuddered as I felt blood start to slide down my face. Apparently, she didn't plan to stab me like I'd originally thought—at least, not yet. With the shallow cut, she only wanted to cause me pain and destroy my face. I was too worried about how to escape to even think about my face. I had to figure out a way to get her to untie me.

"Does it hurt?" Ally asked softly as her eyes followed the drop of blood that had dripped from my cheek to the floor.

"No," I said stubbornly.

"Then, you won't mind if I try the other side."

She held the knife up to my face and made a cut on my other cheek. It was shallow like the first one, but it still hurt. Blood ran down my face and fell to the floor. It was like I was crying blood.

"There—now, you match." She giggled.

"Thanks," I muttered.

She circled me slowly. I turned my head as she went, afraid to let her out of my sight for even a second. There wasn't much I could do if she decided to stab me in the back, but it still made me uneasy to have her right behind me.

"Are you sorry yet?" she asked.

"For what?"

"For ruining everything I had with Jesse. Duh."

"I didn't ruin anything. If he wanted you, he never would have come to me."

"It's not his fault that you tricked him. He's only a guy, and we both know guys never think with their heads. Well, at least, they don't think with the *right* heads."

"You think he was only using me for sex?" I asked incredulously.

"Of course I do. What else could he want from you?"

I didn't even know how to respond to that. Ally was living in her own little world, and nothing I said would change that. There was no point in fighting with someone who couldn't view reality like a normal person.

"I'm hungry, and I need to pee."

"I don't have any food here."

"Fine, but I still have to pee."

"You just want me to untie you. I'm not stupid."

"You're going to look very stupid when I piss myself, and you have to clean it up."

She studied me for a moment. If I could get her to leave me alone in the bathroom, maybe I could escape. If not, maybe I could find a way to subdue her. The thought of me hitting her over the head with my chair was very appealing.

"Straight to the bathroom, and back here," she finally said.

I sighed in relief as she untied my legs from the chair. She was in the perfect position for me to kick her, but I needed my arms free first. It would be useless to kick her and still be stuck to this damn chair.

She moved out of the way of my legs as she untied my arms. "If you try anything, I *will* kill you. Stand up."

I stood up slowly and stretched my arms and legs. They had gone practically numb from sitting in the exact same spot for so long. I yelped more from surprise than actual pain as I felt the end of her knife poke into my back.

"Start walking toward the door. If you try anything, I will put this knife in your back. I don't want to kill you like this, but I will if you force me to."

I don't want to kill you like this...like this. There it was. There was no doubt in my mind now that she planned to kill me. I needed to get out of here and fast. I walked slowly toward the door. I needed a plan.

"Open it," Ally instructed once we reached the door.

I opened it slowly and looked around. The door led into a dimly lit hallway. Another door was a few feet away to the left. On the right was a door near the top of a staircase.

"Which way?" I asked.

"Walk to the one on the right."

I walked slowly, debating on whether or not to run for it. I had no idea how close the front door was to the stairs. If I could get outside, there was a good chance that I could escape or at least scream for help. If she had been telling the truth about still being in Morgantown, I knew that other houses had to be nearby.

"Walk!" she barked.

I had started to slow down since I still wasn't sure what to do. I picked up my pace and walked to the door next to the stairs. I glanced down the stairs to see that the front door was right in front of them. I just had to make it there.

"Don't just stand there. Open the door." She poked the knife into my back a bit.

I opened the door and stepped inside. The bathroom was tiny. Dread filled me when I saw the small window. It was just a little bit too small for me to escape through if she left me alone.

"I'll wait right outside. Hurry up."

I waited until she closed the door. I glanced down at the doorknob, praying that there was a way to lock it. If I couldn't escape, maybe I could at least hide in here for a while. My prayers weren't answered. There was no lock. I glanced around the bathroom, searching for anything that I might be able to use as a weapon.

There was nothing in here, not even a damn plunger. I pushed the shower curtain back to see if maybe she'd left a razor in there, and I found nothing. I tried the cabinet above the sink next, but it was completely empty. I found the same thing under the sink. *Does she even actually live here?* There wasn't even a bar of soap on the sink. I looked into the mirror to see the cuts on my face. They looked horrible, but they were nothing compared to how bad the blood looked. It had dried in streams down my face.

I flushed the toilet and turned on the water, so she wouldn't become suspicious. Nothing in here would help me unless I planned to wrap her in toilet paper, and there wasn't even much of that. I opened the bathroom door to see her leaning against the wall across from it.

"It took you long enough. Did you find my cabinetry interesting?" she asked.

"I have no idea what you're talking about." I stared at her.

She was so close to the top of the stairs. If I caught her off guard and shoved her, I might be able to knock her down them.

"Sure you don't. Go back to your room."

She pushed her weight from the wall as I turned back toward the room. I took a deep breath as I prepared myself. It was now or never. I spun around suddenly and shoved her as hard as I could. She screamed as she fell backward. Everything happened in slow motion, and I watched her eyes widen. Her back hit the top step, and then she went rolling down the stairs. I couldn't move as I watched her roll over and over again. When she hit the first floor, she didn't move.

I forced my legs to move as I ran down the steps. I hoped that she wasn't dead, but I couldn't afford to stop and check. I would find help and call the police. They could check on her. As for me, my ass was going out that door one way or another. I reached the bottom of the steps and ran for the door. My hand was on the knob when her hand wrapped around my ankle. She jerked, and I went down. I scrambled to get up, but she was on me.

She dropped her knees onto my stomach, knocking the breath from me. I was pinned under her weight as I tried to break free. Instead of slapping me first like last time, she wasted no time in landing a punch right in my temple. I raised my hands to shield my face, but it was no use. She punched any part of me that she could reach. Most of her hits landed on my face. I tasted blood in my mouth as I struggled under her.

"You little bitch! You're going to pay for that." She slammed her fist into the side of my head.

For the second time in a matter of hours, I was knocked unconscious.

21

I hummed to a song on the radio as I drove home. I was in an unusually good mood today, and I couldn't wait to get home to Emma. I'd stopped by the local flower shop on the way home to pick up a dozen roses. I wanted to surprise her, and I knew she'd never expect flowers from me.

I pulled into the driveway and grabbed the roses from the passenger seat. I stepped out and walked up to the house. Afraid that she would see them before I had the chance to surprise her, I hid the flowers behind my back as I opened the door and strolled inside.

"Emma? Where are you?" I called from the doorway.

When she didn't answer, I headed back to our bedroom. I expected her to be asleep in there, but she wasn't. I tried the bathroom next, but she wasn't there either. I looked in Ally's old room last. Emma had never so much as stepped foot in there, so I knew she wouldn't be in there before I even looked.

"Where the hell did she run off to?" I asked out loud as I walked back to the kitchen.

I found a glass big enough to hold the roses, and I filled it with water. I put it in the center of the table and stuck the roses inside, so she would see them as soon as she came home.

She'd said that she was going to come straight home to study. Emma always let me know where she was, so I was a little bit concerned. I pulled my phone out of my pocket and dialed her number. I looked around in confusion as I heard it ringing nearby. It stopped ringing before I could find it, so I dialed again.

I finally spotted it on the opposite side of the kitchen on the floor. *What the hell is it doing there?* I reached down and picked it up.

Something felt off. It wasn't just because her phone had been on the floor. It was just a feeling I had. My good mood from earlier all but vanished.

I turned and walked back to the front door. My stomach dropped when I saw her car keys hanging by the door.

Maybe she decided to go for a walk? I stepped outside and made my way down to the sidewalk. I circled the block, looking for Emma as I went, but there was no sign of her.

I called Andy to see if maybe he'd stopped by and picked her up.

"Hello?"

"Andy, it's Jesse."

"I figured that out when your name came up on my screen. What's up?"

"Is Emma with you?" I asked.

"No. I haven't talked to her today."

"Shit."

"Why? What's wrong?"

"I just got home, and she's not here."

"Just call her." He made it sound like it was the most obvious thing in the world.

"I already did, genius. Her phone was on the kitchen floor."

"Maybe it fell out of her pocket?" he asked, sounding unsure.

"I have a bad feeling, Andy. I can't explain it. Something is wrong."

"I'll be over in a few, and we can go look for her."

I kept watching out the window as I waited for Andy to show up. As soon as he pulled in, I walked out to his car.

"No sign of her?" he asked.

"No. I already walked around the block. Let's go to a few of the closer restaurants and see if she's there."

She wasn't, so we went to look for her on campus. We checked her dorm room, the library, and a few other places where she liked to hang out at. We found nothing. When we left campus, I felt sick. Andy seemed as worried as I was. A tightness was around his mouth that wasn't normally there. He could feel it, too. Something was wrong.

We made a quick stop back at my house to make sure that she hadn't come back while we were out. After I checked the house again, we headed back out to keep searching for her. I knew she had a few friends, but she didn't hang out with them much. I had no idea how to contact them.

"Andy, I'm about to freak the fuck out."

"I know. Me, too. This isn't like Emma at all."

"I think we should go to the police."

He nodded as he drove us to the station.

After waiting almost an hour to talk to someone, the cops were absolutely no help. No matter how many times we told them that Emma wouldn't just disappear, they refused to listen. They said something about waiting twenty-four hours before we could file an official missing person report. That meant we had to wait an entire day before the police would help us.

I left the police station feeling more pissed off and worried than I had when I walked in. Andy and I continued our search until almost three in the morning with no trace of Emma anywhere.

"Dude, we've torn this town apart, and there's no sign of her anywhere. I don't know what the fuck to do," Andy said grimly as we pulled up to my house.

We walked into the house, feeling defeated. If something had happened to her, I would never forgive myself. I was supposed to protect her. I couldn't help but worry that Ally had something to do with this. There had been no sign of her for weeks, but she could have come back.

"What are you thinking?" Andy asked.

"Ally. I'm afraid she's done something to Emma."

"I doubt that. She has been gone for a while."

"Something happened, something bad. I can feel it. Emma wouldn't just disappear."

Andy collapsed down onto my couch at the same time I did. "I don't know what the fuck to think. You two didn't get in a fight or anything, did you?"

I shook my head. "No, everything has been great between us. Emma has been so happy lately."

My phone started ringing, and I nearly ripped a hole in my pants as I tried to get to it. I looked at the screen to see who it was. My stomach dropped when I saw *Blocked Caller* flashing across the screen.

"Hello?" I answered cautiously.

"Hey, Jesse. How are you?"

I held my hand over the phone as I cursed. Once I was sure that I wouldn't start screaming at her, I moved my hand away. "Ally?"

Andy's eyes widened when he heard his sister's name.

"Yeah, it's me."

There was no way that it was a coincidence that she was calling while Emma was missing.

"What do you want?" I asked, forcing myself to keep calm. *Maybe if I pretend like nothing is wrong...*

"I just wanted to see how you are doing. It's been a while since we talked."

"I'm doing fine."

"Really?" She seemed surprised.

"Of course. You sound shocked."

"I just thought..."

"You thought, what?"

"I thought...never mind. I thought you might miss...me."

"Ally, I asked you to leave. You messed up—big time."

"I know, and I'm sorry. I just thought you might miss me."

"Where are you right now? If you're close, maybe we can hang out," I said, hoping she would lead me to Emma.

"I'm around. I can't meet up right now though. I'm tied up with a project at the moment." She giggled.

A shiver ran through my body at the way she'd said that, but I pushed it away. I needed to stay calm.

"What has you all tied up?" I asked, pretending to joke around with her.

"Oh, just something I need to take care of."

"I see." I was about to lose my cool. *This bitch is up to something.*

"What's wrong, Jesse? You sound upset."

"It's nothing. I just..."

"You can tell me. I'll listen."

"Emma left me yesterday."

Andy's jaw dropped, but I shook my head. I didn't want him to say something and screw this up.

"Oh, Jesse, I'm so sorry. Is there anything I can do?"

"Unless you can get her to come back to me, no. I miss her so much. I feel so broken. I mean, I knew it was coming, but it still hurts like a bitch."

"What do you mean?"

"We've been fighting a lot lately."

"She never said anything about you guys fighting."

I closed my eyes as I tried not to scream into the phone. *Ally had Emma.* Ally had just admitted it without realizing it. Things with Ally were worse than I could have imagined. She was seriously sick in the head.

"When did you two talk?" I asked.

"Oh, uh…it was a few days ago. I called her to apologize."

"That's so nice of you, Ally. It means a lot that you'd do that. I think…I think once I get over Emma, I'd like to give us a chance again."

I heard her tiny intake of breath.

"I lied before. I've missed you so much since you left. I used Emma to pass the time, but it just isn't the same. I love you, Ally."

"I love you, too, Jesse. We can be together again. I'll come back to you."

"Let me come to you. Where are you?"

She hesitated. "No, it's okay. I need to make a stop, but I'll be at your house in a few hours."

"Why do you need to stop somewhere? Don't you want to see me?"

"I want to see you more than anything. I just need to do something first."

"What? What could be more important than me?"

The line was silent, and for a second, I thought she'd hung up on me.

Finally, she spoke. "I have a problem that I need to take care of."

"How are you going to take care of it?" I asked.

"I'm going to let my problem wash away. I'm going to throw it away and let it disappear with the current," she said simply. "I love you, Jesse. I'll see you soon."

I shouted her name, but the call ended.

"Son of a bitch!" I stood and kicked the living room table in front of me. "Motherfucking son of a bitch!"

I kicked the table over and over again until it busted into pieces in front of me. *This can't be happening. Ally is going to get rid of Emma.* Ally was going to kill Emma, and I still had no idea where Emma was.

"Jesse, calm down. Tell me what she said," Andy said as he grabbed my shoulders. I hadn't even realized that he was standing next to me.

"She said she has a problem that she needs to take care of. She's going to hurt Emma or kill her, Andy." I dropped down to my knees.

I would die if something happened to Emma because of me. *Dear God. Ally is crazy, absolutely fucking crazy.*

"What else did she say?" he asked urgently.

"She's going to let her *problem* wash away. She's going to throw it away and let it disappear."

"Fuck! Did she say anything else? Did she tell you where she is?"

I shook my head. "She wouldn't say. What is she going to do to Emma, Andy?"

He hesitated. "I think Ally is going to drown Emma."

I stood and kicked at what was left of the table. "I'm going to kill Ally. I want to wrap my hands around her neck and watch the life leave her eyes."

"Breathe, Jesse, breathe. We'll figure this out. Were there any sounds in the background when she was talking?"

"Not that I could hear. It sounded quiet."

"Okay, so she's probably still wherever she took Emma then."

"Ally said she'd be here in a few hours. She could have taken Emma hundreds of miles away last night."

"I don't think so. Ally needs time to do whatever it is she plans to do. I think she's still close, Jesse. She has to be."

"We searched everywhere, Andy. I don't know where else to look. The fucking cops don't give a flying fuck about what's happening. By the time they get off their asses to help us, it'll be too late."

Andy started pacing. I kept talking, but he obviously wasn't paying attention. I needed to find Emma. I couldn't just sit here and wait for Ally to show up. By then, Emma would be dead.

Andy stopped pacing and looked over at me. "She said she was going to wash it away. Then, she changed and said she was going to throw it away, right?"

"She said she was going to let her problem wash away. Then, she changed and said that she was going to throw it away and let it disappear—" I froze.

"Jesse, talk to me here. What is it?"

"Let it disappear with the current. Throw it away. I know where she's at—or at least where she'll go."

"And?" Andy asked impatiently.

"You can't really throw a person into water. I mean, you can, but it's not very dramatic, and Ally is all about the dramatics in life. She always has been. The bridge!"

"What bridge?" he asked.

He hadn't lived here very long, so he didn't know the area.

"There is only one body of water around here big enough for her to use—Cheat Lake. They opened up a new bridge last year, but the old one is still up. She wouldn't use the new one because people would be everywhere. She's going to the old one."

"She's going to throw Emma off the bridge?" he asked.

I watched as pure hatred clouded his eyes.

"And let the current wash her away," I said.

"Are you sure?"

"No, but it's the best option we have right now. Let's go." I grabbed my keys and ran from the house.

Andy followed right behind me, and we were tearing down the road in seconds.

"Call the police and tell them what's happening," I instructed as I cut off a car. I ignored the honking horn as I continued to floor it.

I would save Emma. I had to.

22
EMMA

At least I knew where I was when I woke up this time. I held completely still and kept my eyes shut as I listened. If she were in the room with me, I would wait until she left. Maybe that would give me some time to break free. I listened closely for a few minutes. When I was sure she wasn't around, I opened my eyes slowly. I kept my body completely still as I scanned what I could see of the room. I could see that my arms and legs were once again tied tightly to the chair. After my little escape attempt, she had tied me tighter than the last time.

"I see you're finally awake."

I jumped as her voice came from behind me.

Damn it. She'd been behind me all along.

"I am," I said.

She walked around me and crouched down directly in front of me. "Thanks to you, I have one hell of a headache. You're going to pay for that one. I can promise you that."

"Just let me go, Ally."

"Nope."

She held up the knife from before, so I could see it.

"I'm going to play with you for a while before I kill you. I planned to make it a little less painful, but I think you deserve some pain after you threw me down a flight of stairs."

She stood up and grabbed my shirtsleeve. After cutting it off, she ran the knife along the skin of my upper arm. The blade broke the skin but just barely. I almost sighed in relief. I had expected her to hurt me like before.

My relief was short-lived as she pressed the blade against my arm again. I couldn't keep myself from crying out as she sliced deep into my skin.

"Was it worth it?" she asked.

When I didn't answer, she grabbed my hair and yanked my head back. "Was it?"

"Yes. I wish you had died," I whispered as tears ran down my cheeks. My arm felt like it was on fire.

"You're not very nice." She yanked my hair harder.

I bit my lip to keep from crying out.

She walked around and rolled up my other sleeve. She didn't toy with me this time. She dug the blade into my skin and sliced my arm open.

"Please! Stop!" I cried.

She ignored me as she walked back in front of me. I started struggling harder as she pried my knees apart. I was terrified of what she might do.

"Stop moving so much!" she shouted once she had my legs wedged apart. "You'll make me cut something major. I don't want you to bleed out before I'm finished with you."

She dug the knife into my inner thigh. I didn't even try to hold back as I screamed. The pain was unbearable in such a sensitive spot. She finished her cut and then started another one, crisscrossing the first. I screamed again, begging her to stop. I screamed for someone to help me. I screamed Jesse's name as loud as I could. I just wanted the pain to stop.

My throat was raw by the time she finished. I couldn't stand this pain anymore. My leg felt as if she were holding a blowtorch up to it.

"There—now, for your other leg."

"Please, Ally. Please stop. I'll do anything."

"You should have stayed away, Emma. You had your chance before, and you came back around. It's your own fault that you're in this situation."

"Ally, I'll stay away from Jesse. I swear to God, I will. Just let me go. I won't tell him that you did this to me. I'll fly back to California, and you'll never see me again."

"I can't take that chance. If you're still alive, then he'll always hope that you'll come back to him. He'll have to accept that you'll never be his once you're dead. He'll have to move on."

"Ally, I'll tell him whatever you want."

"Nope. You should have just kept fucking my brother. We all could have been happy then."

She sliced into my other leg, and I cried out again. I couldn't scream anymore, only whimper in pain. I wanted to die at this point. Almost every part of my body was screaming out from the cuts or the beatings she'd given me.

"X marks the spot," she said as she finished the cut. "Now, where should we cut next?"

She looked over my body like she was debating on what outfit to put on me, not where she would slice and dice me next.

"Let's do your stomach."

She pulled up my shirt and tucked it into my bra, so it wouldn't fall down. I closed my eyes as I waited for the knife to touch my skin again. She didn't disappoint. A few seconds later, I felt the knife slice across my stomach. She didn't go as deep with this cut as she had with my arms and legs. Or maybe I was hurting so much that my brain just couldn't process the pain. Either way, I was glad. I couldn't handle any more.

"Do you think we should cut anywhere else?" She waved the knife in front of me.

My stomach turned when I saw my blood covering the blade.

"Just kill me, and get it over with," I whispered.

I closed my eyes as I willed my body to shut down. I wanted to pass out again, so I didn't have to feel the pain any longer. She slapped me hard across the face, and my head fell back. I couldn't bring myself to open my eyes or even make a sound at this point. She slapped me again, and I still refused to look at her.

"You're starting to bore me, Emma. I thought you'd be more fun than this."

I stayed quiet as I listened to her footsteps. She walked behind me, and I heard her drop the knife. The room was completely silent for a few seconds. All of a sudden, a cloth was over my mouth.

She's going to smother me.

I struggled against it. It took me a minute to realize what she was actually doing. She'd chloroformed me. I started to feel drowsy, and I stopped fighting her. She'd given me what I'd hoped for. I passed out.

I awoke to the sound of someone calling my name. I refused to open my eyes. All I wanted to do was stay here and sleep.

"Emma! Emma, wake up!"

I knew that voice. My eyes opened to see Jesse running through the door with Andy right behind him. Several police officers followed them into the room. Jesse ran to my side and started cutting away at the ropes holding me hostage.

"Jesse! It's Ally. She's here. She took me."

"We figured that out. Don't worry. She won't hurt you anymore."

"Why? Where is she?"

He pointed to the police officers. "They shot her. She tried to stab me, so they took her down. She's dead."

Tears fell from my eyes as I realized that I was finally safe. Jesse had saved me. He finished freeing my hands and started cutting at the ropes around my feet.

"I was so scared, Jesse."

"God, Emma, you look like shit," Andy said as he crouched down beside me and took my hand.

"I feel like shit."

Jesse freed my legs and held a hand up to my cheek. "I'm so sorry she did this to you. It's all my fault."

"No, it's not. She was crazy."

"She never would have come after you if it wasn't for me."

I threw my arms around his neck as he carefully picked me up and carried me to the door.

"You can't blame yourself, Jesse. None of us knew just how sick she really was."

"I love you, Emma."

"I love you, too."

He carried me through the hall and down the stairs. My stomach clenched as I saw Ally lying at the bottom of the stairs. Her eyes were wide open, but they were lifeless. I turned away from her and buried my face into Jesse's neck. I never wanted to see her again.

I looked up when Jesse cried out. The look of horror on his face chilled me to the bone.

"Jesse? Jesse! What's wrong?"

He lost his grip on me, and I fell to the floor. He dropped to his knees beside me. I screamed in terror when I saw a knife embedded in his back.

"Oh my god! Jesse! Someone help us!"

"No one is here to help you now, Emma. Look what you made me do. Jesse is going to die and it's all because of you."

I looked up to see Ally standing behind Jesse. She was smiling as she watched Jesse struggle to stay upright.

He reached for me. "Emma!" he cried as blood trickled from his lips. "Emma!"

"Wake the fuck up!"

My eyes opened to see Ally standing in front of me.

"Emma! Jesus, you're hard to wake up. You'd think I'd chloroformed you or something." She chuckled at her own joke.

It was all a dream. I started crying as I realized that Jesse was still safe. He was still alive. But he wasn't here to save me. I was still alone with Ally.

"Change in plans. It looks like I'm not going to be able to play with you as much as I wanted," she said sadly.

"Why?"

"Because I have a date with Jesse in just a few hours."

I was still groggy from what she'd done to me, and her words weren't making sense.

"What are you talking about?"

"I just talked to him on the phone a few minutes ago. He couldn't be happier that you're gone, and he wants me back. Oh, Emma, I'm so excited. We need to hurry because the sun will be up soon, and I don't want anyone to see where I'm taking you."

"You talked to Jesse?" I asked, unable to believe what she was saying.

"You're a bit slow, aren't you? Yes, I talked to Jesse."

I felt a small ray of hope fill me. If she'd talked to Jesse, maybe she had slipped and told him where she was. Maybe he was on his way over here right now. I knew that he had lied when he said he wanted her back. He had to know that she'd taken me, and he'd simply been playing along, so he could find me.

"You can have him—really. Just let me go, and then you can skip off into the sunset with him."

"I already told you that I'm not going to let you go. Now, let's get you untied, so I can get rid of you."

I sat still as she slowly untied my arms. Once they were free from the arms of the chair, she jerked them behind me and retied them. My legs were next. She untied them from the chair and made me stand. Between the pain coursing through my body and the fact that I couldn't use my arms, she had to help me up. Once I was standing, she tied my legs together so that I could walk slowly but not run. Every time I moved, I wanted to cry out in pain.

"Walk," she said as she pushed me forward.

With my legs tied, I could barely walk. It seemed like forever before we reached the stairs. She had to help me as I practically crawled down them. When we reached the front door, she grabbed a roll of duct tape from the table beside it. She ripped a piece off and covered my mouth.

"I can't have you screaming bloody murder and waking up my neighbors." Satisfied with her work, she turned and opened the door to look out. "There's no one around. Hurry up."

I couldn't have hurried if I tried. She practically dragged me to a car sitting a few feet away from the front door. She stopped at the back of the car and opened the trunk.

"Get in."

My eyes widened, and I shook my head. There was no way I was getting in there.

"Fine. I'll shove you in."

She grabbed my upper arm right where she'd cut me, and I screamed against the duct tape. Her fingers dug in until I gave in and climbed into the trunk. She smiled sweetly, and then she slammed the trunk down.

I tried to stay calm as darkness surrounded me. The car started a few seconds later, and I could feel us moving. I closed my eyes, trying to block out the pain. I couldn't believe that I was spending my last few minutes alive stuffed in the trunk of a car.

What did I ever do to deserve this? I loved Jesse.

Despite my situation, I wouldn't trade a moment of our time together for anything. It saddened me to realize everything I was going to lose. I let my tears flow freely as I gave up. There was no way that I would come out of this alive. She'd won. I only prayed that Jesse would never find comfort in her.

23

"I think we were wrong," Andy said as he stared at the main road.

"We've been here forever, and there's no sign of them."

"We've been here for forty-five minutes. That isn't forever."

"It feels like it. What if this isn't the place? We could be out searching for Emma instead of hiding behind trees."

I shook my head. "This has to be it. It just feels right."

And it did. The same nagging feeling I'd had when I discovered that Emma was missing was back. It told me that this was the right place. We just had to wait. I still couldn't help but feel a twinge of uncertainty though. If I were wrong, Emma could die because of my mistake. I couldn't even think about that. I wouldn't.

"Where the fuck are the police?" Andy asked.

"Probably eating doughnuts."

It had taken most of the ride over here for Andy to convince the police that he wasn't trying to pull some kind of prank. The officer had said that he would send someone to check it out. As far as I was concerned, we were on our own. The police were too busy trying to bust minors for drinking than worrying about something that was actually important.

We waited for another fifteen minutes with no sign of Emma or Ally. I was starting to doubt myself. *Maybe I was wrong. Maybe this wasn't where Ally was taking her. She could be miles away right now.* I closed my eyes as I tried to block out the images filling my mind—Emma in pain, Emma dead. Those were not things that I wanted to see.

I couldn't lose her. We'd just barely found each other again. I wasn't ready to let her go. This wasn't how life was supposed to happen. We were supposed to live happily ever after until we were old. Then, we'd die together at the exact same moment, so neither of us had to suffer the loss. Anything else was too painful to think about.

"Dude, look," Andy whispered.

I'd been so caught up in my thoughts that I had missed the car quickly approaching us. It had turned off on the same road we had. This road only led to the old bridge, so I knew that it had to be Ally. At least, I hoped it was.

Andy and I had hidden my car on an old four-wheeler path a few feet off the blacktop road. After we'd made sure that it wasn't noticeable, we'd hidden next to several large trees. We were camouflaged enough that I wasn't worried Ally would see us or my car and run for it.

The car passed us and stopped a few feet away from the bridge. I watched silently as Ally opened the driver's door and stepped out. I'd been right about this being the right place. I sent a silent prayer of thanks toward the sky.

Ally closed her door and walked to the bridge. Andy and I exchanged looks as we watched her walk halfway across it, and then she looked down to the water below.

Where is Emma? I didn't see her in the car. My stomach dropped. *Maybe Ally already killed her. Dear God, I can't even think about it.* I refused to believe that we were too late.

Ally stared down at the water for a few seconds more before she turned and walked back to her car. She walked to the trunk and opened it. I held my breath as I watched her reach inside.

Please don't let Emma be in there. Please don't let her be dead, I begged silently.

It was taking every ounce of willpower I had not to jump from my hiding spot and tackle Ally, but I couldn't. If she didn't have Emma with her, I didn't want to tip her off that we were here. Instead, we would follow Ally when she left.

I could hear Ally cursing as she struggled to pull something from the trunk. I nearly lost it when I saw her drag Emma from the back of the car. Emma fell to the ground and didn't move. She was dead.

"No, no, no, no," I whispered. *She can't be dead.*

"Come *on!*" Ally shouted as she kicked Emma in the stomach.

I stood from my crouching position and was about to run out to them when Ally finally managed to get Emma to her feet.

"She's alive," Andy hissed from beside me.

I couldn't breathe as I watched Emma struggle against Ally. Emma's hands were tied, and it looked like her feet were, too. Ally practically carried her toward the bridge. It was now or never. I ran from my hiding spot and headed directly toward them.

"Ally! Stop!" I shouted.

She turned to look at me just as they reached the bridge. I ran as hard as I could, but I knew I'd never make it to them in time. I could hear Andy right behind me.

"Jesse?" Ally asked.

"Let her go!" Andy yelled from behind me.

"Both of you, stop right now! I'll throw her over if you come any closer," Ally screeched.

I stopped dead about fifteen feet away from them. Andy didn't get the message in time and nearly knocked me down as he plowed into me. I couldn't take my eyes off of Emma. She was hurt badly. Dried blood covered her face, arms, and legs. The front of her shirt was also soaked with blood. Both of her eyes were blackened, and even from this far away, I could see a large bump on her forehead. Her mouth was covered by a piece of duct tape.

But it was her eyes that did me in. What little I could see of them was clouded with fear and pain. She didn't even struggle as Ally pushed her up against the edge of the bridge. It would only take a second for Ally to throw Emma over the side to the dark water below. It was obvious that Ally had made Emma suffer as much as possible before bringing her here.

"Ally, what are you doing?" I asked quietly.

"You weren't supposed to see this!" she cried out as if it were *her* in pain.

"Let her go. You don't want to do this." I fought to keep my voice calm, afraid that she would toss Emma over if I shouted like I wanted to. I'd never wanted to hurt someone as much as I wanted to hurt Ally right now. I wanted her to feel just as much pain as she'd inflicted on Emma.

"I don't want to, Jesse. I have to."

"You don't have to do this," I reasoned.

"Yes, I do."

"Why?"

"Because you'll never let her go if I don't! She'll always be in our way!" She screeched.

I had to think fast. I needed to make Ally believe that Emma wasn't a threat. If Emma weren't a threat to her, then maybe Ally would let Emma go. I didn't see any other option unless I could get closer to them. Even then, I doubted if I could reach them in time to catch Emma.

"She's not a problem, Ally. I already told you that earlier."

"You'll change your mind. Then, I'll be left with nothing while you go crawling back to her."

"Ally, think about it. What I had with her is over, and I'm ready to move on with you. Sure, she was fun for a while, but it's over now. I got bored."

"You say that now, but what about later? You've spent so much time pining away over her that you'll start to miss her."

"I've never pined away for her, Ally. She's pretty, and I wanted to fuck her. I did, and now, I'm over it." I slowly took a few steps closer to Ally and Emma. "Don't you trust me?"

Ally bit her lip as she watched me. It was obvious that she was too lost in her thoughts to notice that I'd moved closer to her.

"You were so mad at me," Ally said.

"I was, but I'm not now. You lied to me, Ally, and you hurt me. Wouldn't you be angry if I had done that to you?"

"Yeah, I guess. I only did it because I love you. I just wanted you to give me a chance. I wanted you to love me back."

I pretended to hesitate. "Ally, I've thought about you a lot since I made you leave. I've missed you so much. I've tried to push my feelings for you away because you've always been like a sister to me, but I can't do it anymore. I'm falling in love with you, no matter how many times I tell myself that I shouldn't."

"Why shouldn't you?" she asked breathlessly.

She was obviously buying everything I'd said.

I took another step forward, careful not to even glance at Emma. I couldn't let Ally figure out what I was doing.

"Because I feel guilty for feeling this way about Andy's sister. I'm supposed to help protect you. Instead, I want you."

"I want you, too."

"Then, it's settled. Leave Emma here, and come with me. We'll leave this town and start over in someplace new. No one will ever find us."

She smiled. "I'd like that, but I can't let Emma live. If I do, I'll always worry that she'll ruin everything. Once I take care of her, my mind will be free."

I sighed. "It hurts that you don't trust me."

"I do trust you, Jesse. It's her that I don't trust."

It killed me not to glance over at Emma. I wanted to look at her and tell her that everything would be okay. I wanted to comfort her. I hoped that Andy was passing the message along with his eyes since I certainly couldn't. Emma had to know that I'd get her out of here. It killed me to pretend to love Ally when I could barely stomach the sight of her.

"She doesn't matter, Ally. You have to realize that. I mean, think about it. What chance does some rich snob who I wanted to bang have against you? I've known you my entire life. We grew up together in that shithole of a trailer park. We're from the same world, Ally. Emma could never relate to me like you can."

I took another step closer. I'd managed to get within a few feet of them. Ally didn't seem to notice as she thought about what I'd said. I chanced a glance at Emma. Her eyes were still filled with fear, and she was visibly shaking. I wasn't sure if it was from fear or from the chilly predawn air.

"I don't know..." Ally trailed off as she turned to look at Emma.

It was now or never. I lunged for Emma while Ally's back was turned, but Ally saw me coming at the last second. I watched in horror as she shoved Emma hard. My fingertips brushed Emma's arm as she fell over the side of the bridge.

With the duct tape over her mouth, she couldn't even scream. I watched as she fell in slow motion to the dark water below. Her hands and legs were still tied, so she wouldn't be able to swim. I wasn't sure if she would have been able to swim even without the restraints. She was hurt too badly.

"You lied to me!" Ally screamed.

Emma hit the water and disappeared below the surface. I jumped on the railing and dived in after Emma. I heard Ally cry out as my foot connected with her when I pushed away from the railing. I couldn't have cared less. I only cared about getting to Emma.

The breath was knocked from me as I hit the frigid water. I broke the surface and kicked back up to grab a breath. I took a deep breath and dived back under in search of Emma. The water was so black that I couldn't see a foot in front of me. I reached around, trying to feel for her. Nothing was there, so I dived deeper. My body felt numb as I continued to search, but I refused to give up.

When I couldn't hold my breath any longer, I kicked to the surface. I took another deep breath and dived under again to continue my search. With every second passing, I felt more and more helpless. I had to find her. I wouldn't stop until I did.

I continued to search until I ran out of air again. Just as I was about to push back to the surface, my hand connected with something hard. I grabbed it and pulled it to the surface with me. I nearly cried when I saw that it was Emma. I kicked my way over to the edge of the water and pulled Emma out. Her eyes were closed, and she wasn't breathing.

"Emma! Emma!" I shouted as I shook her. Terror filled me when her eyes stayed shut. "Think, Jesse, think!"

I needed to give her CPR. I'd taken the class my freshman year of high school, but that had been years ago, and I'd barely paid attention. I'd never thought I would need it. *Well, I sure as hell need it now.* I tried to remember what I was supposed to do. I needed to tip her head back. *Yeah, that's right.* I gently pushed her head back. I ripped the tape off and opened her mouth. I plugged her nose and pressed my lips against hers. I breathed air into her lungs.

"Come on, Emma!" I said after a few breaths.

I needed to do compressions. I put my hands together and put them on her chest. I shoved down gently, afraid that I would hurt her. I pushed a few times before stopping to blow air into her mouth again. I repeated the compressions, pushing harder this time.

Breath. Breath.

Chest compression. Chest compression. Chest compression.

Breath. Breath.

I continued to work on her, refusing to give up.

"Emma, please breathe. Please, baby. Open your eyes," I whispered as I pushed on her chest.

I would do anything, I would give anything to see her open her eyes. Tears ran down my face as time passed. I wasn't doing something right, or she would be breathing by now.

Finally, Emma coughed, and water poured from her mouth. My heart leaped to my throat as I helped her roll over. She tried to suck in a breath, but she couldn't because the water was still coming out of her mouth.

"Get it out, Emma. Come on, baby, breathe."

She coughed again and then sucked in a breath. She coughed a few more times.

"Emma, are you okay?" I asked as I held her to me.

"My lungs hurt," she managed to gasp out. "I hurt everywhere."

"I know, I know. I'm here now. She'll never hurt you again."

I could hear police sirens in the distance. I prayed that Andy had managed to keep Ally on the bridge once I'd dived off of it. I wanted to watch as the police loaded her into the back of a cruiser to cart her ass off to jail. She could rot there for the rest of her life. I would make sure she stayed there. I'd never let her hurt Emma again.

I looked down at Emma and saw her, really saw her, for the first time. "Oh god, Emma."

Her shirt was pushed up enough that I could see her stomach had been sliced open. Her arms and legs were covered in the same knife marks as well as both of her cheeks.

"She cut me."

"I can see that. I'm so sorry, Emma."

"Not your fault," she whispered. She closed her eyes and laid her head against my chest.

The sirens were closer now. They sounded like they were almost to the bridge. I looked up to see if I could spot Andy, but he wasn't anywhere in sight. Off to my left, I heard someone gasp. I looked over to see Andy emerging from the water.

"Andy? What the hell?"

"You hit Ally in the head with your foot when you dived in. You knocked her out, and she fell over the side, too. I tried to find her, but I couldn't. Oh god, I couldn't find her. She's my sister, Jesse."

I didn't know what to say. Even though she was crazy, she was still his sister. He had to be hurting, but I couldn't worry about him or Ally right now. I glanced down at Emma to see that she'd passed out in my arms. I had to focus on her. I had to protect her. Nothing else mattered.

The sirens were blaring on the bridge now. I looked up to see two police officers staring down at us. They hadn't bothered to show up when we actually needed them. No, they'd waited until everything went to hell.

"We need an ambulance down here!" I shouted.

Emma moaned, and I pulled her closer to me. I wanted to protect her from the world.

"Everything will be okay. I've got you now, and I'm never letting you go again."

24
EMMA

I didn't want to wake up. When I did, *she* would be there, waiting for me. I kept my eyes firmly shut as I willed myself to fall back asleep. My body felt strangely painless, and I didn't want to know why. All I could remember from before I fell asleep was pain. It was everywhere. It had surrounded me like a fog, closing me off from everything else in the world. I didn't want to feel it anymore. I knew it couldn't be good that I felt nothing, but I embraced it.

Maybe I'm dead. Maybe that was why I felt absolutely nothing right now. If this were death, I welcomed it. The only regret I had was that I'd left Jesse behind. I'd also left without telling Andy, Lucy, or my dad good-bye. They would be so angry with me for leaving them like that, but I hadn't had a choice. Surely, they would understand why I let go. The pain from her blows, the struggles, and her knife had just been too much to bear. No one should have to feel a blade slice through the skin over and over.

I hoped that Jesse never found out what she'd done to me. I knew him, and he was probably already beating himself up for my disappearance. That was just how he was. He pretended not to care about anyone or anything, but he did. He cared so much that the pain and guilt crushed him. This would cripple him. It would destroy him. I could only hope that Andy would help him through it. Both of them were so kind despite how they portrayed themselves to others.

Jesse's face flashed before my eyes, and I smiled. He was so beautiful, and he had been mine. My smile slipped away as I realized that I no longer had a claim on him. Someone else would come along and take away his pain and guilt over me. He'd be whole again one day, and it wouldn't be because of me. I prayed that he wouldn't find comfort in Ally. He had to know that she'd had something to do with my disappearance.

I wondered if my mother would even care that I was gone. Would she cry when they told her I was missing? Would she cry when she finally found out that I was dead? I doubted it, but I hoped that she would miss me. Even if it were for only a day, an hour, a second, I just wanted her to feel *something, anything* for me. I regretted our last conversation. I wished that I had told her that I loved her. As much as I hated her, I loved her, too. She was my mother.

I hated the darkness surrounding me. Wasn't there supposed to be a light that I followed into a peaceful oblivion? Had I missed it? I didn't want to be stuck in this darkness forever. I wasn't sure I could handle that.

"Her eyelids fluttered. Did you see that?"

I heard a voice. I could have sworn it belonged to my mother. It was muffled and sounded like it was far away. Maybe someone was here to take me from the darkness and lead me into the light.

I knew I hadn't been a saint, but I couldn't think of a thing I'd done to deserve this darkness. I'd never been particularly religious, but surely, if he existed, God wouldn't send me to hell. I'd already been there, thanks to Ally. I just wished that if I were in hell, I could bring her with me. In my opinion, she deserved it more than I did.

"Emma, can you hear me?"

That sounded like Jesse. I smiled. If I could hear his voice, then this darkness wasn't hell. It couldn't be.

"Emma, it's Daddy. Open your eyes, baby girl. We miss you."

I really must be dead. There was no way that my mom and dad were both talking to me. For that to take place, they would have to be in the same room together. That hadn't happened since right before they separated when I was younger.

"I just saw her eyes move again. Someone get the doctor." My mom's voice echoed through my head.

"It's time to wake up, Emma. Come on, baby. You're safe here. No one will hurt you."

There was Jesse's voice again.

I didn't want to open my eyes, but I wanted to see him. It was probably just a trick of Ally's, but it didn't matter. I'd do anything just to see him again for a minute. I didn't care if he wasn't real.

I tried to open my eyes, but they refused to cooperate with me. They weren't ready to face the world just yet. I decided that I wasn't either. I'd much rather stay dead and never face the pain again. I let myself relax as I slipped into a peaceful oblivion.

"It's been a week. Why isn't she awake yet?"

"Emma went through a lot, Mr. Daniels. She needs time to heal, both mentally and physically. When she's ready to wake up, she will."

"You're sure that nothing is wrong?"

"We ran tests when we brought her in. As you're well aware of, she was beaten. Despite the condition of her body externally, she has no internal injuries. She had a concussion, but that was it. Everything else came back normal."

"I just want her to wake up. I don't know what I'm supposed to do to make that happen."

"There's nothing you can do, Mr. Daniels. You just have to wait for her to be ready. She has to want to come back to you. She'll be ready one day.

It could be tomorrow, next week, next month, but eventually, she will. I imagine that she's trying to shut everything out to protect herself from what happened to her."

"Emma, if you can hear me, I need you to wake up. You're starting to scare me. I just want to see those beautiful eyes of yours."

Jesse. It sounded as if his voice was muffled, like I was underwater. I tried to concentrate on it to break the surface. I just wanted to see him. That wasn't too much to ask. I clawed my way out of the darkness. *I have to see him.* The darkness had protected me, but I was tired of it. *I want light. I want him.*

My eyes slowly opened. I blinked a few times as I tried to adjust to the brightness. After spending an eternity in darkness, the light was hard to accept.

"Jesse?" My voice came out as a hoarse whisper.

"Emma! You're awake."

His features slowly came into view as he hovered over me, blocking some of the light. All I could do was stare at him. He was the most beautiful thing I'd ever seen.

"Where am I?" It hurt so much to talk. I felt like gravel was embedded in my throat.

"You're in the hospital. You've been here for almost two weeks."

I closed my eyes as I tried to remember how I'd ended up here. I could remember nothing besides the chair Ally had tied me to. My eyes squeezed shut as I relived her hitting me, cutting me.

"Ally?"

"She's gone. She fell off the bridge at the same time you did. Andy tried to find her, but he couldn't. The water was too dark. It's a miracle that I found you."

Bridge? Water? I tried to force my memories to appear, but still nothing came to me.

"I don't remember the bridge," I whispered.

"What do you remember?" he asked softly.

"Water, first. Please."

His eyes widened. "Of course. I'm an idiot. Let me find the nurse."

He was gone a split second later. Before I could even process the fact that he had disappeared, he was back. A woman appeared with him, carrying a pitcher. She smiled down at me.

"Emma, my name is Adrienne. How are you feeling?"

"I need water."

"Of course. I'm sure your throat feels raw."

I nodded as I watched her pick up a small cup from the table and then pour water into it. She pushed the button on my bed, so I was almost in a sitting position. I opened my mouth and sucked the water through a straw. I'd never felt something so amazing in my entire life. When the cup was empty, she poured more water and held the cup as I drank.

My throat still hurt, but it was bearable now. "Thank you."

"You're very welcome. How do you feel?"

"I hurt everywhere, but it's not as bad as it was when I went to sleep."

"You had several injuries when you came in, so we have an IV in with pain medication to help you."

"What did she do to me?" I asked. I was terrified of what I *didn't* remember.

The nurse frowned. "What do you remember, Emma?"

229

"A chair and a...a knife. She cut me. I remember her hitting me when she came to Jesse's house and then later when I pushed her down the stairs."

The nurse's eyes widened.

"I was trying to get away. I didn't mean to hurt her."

"You were trying to protect yourself. Given your condition, it's obvious that she deserved it." She smiled. "That's off the record, of course."

"Thank you."

"Do you remember anything else?" Jesse asked from beside me.

I struggled to see through the fog that clouded my thoughts. I *needed* to remember. I needed to know what else she'd done. She'd put me in a car trunk. I recalled the movement of the car as it drove over potholes. I remembered cold and darkness.

"My mouth was covered, so I couldn't scream. I remember the trunk of a car, but then I can't recall anything else."

"Take your time, Emma. You went through a lot," Jesse said as he took my hand in his.

I looked down as he joined our fingers together. I closed my eyes as I tried to remember the source of the coldness I'd felt.

"You were there. You tried to help me."

He nodded. "I was."

"Andy, too. She made me get out of the car even though it hurt. It hurt so much," I whimpered as I remembered the pain. "My shoulder took most of the impact when she dropped me to the ground. We were on a bridge. She pushed me to the edge when she saw you and Andy. You tried to reason with her, but she wouldn't let me go. You ran toward me, but she pushed me over before you could get to us in time. The water was so cold. I don't remember anything after that."

Jesse lifted my hand to his lips and kissed it. "I went in after you, but I couldn't find you. I thought I was too late. Ally fell in, too, and Andy tried to save her, but he couldn't find her. When I finally found you, you weren't breathing. I almost lost you, Emma. I almost lost you."

Tears ran down my cheeks as I stared up at him. We'd almost lost each other. Why had Ally done these things to me? Why had she hurt me so much? I remembered the cuts on my face. Unable to stop myself, I turned away from Jesse.

"Emma? What's wrong?"

"My face," I whispered. "She cut me. I must look horrible."

He cupped my face and gently turned my head. "The cuts on your face were a lot shallower than the other ones. You still have black eyes, but the cuts have healed a lot while you've been asleep."

"I'll have scars."

I wasn't a particularly vain person, but the cuts bothered me. For the rest of my life, I'd see them every single time I looked in the mirror. They would be a reminder to both Jesse and me of what she'd done to me.

"No, you won't, and even if you did, it wouldn't matter. I love you, Emma. Nothing could change that, especially not something as superficial as scars."

"I don't want to remember."

"You don't have to if you don't want to. You've been through so much, and you deserve to forget."

"Emma! Oh, thank God!"

I looked up to see my mother rushing into the room. She pushed the nurse aside, and then she hugged me gently.

"Mom? What are you doing here?" I asked.

She was the last person I'd expected to see here.

"Jesse called me. He called your father, too. We've been here since they brought you in. You terrified us, Emma. We thought you'd never wake up."

"Where's Daddy?"

"He had to make a phone call, but he'll be back soon. I'm so glad you're awake."

"I'm sorry for what I said on the phone."

"Don't even think about that. I want you to concentrate on getting better."

I couldn't even begin to process the fact that my mom was here, and she was worried about me. She never worried about me. She'd barely noticed me most days.

"Why are you here?"

She gave me a puzzled look. "Why *wouldn't* I be here? You're my baby, Emma."

"I didn't think you'd care." It hurt to say it, but it was true.

She closed her eyes for a moment before opening them to look at me. "I've messed up a lot when it comes to you, Emma. Jesse made sure to point that out to me when I showed up. I love you. I'm sorry if I made you feel like I didn't. I'm just... I'm not good with feelings. I drove your father away first and then you."

"You hurt me."

"I know, and I'm sorry, Emma. I will do everything in my power to make it up to you. You mean the world to me. I've missed you so much since you left. I just couldn't bring myself to beg you to come back after I threatened you. I never expected you to be strong enough to leave."

"I am strong, stronger than I thought."

She smiled. "You are. You're stronger than anyone realized. Jesse told me everything that happened, both before he left California and then over the past few weeks. I'm sorry that I made you think you couldn't talk to me about the things happening in your life."

"You never wanted to listen. I didn't tell you about Jesse because I knew you'd push him away. He wouldn't be good enough for you."

She looked over at Jesse. "I admit that I would have before. Seeing you in this bed and knowing he's the reason you're here and not at the bottom of a river made me realize that I owe this young man a lot. You're an adult now, Emma, and I couldn't keep you two apart even if I tried. I don't want to though. I've watched him, and I know that he loves you."

"Thanks, Mom."

She smiled down at me. "You're welcome."

It was a start. My mom and I still had a long way to go, but we might be able to have something close to a normal relationship one day. It would take more than one apology to forget everything that she'd done to me. But if Ally had accomplished anything, it was to show me just how unpredictable and short life was. I had to let go of the hate I felt for my mother and start over. I couldn't spend my whole life hating her.

The past two weeks had been pure hell. I'd sat helplessly as I watched Emma lay unconscious in her hospital bed. I'd never felt so worthless in my life. I would have given anything to see her open her eyes.

I'd only left to shower and shave. Andy would bring me food every morning and evening when he came in to check on her. I'd even slept in the damn chair in her room, so I would be there when she woke up. I had felt terrified that she'd wake up alone and scared. I never wanted to leave her alone again.

I'd had words with her mother when she arrived. I hadn't wanted to call her, but I'd known it was the right thing to do. Her number wasn't in Emma's phone, so I had called Lucy to get it. Of course, Lucy had freaked out the minute I explained why I needed it. She'd wanted to come out, but she couldn't due to her classes. I'd promised to call her as soon as anything changed.

Her mom had been cold to me at first when I called her. It had been obvious that she'd felt like I was wasting her time. Once I'd told her about Emma, her attitude had changed. She'd gone from cold bitch to terrified mother in two seconds flat. I hadn't expected that reaction from her. She had shown up a few hours later, crying and holding Emma's hand.

I couldn't help but snap when I had seen her reaction. *Why did Emma have to almost die to get that kind of attention from her own mother?* I'd called Emma's mother out on her pathetic attempts at parenting. There had been a lot of shouting. Emma's dad had walked in right in the middle of it. The look on her mom's face when he'd strolled over to me and hugged me was priceless. Up until that point, her mom hadn't even bothered to ask who the hell I was. All she knew was my name and that I was one of Emma's *friends*. When her dad had explained that I'd been with Emma for years, her mother had been speechless. She'd finally managed to thank me for what I'd done, but we were still uneasy around each other.

As far as I was concerned, two weeks of good parenting didn't make up for nineteen years of nothing. She still had a long way to go in my opinion. I was just glad that she'd actually shown up. Emma was going to need a lot of support when she woke up.

I'd watched each day as the bruises and cuts slowly started to heal. Once I had calmed down enough to see the extent of Emma's injuries, I wanted to kill Ally all over again. She'd tortured Emma. Ally had beaten Emma and cut her over and over again in less than twenty-four hours. I didn't even want to think about what Ally might have done if she'd had more time. I didn't want to think about watching her push Emma over the side of the bridge. I didn't want to think about Ally ever again. I didn't want to think period.

The doctors had assured us that Emma would wake up. She'd needed time to heal, both mentally and physically. But as one day had turned into two and then three, I'd started to wonder if she'd ever come back to me. *Would she want to?* It was my fault that she'd suffered so much. If it weren't for me, she never would have even met Ally. I couldn't blame Emma if she hated me for everything that had happened to her.

Andy had tried to make me feel better, but it had been no use. Until Emma's eyes had opened, I'd known I would never find peace. While I'd blamed myself, Andy had put the blame on himself as well. He'd kept saying that Ally was his sister, and he should have known something wasn't right with her. I wasn't sure which of us had felt worse.

Emma's dad had been silent most of the time. For a rock star, he was certainly the quiet, thoughtful type. He'd taken time off from the recording studio to stay with Emma in the hospital. The nurses had brought in extra chairs, so her mom, her dad, and I would all have places to sit. Her parents had stayed with her all day just like I had. When nighttime had rolled around, they would both go to their hotel rooms, only to return first thing in the morning.

My mom had stopped in twice to see how Emma was doing. She'd known nothing of what had happened with Ally before we left California or what Ally had done to me recently. My mom had been shocked to learn that the little girl who had practically grown up at our house had become the ruthless person who tried to kill Emma. When I'd told her everything, my mom had cried for both Emma *and* Ally. She'd cried for Emma because of everything that she'd gone through, and for Ally because it was obvious that she had been very sick, and no one had noticed. Maybe if we had, things could have ended differently for her. Maybe she would still be alive.

I'd never wanted my mom to know what had happened, but I'd had no choice since I refused to go to class. The university had called her when they couldn't reach me. She'd called me and demanded an explanation, thinking I was just skipping. She hadn't expected for me to tell her that I was in the hospital with Emma. She'd called the school and let them know that I wouldn't be back for a while before rushing to the hospital.

When she had seen Emma unconscious and battered in her hospital bed, she'd lost it again. I knew she always liked Emma, but I hadn't realized how much until I'd seen the fear in her eyes. She had felt as terrified as I had that Emma would never wake up.

The day Emma opened her eyes was the single most important day of my life. I'd thought I'd imagined her eyelids fluttering, but when I'd begged her to open them, she had. It had been obvious that she had been in a lot of pain, but she had woken up. She would be okay, just like the doctors had said she would. The weight that had been sitting on my chest lifted as soon as she had spoken.

Emma's mother wanted her to come back to California, but she refused. She said that West Virginia was her home, and she wasn't leaving. Her mother finally caved after I told her that I'd take her to my house to watch over her. I thought I was slowly starting to grow on her. She'd promised to visit at least once a month, but I had no idea if she really would, and I didn't care.

Her dad left the day after her mom went home. He wanted to stay, but was forced to fly back only a few days after Emma woke up. The band was three weeks behind schedule, and their label was pressuring them to get their latest album recorded. I promised to keep him informed on how Emma was doing.

Her dad had called the school and informed them of the situation before he flew back to California. She was pulled from all of her classes for the semester, and I went to her dorm room to pack the rest of her things. Only a few things were left there since she'd slowly started bringing her stuff to my house before everything had gone to hell. I packed what was left and brought all of it back to my house. I hoped that having the rest of her stuff with her would help her feel safer once she was back home.

We spent another week in the hospital before Emma was released with strict orders to rest. The doctor gave me a list of psychiatrists in case she needed to talk to someone about what had happened. She'd refused to speak with any of the doctors or nurses about what she'd gone through while she was with Ally.

The day I took her home, Andy helped me get her into my car, and he followed us back to my house. Emma was still sore and extremely weak after three weeks in a hospital bed. We had to help her inside and sit her on the couch. The doctor had prescribed her painkillers to help while she healed.

I had Andy stop by my house to change the locks the day before Emma came home. I didn't want to take a chance that Ally would come back to hurt Emma again. We would never have closure until Ally's body was found, and there was no certainty that it would be. I hated that Emma would always be looking over her shoulder. I knew deep down that Ally was gone, but it would be a long time before I stopped looking for her everywhere. I refused to let her or anyone else hurt Emma ever again.

Andy or I stayed with Emma constantly the first few days. Andy was sleeping in Ally's old room, so he could help out. He would leave for work, but that was it. The guilt that tortured me was also eating him alive. We both felt responsible for what had happened.

Emma and I had never had a chance to talk about the events of that night while she had been in the hospital. Someone had always been around. After she came home, it seemed like Andy would appear anytime I tried to talk to her about it.

She was quiet for the first few days after she had been released from the hospital. She would spend hours on the couch, staring at the wall. I knew she needed to talk about what had happened, but I wasn't sure how to get her to open up.

I slept on the couch while she stayed in my bed. I missed sleeping beside her, but I was afraid that she didn't want me there. I didn't want to push her when she was so fragile. I wouldn't be the one to break her.

She had nightmares almost every night. She would wake up screaming, and I'd rush to her side. I could never get her to talk about them. Instead, I'd hold her as she cried.

Weeks passed by in slow motion as Emma's body slowly healed. Once she was fully healed, Andy moved back into his apartment. I wasn't sure if he had done it to give us space or for the simple fact that he couldn't stand to look at her blank face anymore. She only spoke when we would ask her a question. The rest of the time, she was silent.

I finally reached my breaking point one afternoon when I came home to see her sitting in the exact same spot she'd been in when I left hours before. She hadn't moved a muscle. I couldn't take this any longer. Either she opened up to me, or I would call her dad. Maybe he could get her to talk or at least set her up with a therapist. She needed to talk to *someone* even if it wasn't me. She couldn't keep living inside of herself.

I slammed my books down on the bedside table harder than I'd meant to. She jumped and looked up at me. I didn't think she'd even noticed that I'd come home until then.

"Emma, this has to stop." I sat down next to her on the bed.

"What?"

"You can't keep living like this. It isn't working for either of us."

"You're right," she said quietly. "I'm sorry that I came here. I never meant to bring you into this."

"What are you talking about?"

"You want me to leave. I understand why."

"Emma, I don't want you to leave. I want you to talk to me."

"I don't understand. You've been sleeping on the couch, and you barely talk to me."

"I'm on the couch because I thought it was what you wanted. I thought you needed space. And I've tried to talk to you, but it's kind of hard when you only give me one-word answers. You've been living in your own head for weeks, and I have no idea what you're thinking. You have to help me understand what's going on in there. I want to help you in any way I can."

"I don't want to lose you, but I feel like you're slipping away, and there's nothing I can do to change that," she said.

"I'm not going anywhere unless you want me to. I've been trying to give you space, so you can figure things out."

"I'm so scared of everything. I keep reliving everything that she did to me," she said as tears filled her eyes.

"She's gone, Emma. She can't hurt you anymore."

"Part of me knows that, but the other part wants to hide under the bed. I keep waiting for her to show up again."

"You're safe. She will never touch you again."

"I kept picturing you every time she would hurt me, you know. I willed myself to be strong enough to overcome it, so I could see you again." She took a deep breath. "I tried to fight back when she showed up here. I wasn't strong enough though. She won without even trying. Then, I tried to get away at the house where she was keeping me. I pushed her down a flight of stairs, Jesse. What kind of person does that make me to do something like that to another human being?"

"You were trying to protect yourself. No one thinks badly of you for it."

I hated how much this was hurting her. Anyone else in her position would have done the exact same thing. Emma was one of the few people in this world who would feel guilt from causing pain to her would-be killer.

"She made me pay for that. That's why she cut me. She said she wanted to hurt me because I'd hurt her. The pain was horrible, Jesse. I wanted to die when she sliced through my skin."

I could barely stand to sit here and listen to her talk about what Ally had done, but I knew I had to. Emma had to talk to someone. She had to get it all out. That didn't make it any less painful for me though.

"I've never felt anything like that. She did it slowly, so I felt every centimeter."

"I'm so sorry that you had to go through that, Emma," I choked out.

"It's not your fault."

"But it is. If it weren't for me, you never would have had to go through that. I'm so sorry."

"None of us realized just how sick she was. She loved you so much that it drove her crazy—literally. She kept telling me that once I was gone, you'd finally let me go and realize that you loved her back. She thought that you loved her but didn't know it. She blamed me for the fact that you refused to love her back."

"Maybe if I hadn't been so cruel to her, then she would have reacted differently."

Emma shook her head. "I don't think so. I don't think there was anything you or I could have done to help her. She was too far gone, lost in her own mind. It didn't matter what I told her. She refused to listen. Whatever you said to her that night on the phone saved my life. She'd planned to keep me for a while, but then she said she didn't have time for all the stuff she had planned because she had to meet with you. If you hadn't talked with her, she would have tortured me and killed me slowly."

"I told her that I loved her."

Emma smiled weakly. "She obviously believed you. I just wish that I could make myself forget all of it. I'm so tired of replaying it over and over in my head."

"Is that what your nightmares are about?" I asked.

"Sometimes, I dream about what happened. Other times, I dream about what would have happened if she'd had the time. Occasionally, it's about her sneaking in while you're asleep on the couch, and then she smothers me in your bed." She shuddered. "When she knocked me out, I had a dream that you saved me, but she killed you for it. I've never been so scared in my life. I thought it was real. I thought that I'd lost you."

"I'm not going anywhere, baby. Don't worry about that. If it's okay with you, I'd like to sleep beside you again. Maybe it will help with the dreams if I'm with you."

"I'd like that," she whispered.

I pulled her into my arms. It felt so good to hold her again. "We'll get through this, Emma. I swear, we will."

"I hope so."

"I think you should see someone. You need to get it all out."

"A therapist?"

I nodded. "Yeah, the doctor gave me a few names when you were in the hospital. Will you let me call one of them for you?"

She was silent for a moment. "I'll try to talk with one of them, but I can't promise that it'll help."

"I think it will. I'll call first thing tomorrow. Tonight, I just want to hold you in my arms."

I stood and picked her up. She smiled for the first time in weeks as I carried her to my bed and laid her down. I crawled in next to her and pulled her close. I'd missed this. I'd missed her.

Things would work out. They had to. I wouldn't let her go without a fight.

Three Months Later

Emma was healing. I could see the changes daily. It took a couple of weeks for her therapy sessions to start helping her, but I noticed the changes as soon as they happened. It was hard not to notice when I was watching her every move. I was terrified to let her out of my sight.

The only time I left her side was when I was in class or grocery shopping. I would make sure to stock up on enough food, so I only had to go to the store once or twice a month. Hell, I was even learning to cook a few things. It was a big change after living off of cereal most of the time.

The changes in Emma were small at first, beginning with a smile here and there. She started to talk more, and then the nightmares stopped coming every night. She still had them, but instead of being a constant in her life, they slowed to once or twice a week.

I nearly dropped my bag on my foot the day I came home to hear her talking to her dad on the phone. Up until then, she'd refused to talk to anyone. Instead, I was forced to tell them how she was doing.

Andy came over a couple of times a week for dinner, but he stayed away more often than not. When I asked him why, he told me that he couldn't stand to look at Emma after what his own sister had done. The guilt was killing him inside. No matter how many times I explained to him that it wasn't his fault, he refused to believe it. Emma noticed his absence and asked what was wrong. I lied and told her that he was working more hours. She had enough to deal with without adding Andy's guilt to her conscience.

Valentine's Day had been almost nonexistent in our house. In an attempt to cheer Emma up, I offered to take her out for dinner. She refused, saying that she wasn't in the mood to celebrate any kind of holiday. I agreed not to go out, but I still bought her a present. Instead of being excited when I handed her the small box with a necklace inside, she was upset that she hadn't gotten me anything. I told her that it didn't matter, but she refused to listen. A few days later, a package showed up for me with a new CD. I couldn't help but laugh at her choice of music. She was trying at least.

Emma was meeting with her therapist three times a week. When she first started seeing him, she refused to talk about her sessions with me. I hated that. I felt like she was trying to keep me away. I didn't want her to push me away or protect me from what was going on inside of that head of hers. I wanted her to feel like she could trust me. She finally started opening up to me a few weeks after she'd started. Even though she didn't share much, she was still sharing. I'd take anything I could get at this point. I wasn't picky. I just wanted in.

She decided to start going to school again. She only took a few classes, but they were enough to keep her occupied. Before then, the only time she would leave the house had been for her sessions. It was good to see her out again. I even convinced her to go watch a movie with her friend, Abby.

Emma was slowly coming back. The only thing that wasn't healed was our relationship. I knew she was trying, but it still felt strained. I was afraid that we'd never be the same again. I didn't want Ally to win. I wanted to show Emma how much I still loved her.

I decided to do something special for her. I'd racked my brain for days, trying to come up with an idea that would mean something to her. I wished that we were closer to the beach, so I could take her surfing. Since that was out, I had to come up with another plan. I was getting a lot better at cooking, so I decided to do a romantic dinner. I even went as far as picking up a dozen roses, and I bought enough candles to put the store out of stock. I just hoped that my plan would work.

I hurried home after class to set everything up. Emma had a late class, so it gave me enough time to make dinner and get everything ready. I put the roses in a vase at the center of the table and covered every surface in the kitchen with candles. We were at the very end of winter, so I could count on the sun setting early enough to make sure we had a dark candlelight dinner to set the mood. I wanted to be the most ridiculously romantic guy in the world for her.

Everything was ready when she finally made it home. I was sitting at the table, waiting for her, when I heard her keys unlocking the door. I held my breath as I listened to her throw her bag down by the door before heading to the kitchen. I prayed that this would work. I *needed* this to work.

"Hey, I'm home," she called out as she entered the kitchen. She stopped dead when she noticed the candles everywhere.

"Welcome home."

"What's this?"

"It's…" What is it? A peace offering? Kind of. An attempt to show her how much I still love her? Definitely. "It's a dinner," I said lamely.

"I can see that. But why?"

I stood and walked over to her. I grabbed her hands and pulled her closer. "Because I love you. I want things to go back to the way they used to be with us."

Her eyes widened in shock. "I don't know what to say."

"You don't have to say anything right now. Let me talk while you eat."

I pulled her over to the table and pushed her gently into a chair. I lifted the foil off the top of the lasagna and grabbed her plate. After filling it and placing it back in front of her, I did the same with mine. She was quiet as she watched me. I ignored her stare as I sat down and picked up my fork. I wanted her to relax before we started talking about everything. Tonight would decide everything for us. It was now or never. We couldn't keep living the way we had been. I couldn't take it anymore.

"I thought you wanted to talk," she said as she stared at me.

I hesitated. "I do. I just don't know where to start. I had all of this planned out in my head, but you walked through the door, and now, I'm blank."

"Jesse, just say what you want to say. You won't hurt me."

"I can't keep living like this. I love you, Emma, but it's killing me. You're doing so much better in every aspect of your life, except with me. I'm not sure if you're still having a hard time with everything or if you just don't feel what you used to feel when it comes to me."

"I'm hurting you." It was a statement, not a question.

I nodded. "I know you're not doing it on purpose, but you are. I just want to know where we stand. I want things to be okay between us again. If you still want to be with me, tell me how to fix us, and I swear that I will."

"I still love you, Jesse. It's just that I still can't get over what Ally did to me. I'm not in a good place right now. Granted, I'm a lot better than I was a month or two ago, but I'm still not me, not entirely. I don't want to drag you down with me."

"You're supposed to drag me into it. It's my job to be there for you when you need someone to talk to."

"I don't want to bother you," she whispered.

"You could never bother me. I want you to feel like you can talk to me."

She bit her lip as she stared at me. "I'm so scared...of everything. I'm starting to move past what she did to me, but I'm still terrified that she's going to come back. I'm afraid that you'll leave me, and I'll be on my own. I don't think I could handle that."

I pushed my chair back and walked over to her. Her eyes were full of tears as she looked up at me.

"I will *never* leave you—never. I love you, Emma. I just want us to go back to the way things were."

"I want that, too, but I'm afraid of what you'll think of me if I tell you everything that goes on inside of my head."

I grinned. "With the exception of you thinking about Andy naked, nothing could scare me away. Will you talk to me? Please."

She studied me for a moment before nodding. "I can try. I just don't know where to start."

"It doesn't matter."

"Huh?" she asked.

"It doesn't matter where you start. All that matters is where we're at when you're done."

She smiled at me. "I know where I want to end."

We finished dinner in silence. I wanted to give her space to figure out how she wanted to start. I didn't want to pressure her or scare her into telling me. She had to do it on her own.

Once we were finished, we put our plates in the sink and cleaned up.

"Do you want me to put out the candles now?" I asked, unsure of what would happen next.

"No, leave them, but I want you to come with me."

I raised an eyebrow as she took my hand and led me back to the bedroom. Now, I really had no clue what was going on inside her head. She walked into the bedroom and stopped next to the bed.

"I love you, Jesse."

"I love you, too."

"I want to ask you to do something for me, but only if you're okay with it."

"I'd do anything you asked me to do."

"I want you to make love to me."

That definitely wasn't what I'd expected to hear. I stood frozen as I tried to process what she'd just said.

"I…"

"You don't have to if you don't want to," she said.

"Emma, I can't think of a time when I'd ever turn down *that* request. I just don't understand where this is coming from."

"I just…I need you."

"I need you, too. I just don't want you to do this and regret it. I want you to be okay first. I can wait for this as long as you need me to."

"Being with you will help me get a little closer to okay. I've needed it since the beginning."

"Why didn't you say anything?" I asked.

I reached up and ran my thumb along her cheek. She closed her eyes as I continued to run my thumb back and forth across her skin.

"I didn't know how to ask."

I leaned forward and brushed my lips against hers. The simple gesture caused a shudder to run through her. I pressed my lips harder against hers. She wrapped her arms around me as she pulled me closer. I wanted this badly, but I was afraid that she would regret it later.

"One more time before we get too far into this—are you sure?"

"I'm sure," she whispered.

I picked her up and laid her gently on the bed. I slowly crawled on top of her, afraid to make her uncomfortable or uneasy. I didn't want to do anything to screw this up for her. If she was willing to take this step with me, I wanted it to be perfect.

I kissed her lips again before moving to her jaw. She moved her head to the side to give me access to her neck. I kissed there, too. It had been so long since we'd been together, and it was killing me to go slow. I wanted to rip off her clothes and bury myself deep inside her right now. I held back as I peppered her face and neck with butterfly kisses. I wouldn't let my dick control me. After everything she'd been through, she deserved better than that.

She sat up and slipped her shirt over her head. I lifted my arms as she pulled my shirt off next. She reached behind her and unclasped her bra. I clenched my hands into fists as she lay down to keep from reaching out for her. I had to go slow.

She smiled shyly, and I was transported back to our first time together. She'd been so sweet and innocent then, and she still was even now. She'd been through hell, but she would *always* be my Emma. I ran my fingers down her cheek before continuing down to the swell of her breasts. Her chest rose and fell rapidly. I wasn't sure if it was from nerves or excitement.

"You okay?"

"Better than okay."

I smiled as I trailed my fingers between her breasts and down her stomach. I loved her softness. I'd missed touching her like this. I leaned over and ran my tongue over one of her nipples. She sucked in a breath as her hands grabbed my shoulders. I took that as confirmation that it was okay, and I did it again to her other nipple. Her back arched off the bed as I took one in my mouth and sucked gently.

"Oh god, that feels so good," she moaned. "Don't stop."

"I won't." I didn't think it was possible for me to stop at this point even if I wanted to.

This time was different from any of the others. It wasn't just sex. It was a way for her to heal.

I reached between us and unbuttoned her jeans. I pulled them down just a bit and ran my fingers across the top of her underwear.

Her breath hitched, and she wiggled underneath me. "Take them off."

I stood at the foot of the bed and slowly pulled her jeans and underwear down her legs. I couldn't help but stare at her naked form on the bed. She was beautiful.

I pulled my jeans and boxers off before getting back onto the bed. I started kissing her ankle, working my way up her leg with light kisses. When I reached her knee, I pushed her legs apart. The scars were faint from where Ally had cut her, but I could see them. I kissed my way up first one scar and then the other.

"Does it bother you?" she asked as she stared down at me.

I shook my head. "Not at all."

"I just wish they would go away. I don't want you to have to look at them."

"Emma, they don't matter to me." I eased up her body to where the thin scars went across her stomach. I kissed them, too. "You're the only thing that matters to me."

"Thank you," she whispered as tears filled her eyes.

We didn't speak after that. My lips moved against her skin as I kissed back down her body. I ran my fingers across her hips, slowly making my way down. She gasped as I ran my finger between her folds, stopping on that one spot that drove her crazy. I stroked her clit slowly, building her up, as I kissed my way back up to her breasts. I sucked on one before biting down gently. I started rubbing circles around her clit as she moaned and raised her hips up against me. I released her nipple and bit down on my lip as I tried to stay in control. I was hanging on by a thread and touching her naked body wasn't helping. I pulled my hand away, and she cried out in displeasure.

"Don't stop!"

"I'm not." My voice was gruff as I pushed her body down onto the bed and positioned myself over her.

I couldn't wait anymore. I had to have her. I slid into her slowly, afraid that I would come before we even started. Every part of my body demanded that I take her hard and fast. We hadn't been together in months, and she was tight. I moaned as I filled her completely. Nothing in the world could compare to this.

"I love you, Emma."

"I love you, too."

I pulled out and pushed back inside, going slow to make sure that I didn't hurt her. I wanted everything about this to be perfect for her. She wrapped her legs around my hips, pulling me deeper inside her. I groaned as my thrusts became harder. I couldn't contain myself any longer. The need to be with her took complete control of me, and I let go.

"I'll never leave you. I swear it," I said as I continued to pound into her.

She moaned in response and squeezed her legs tighter around me. My thrusts became erratic as I tried to keep myself from coming. I wouldn't come until she did. I leaned down and sucked her nipple into my mouth. She cried out, and I felt her body tense as she came. I continued to suck and thrust my hips, prolonging her orgasm as long as possible.

I gave one final thrust and exploded inside of her. Unwilling to let her go just yet, I rested my weight on my elbows and stared down at her. She looked beautiful, even more so than normal. Her lips were swollen from our kisses, and I leaned down to kiss her again, unable to stop myself. I felt closer to her now than I had in a long time.

"Thank you for that," I whispered.

She smiled up at me. "No, thank you. It sounds stupid, but I needed that. I needed to feel close to you."

I forced myself to pull out, and I rolled over to lie beside her. "That's about as close as you can get."

She laughed. "I guess it is."

"Will you talk to me now?"

She bit her lip as she looked over at me. "Yes, I will. Just bear with me."

"Take your time, babe. I'm all yours."

I listened as she started at the beginning and continued from there. I let her get everything out that she needed to say. I held her as she cried for not only what had happened to her but for Ally as well. We lay together for hours after she was finished. I held her tightly in my arms until she fell asleep.

She still had a lot of healing to do, but she was definitely getting there. I was willing to wait for her and help in any way I could. We would figure things out together.

At the end of the day, love is not perfect. It doesn't protect us or save us from the darkness surrounding our lives. Instead, it is the light that shines through to help us. Without it, we would be consumed by the darkness.

Life was the craziest journey that a person could ever take. I had no idea where Emma and I would be ten months or ten years from now, and I didn't care. All I knew was that she would be with me wherever I ended up at in life.

After all, we'd been to hell and made it back alive.

EPILOGUE

Five Years Later

I knew something was up the minute Emma walked through the door. She was trying her hardest not to smile, but she was failing miserably. She'd always been terrible at keeping secrets.

"What's up with you?" I asked.

"Nothing. Why?" she asked innocently.

I wasn't buying it. "Bull. You can barely contain yourself. What did you do?"

"Promise me that you won't be mad first, or I won't tell you."

I raised an eyebrow. I couldn't remember the last time that I'd been mad at Emma. She never gave me a reason to be mad. She made my life perfect.

"I promise," I said slowly.

"Okay, so you'll have enough hours to become certified soon, right?"

I nodded. "Yeah. Why?"

I'd finished college over a year ago with a bachelor's degree in business. My mother had been thrilled until I told her my plans to get an apprenticeship at a local tattoo shop. She couldn't understand why I would waste four years of my life at college if I hadn't planned to use my degree for anything. She thought I was throwing my life away instead of bettering myself like she'd hoped. I'd never seen my mom so angry with me as when I told her I only went to college for her. I'd explained that I had done it to make her happy, but a desk job just wasn't for me. I wanted to tattoo. She'd cried and begged me to reconsider, but I'd held my ground.

In the back of my mind, I think I always knew that I would go back to tattooing. Or maybe I would have done what my mom had wanted if it wasn't for Emma. She'd convinced me to go after my dream. I'd told her no over and over at first. I knew I wouldn't make a lot of money tattooing, and I wanted her to have the best of everything.

Emma had laughed at me every time I'd told her that. She'd said money didn't matter to her as long as we were together. I knew she meant what she said, but she'd never lived without money before. It was a completely different thing to actually live that kind of life rather than talk about it.

I'd finally caved a few months before I graduated college. The closer we had gotten to graduation, the more depressed I'd become. I knew once I had my diploma in my hand, working life would become a reality, and I'd need to find a job within my chosen career path.

I knew I couldn't spend my entire life doing something I hated, so I took a chance and walked into a local tattoo shop for the first time in years. I hadn't known how much I'd missed it until I was back in one. There was just something about the sound of a tattoo gun and rock music playing somewhere in the shop that felt like home. I'd been lucky and caught the owner at the shop when I stopped by. He was a nice enough guy, and he'd agreed to give me a chance.

I'd started by working at the shop part-time while I finished college. Once I'd had my diploma, I'd started taking the courses I needed before I could start my official apprenticeship. Once I had finished them, I'd started my apprenticeship. I was paid next to nothing, but I loved every minute of it.

Emma and I had moved into another house right before we started our sophomore year of college. Neither of us could stand to be in the house that was tied to Ally. The new house was smaller, but it worked fine for us. I tried to find another part-time job to help with rent and bills, but Emma wouldn't have it. Instead, I felt like the biggest ass ever as Emma paid for everything.

"You know what? I think I'd rather show you instead of telling you. Come on," Emma said as she grabbed my hand and led me out of the house.

"Where are we going?" I asked.

"Shush. You'll see soon enough," she teased.

I was silent as Emma drove across town. I had no idea what she was up to. Usually, I could tell what she was thinking but not this time.

She pulled up to an empty building close to the college campus. "We're here," she said excitedly.

"Where is here exactly?" I asked.

"Come on."

I stepped out of the car and followed her to the empty building. I noticed a sign in the front window that had *For Sale* written across it.

"Emma, what did you do?"

She laughed as she unlocked the door and walked inside. I followed her in as she flipped on a light switch. The building was large but completely empty. The walls had a nasty-ass wallpaper on them that looked like it'd been around since before I was born.

"What is this?" I asked.

She walked to the window and pulled the sign off the glass. "This is your new tattoo shop."

"Huh?"

"Remember a long time ago, I said I wanted to help you get started with a shop of your own?"

I nodded.

"Well, here it is. I bought the building today."

"Emma, you didn't!"

She laughed. "I did. I know it doesn't look like much now, but we can decorate it and paint the walls. We can build a wall across this room and make it a lobby. There are rooms in the back that we can use for clients. I'm sure Andy will help us. He can design a few skateboards to hang on the walls and maybe even a few pictures."

After everything had happened with Ally, Andy had decided to go back to California. I had seen Emma talking to him one night, a few days before he planned to leave. I wasn't sure what she had said to him, but he'd finally changed his mind and agreed to stay in Morgantown with us. I hadn't asked, and I hadn't wanted to know. He'd claimed that there was nothing in California for him anymore, but I wasn't buying it. I knew Emma was the reason that I still had my best friend around.

After the night of their talk, Emma and Andy had become even closer. Andy was still my best friend, but I understood that they had a special bond. I wasn't jealous of it. Instead, it made me happy. I wanted both of them to be happy.

The guilt that Andy and I had both suffered from after what had happened to Emma had slowly started to fade away. Both of us had finally realized that Ally had truly been sick, and there wasn't a thing that we could have done to help her. We'd let go of our guilt once Emma came back to herself. It had taken a very long time for her to do it, but looking at her now, I would never know that something so traumatic had happened to her. She was my Emma once again.

Andy's boss had fired his brother, Sam, after he caught Sam stealing money. His boss had asked Andy to take over as manager from that point on. He pretty much ran the shop by himself. He'd also started fooling around with photography. He was damn good at it, and he did it as a side job for some extra cash. Andy wasn't the richest guy out there, but he was happy. He still got into trouble occasionally, but he was slowly becoming grounded.

I was glad to see that he'd found his place in life. I just wished that he would settle down and find a girlfriend. Even after all this time, he still refused to give up his playboy ways. He laughed every time I mentioned it, and he would say that he didn't want to be a lovesick idiot, like Emma and me. I couldn't wait until he found a girl who knocked him on his ass. Whoever she was, she would have to have balls of steel to deal with his ass on a daily basis.

"I'm sure he'll help us out," I said as I looked around the building. "Why did you do this, Emma?"

"Because it's your dream," she said simply.

"What if it fails?"

"It won't. You have a passion for tattooing, and you have the knowledge of how to run a business. We'll get this place ready to go, hire a few guys, and watch your dreams come true."

"I'll agree to this on one condition," I said stubbornly.

"And what would that be?"

"You work here, too. I want this to be our dream—together."

Emma had ended up majoring in accounting. I'd found this hilarious since she'd hated math in high school. When I'd asked why, she'd shrugged her shoulders.

She'd said, Math became my favorite subject the day you walked into my class. I figured if it brought us together, I might as well stick with it.

"I was hoping you'd ask me to," she said as she walked over and threw her arms around me. "I wouldn't feel safe with you tattooing girls if I weren't here. You might run off with one of them or something."

I laughed, and I pressed my lips against hers. "I only have eyes for you. I'd like you to be my first official client when we open up."

"I'll think about it. So, be honest, are you excited? You don't have to hold it in if you are."

I pretended to think for a minute. "Maybe a little."

"I'll take it. Come on, I want to show you the back rooms."

I followed her as she showed me each room. I couldn't help but smile at her excitement. She was more excited than I was. She had no idea how much this meant to me. She was giving me a chance to follow my dreams.

We'd been through hell and back. We'd started out as two high school kids who knew nothing about this world, and we'd slowly grown up together.

Now, I couldn't wait to see what would happen to us next. The future no longer scared me when I thought about it.

I smiled as I thought about the ring I had back at the house. I hadn't had the nerve to ask Emma to marry me just yet, but I would—soon. I wanted everything with this woman—marriage, kids, growing old together. I wanted all the sappy shit they write about in books and show in movies.

I wanted everything—and I had it with her.

The End

A NOTE TO READERS

I'm sure your head is spinning from Ally. I know mine is. Ally took me to a place where I hadn't known I was capable of going. I'm sure you're all sitting there, wondering what happened to Ally.

Is she alive? Will she come after Emma and Jesse?

That's for you to decide.

Emma and Jesse's story is finished though, so I hope that gives you some peace of mind.

Hugs,
K.A.

Enjoy this excerpt from
K.A. Robinson's

BREAKING ALEXANDRIA

Coming April 2014

Chapter One

I groaned and rolled over to escape the sun shining through the window of Joel's bedroom. My body tensed as I realized for there to be sunlight, then it must be day. My eyes opened, and I grabbed my cell phone from the table beside the bed to check the time. *Shit.* It was almost three o'clock in the afternoon, and I had a ton of voice mails and missed calls. I was so fucked.

I sat up and pulled the blanket up to cover my naked body. I had snuck out of my parents' house last night after they grounded me for fighting in school again. I'd thought I could sneak back in this morning before they woke up, but that obviously wasn't going to happen now.

My eyes traveled to Joel as he snored lightly beside me. The sun was directly on his back, showing off the skull and crossbones tattoo that covered most of the area. His normally guarded expression was gone while he slept. Joel looked like the typical badass, but he was so much more. His body was covered in tattoos. And when I say covered, I mean, covered. There was barely an inch of him that didn't have ink with the exception of his face. His hair was a dark brown color, and he kept it just a bit shaggy. His eyes were a startling green color that made people stop and look twice. His cheekbones and overall face structure would make any male model jealous.

I smiled dreamily as I thought about our night together. At twenty-two, he was five years older than me, but our age gap never seemed to bother him. We'd been together for almost a year now, and I couldn't be happier. I'd met him at my cousin's graduation party two years ago, and I'd instantly developed a crush on him. He hadn't paid me any attention then, but when I started hanging out with some of his younger friends that were in high school with me, I'd finally gotten him to notice me.

I'd been drunk that night and braver than usual. He had been surrounded by girls much older than me, but I had shoved through them and walked straight up to him. He'd raised an eyebrow when I stopped in front of him, but I'd simply hopped on to his lap and kissed him until I couldn't breathe. After I had finished, I'd stood up and walked away.

We'd been together ever since. My parents weren't happy that I was dating someone so much older who was covered head to toe in tattoos, but I'd sworn to them over and over that we weren't having sex. Obviously, that was a lie, considering where I woke up at just now, but they didn't need to know that.

Joel was trouble. I'd known that before I got with him, but I'd still taken a chance, and I was glad that I had. Everyone knew he was the son of the town drunk, and it showed. Joel had one hell of a mean streak. Even when he had been in high school, everyone had been terrified of him. He had been kicked out for fighting more times than I could count. On top of that, everyone knew he was the go-to guy if someone needed a fix. He'd later explained to me that he'd started selling drugs to help pay the bills that his dad never worried about. Joel was good at it though, and he'd stuck with it even when he could have left this town and started fresh.

He was already living on his own by the time we'd met, and I was glad. I wasn't sure how I would handle seeing the man who had abused Joel for years. I'd want to cause Joel's father as much pain as he had done to Joel. I knew it had been years since Joel had talked to his father, but it still bothered me.

"Joel, wake up. I need to leave," I said as I nudged his shoulder.

He groaned in his sleep, but he refused to open his eyes. I sighed as I started hitting his shoulder harder. His eyes finally opened when I started smacking him on the ass. He shielded his eyes as he rolled over to look at me.

"What?" he grumbled.

"I need to go home, like right now. We slept in." I stood up and started looking for my clothes.

"You're already in trouble. Why hurry home to be yelled at?" he asked as he sat up.

He didn't bother to cover himself, and I couldn't bring myself to look away from his naked body. I loved the trail of black hair that led down his stomach…and to other places. His nose was a bit crooked from being broken more than once, but it didn't take away from his appearance. If anything, it made him look sexier and dangerous. His eyes were his best feature by far though. They held a vulnerability in them that made me want to crawl into his arms and try to make everything better.

He was in great shape. I guessed he had to be when he dealt with strangers who were high and desperate for their fix on a daily basis. The muscles in his arms were well-defined, and his chest was as hard as a rock. I loved curling up in his arms. I always felt like he could protect me from anything.

"I don't want to make it worse," I said as I located my clothes.

They were next to the door, making it obvious as to how they had come off. We'd barely made it to his room before he started stripping me.

"Your parents suck. Why do they care about you fighting so much? At least they know their kid can defend herself. Personally, I'd be proud," he said as he stretched.

"They're sick of me getting kicked out of school. Something about college and doing something with my life."

"I fought, and look at me. I'm living the high life." He grinned at me.

I rolled my eyes even though I knew he had a point. He used drugs occasionally, but he sold more than anything, and he'd made quite a lot of money doing it.

"I'm sure they'd be so proud of me if I decided dealing drugs was going to be my career choice in life. I might even get the Daughter of the Year award."

He grinned as he watched me pull on my shorts. I still couldn't find my underwear, so I decided to skip them.

"Looking for these?" he asked as he held up my underwear.

I walked over to the bed and held out my hand. "Come on, I need to hurry. Give them to me."

"Make me," he taunted.

I grumbled as I reached for them, but he held them just out of my reach.

"Damn it, Joel."

He reached up and pulled me back onto the bed. "Maybe I don't want you to go home. Maybe I should hold your underwear for ransom, so you'll stay."

"Keep them. I'll get them another time."

I tried to sit up, but he kept me pinned against him.

"Stay for a little while longer. We can light up and have some fun."

"I can't go home stoned. That's just asking for trouble."

"But you could go home thoroughly fucked," he said as he ran his fingers down my back.

I shivered. "I could, but I need to leave."

"I'll make it quick." He started pulling my shorts down my legs.

"Joel…"

"Shh, you know you want to."

Of course I wanted to, but I was already in so much trouble.

He silenced my protests as he rolled me onto my back. His naked body was tight against mine, and I could feel just how much he wanted me. He tweaked both of my nipples with his fingers, making me moan.

Fuck it. Going home will have to wait.

"Oh fuck," I said as he nudged my opening with his dick.

He leaned down and ran his tongue across my throat and then across my breasts. I arched my back, trying to get as close to him as possible. His hands traveled down my body to my core, and he started rubbing my clit. His dick was still at my entrance, teasing me. I tried to adjust my body, so he would enter.

"I thought you had to go home," he taunted.

"I do, but I thought you said you wanted to fuck me."

"Oh, I do. Grab the bedposts."

I did as he'd said, preparing myself for his entry. He didn't disappoint. He slammed into me hard enough that I had to hold on to the bedposts to keep myself from moving up the bed. I gasped out his name as he pulled out and ran his thumb along my clit.

God, I'm going to kill him for torturing me.

"Again," I said as I shifted, trying to force him to enter me.

"You like it rough, don't you, baby?" he teased.

"You know I do," I groaned.

He ran his hands over my body before grabbing my hips and thrusting into me again. Over and over again, he slammed into me until I was gasping for breath. He wasn't gentle, and I hadn't expected him to be. It was just the way we were. He liked rough sex, and I was happy to oblige.

I wrapped my legs around his waist to allow him to go deeper as I met him thrust for thrust. His grip on me tightened as he came closer to his release. I couldn't hold out much longer either. I was *so* close. He continued to pound into me as he reached between us. He flicked my clit and sent me screaming into my orgasm. My legs clamped tighter around him as I came. His thrusts became harder and more erratic as he came with me.

My body went limp, and I could see again once my orgasm left me. Joel was panting above me with his forehead resting against mine. Once his breathing returned to normal, he slipped out and rolled over to his side.

"I told you I'd make it quick," he said as he grinned over at me.

"Yay for you." I stuck my tongue out at him.

He continued to grin as he leaned over, and then he kissed me. "Come on, let's get you home."

We both dressed quickly, trying to hurry. Now that I wasn't staring at Joel's naked body, the need to get home was strong. I knew I was in trouble, but I just didn't care. I was tired of spending all my time trying to figure out ways to get around my parents' rules.

I knew fighting didn't solve anything, but it sure as hell made me feel better. Since Joel and I had become a couple, I'd made quite a few enemies, especially from the female population, but I didn't really give a fuck. He was mine, and if people tried to come between us, I'd take care of them.

I wasn't the sweet and innocent girl who I'd been before I met Joel. He'd changed me—but for the better. Before him, I rarely drank, and I never got into trouble. Now, I did what I wanted, and I didn't care what anyone thought of me. I had no friends of my own. I only hung out with his. It didn't bother me though. I hated girls. My solitude and bad attitude usually led to rumors that I was on drugs or helping him sell them. And both rumors were true, so it didn't bother me either.

It made most people leave me alone, but there was always some dumb skank who thought she could talk about me or try to push me around. Joel had taught me how to fight since he would bring me along to deals or he'd even send me out to do them on my own if he was busy. I knew how to take care of myself. The girls who talked about me or tried to start fights with me always ended up with blood dripping down their faces as they cowered on the floor.

Most people who were aware of the fact that I was helping Joel deal thought I was nuts, but I considered it a normal part of our relationship. Besides, he never sent me out on deals that were dangerous. He always handled those on his own. I would try to help him as much as possible. I knew that if I got caught, I wouldn't end up in as bad of a situation as he would since I was under eighteen.

I never used drugs—with the exception of weed. While I had no problem dealing, I didn't want to end up like one of the addicts who I supplied. They were gross and pathetic. Joel smoked weed a lot, but as far as I knew, that was the only thing he did. We both knew that if he started using, his profits would disappear.

We walked down the steps from the house to where his Harley was parked outside. He was the only guy I knew who was confident enough in his badass reputation to leave his bike out on the street all night. I grabbed my helmet and put it on before climbing on the bike behind him. I wrapped my arms around him as it came to life, and we tore down the street. The ride was short but exhilarating. I loved being on his bike more than anything else. I'd made him promise me that we would go on a road trip the summer I turned eighteen. I wanted out of this town and away from my parents. I just wanted to be free.

We arrived in front of my house faster than I would have liked. While I was in a hurry to get home, I hadn't taken the time to mentally prepare myself for the fight that was sure to ensue. Sure enough, the front door flew open as soon as Joel parked. My mother stomped down the sidewalk to where we were sitting before I even had the chance to take off my helmet.

"Get. Inside. Right. Now!" she shouted.

I sighed as I pulled off my helmet. *This should be fun.*

"I can explain—" I started.

She held up her hand to stop me. "I don't want to hear it. Inside the house—now."

I kissed Joel's helmet and hopped off the bike. He started it back up and left, leaving me to deal with my mother alone.

Asshole.

"Mom, let me explain," I started again, hoping that she would let me talk. "I just wanted to see him for a little bit. I planned to stay with him for only an hour or two, but I fell asleep when we were watching a movie. I woke up and started freaking out."

"You never should have gone to him in the first place. You're grounded."

"You can't keep us apart. I love him, and he loves me!" I shouted.

"You have no idea what love even is, Alexandria! You're still a child."

"Yeah, I do. I know what I feel for him is love, and there is nothing you can do to change that."

I stomped past her, focusing on the front door in front of me. Once I made it inside, I hurried upstairs to my room. She followed, obviously not finished with me.

"You are not to leave this house for a week. You were kicked out of school for the rest of the week, and since you don't need to be there, you don't need to be anywhere."

"What does it even matter? This is the last week of school anyway. If I hadn't been suspended, I would have skipped anyway."

My mother shook her head. "I will never understand you, Alexandria. You're not my baby girl anymore, and I have no idea what happened to you. I'd blame Joel, but this attitude of yours started long before him. If things don't change, I'll—"

"You'll, what? You might as well figure out what you'll do to me because this is me, and I won't change who I am to make you happy."

"You're destroying yourself, Alexandria. Look at you—you're as thin as a twig. You've dyed your beautiful blonde hair black and put red through it. You won't listen, and you have no respect for your father or me." She glared at me. "And don't even get me started on those piercings in your lip and nose. They look horrible."

"Don't forget about my tattoo. I know how much you love it," I said sarcastically.

I'd come home almost three months ago with a tattoo on my left arm. It covered most of my inner arm from my elbow to my wrist. I wasn't eighteen yet, but Joel's friend was a tattoo artist, so he had done it for me. I'd wanted a tattoo forever, so I'd jumped at the opportunity to get one. I had drawn the design myself. At the top was a skull that ended with partial butterfly wings. Below that was a blue rose. I loved it even though I'd ended up being grounded for a month when my mother saw it.

I really wasn't sure why she was still so angry over it. I would come home with new body modifications all the time now. I would have thought she'd be used to it by now. Currently, I was rocking a septum piercing and a piercing in my nose along with looped snakebite piercings.

"I'm tired of your attitude, Alexandria. Enough is enough."

"I love you and Dad, but I'm tired of you both looking down at me. This is my life, and I'll live it however I want to. I don't have an attitude. I just can't handle how you freak out over every little thing."

My mother's nostrils flared as she tried to control her temper. She closed her eyes, and I watched as she counted to ten under her breath. Her entire body sagged the second she hit ten. It was like someone had dropped a ton of bricks on her shoulders.

"I don't know what you expect from me, Alexandria. I refuse to just sit here and watch you self-destruct."

I stared at my mother as she spoke. She looked tired, the kind of tired that came from worrying. Her blonde hair was hanging limply around her face, and there were lines around her mouth and eyes that I hadn't noticed before. Her hazel eyes that were identical to mine had fear in them. I felt a twinge of guilt for causing her any worry, but I pushed it away.

"I don't expect a damn thing from you."

ACKNOWLEDGMENTS

To me, this is the hardest part of a book to write. There are so many people who have helped me, and I know I will miss a few.

To my husband—Without you, none of my books would have been finished. You're my rock.

To my parents—You listen to me and help me with everything I need. I wouldn't be who I am today without you.

To my blogger friends—Gah! I can't say thanks enough times to all of you. You're not *just* bloggers to me. You're my friends. Without you, no one would even know who K.A. Robinson is. No one would know who Drake and Jesse are. (That would be a damn shame right there, wouldn't it?) Your support means so much to me.

To my "real-life" friends—Thank you for dealing with my constant absence. I know it's hard to get a hold of me. I get so into writing that I forget to live sometimes, but you're always there to drag me back to reality. I love you!

To my author friends: Tabatha, Katelynn, Sophie, Tijan, and several others I know I'm forgetting—I love you. Seriously. You guys keep me calm, help me when I need it, and remind me to eat. I feel so blessed to call you my friends.

To my readers—Your response to both of my series has been overwhelming. I *never* imagined that so many of you would care about these two characters the way you do. You guys continue to rock my world on a daily basis. I love you all to pieces.

To Letitia—You make the best covers ever. Thank you!

To Jovana—You deserve a medal for dealing with my crazy self and for reading the unedited mess of a book that I send to you. You rock!

ABOUT THE AUTHOR

K.A. Robinson is twenty-three years old and lives in a small town in West Virginia with her toddler son and husband. She is the *New York Times* and *USA Today* bestselling author of The Torn Series and The Ties Series. When she's not writing, she loves to read, usually something with zombies in it. She is also addicted to coffee, mainly Starbucks and Caribou Coffee.

Facebook: www.facebook.com/karobinson13

Twitter: @karobinsonautho

Blog: www.authorkarobinson.blogspot.com

CPSIA information can be obtained at www.ICGtesting.com
Printed in the USA
LVOW10s1850290914

406396LV00004B/296/P